"Hello, Nkrumah," I said, real friendly-like.

I never saw somebody jump like that. "Annie! Nan! Stations!" Suddenly one hooker came up with a pistol, and the other showed a real nasty-looking M-16 rifle.

"Now, is that any way to treat two old friends and ex-employees?" I asked.

Little Jimmy Nkrumah stared at me. "Horowitz? Is that really you?" He started to relax, then tensed again. "No! Nobody grows a beard like that and drops fifty pounds in a few days! You're not Horowitz—you're one of them!"

"Little Jimmy," Brandy sighed, "for a man with smarts you sure been actin' stupid of late."

I could see in his eyes—the man was scared to death. "You—you're not the Brandy I knew!"

"Still wrong," she replied. "You hired us, you fired us—only after we got canned we got taken for a ride. Right outta this world."

I grinned. "But now we're back."

Look for all these TOR books by Jack L. Chalker

JACK L. CHALKER

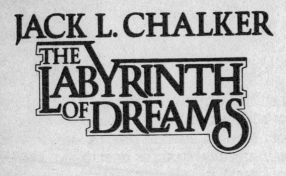

THE LABYRINTH OF DREAMS

G.O.D. INC. NO. 1

TOR

A TOM DOHERTY ASSOCIATES BOOK

THE LABYRINTH OF DREAMS

Copyright © 1987 by Jack L. Chalker

First printing: March 1987

A TOR Book

Published by Tom Doherty Associates, Inc.
49 West 24 Street
New York, N.Y. 10010

Cover art by Tim White

ISBN: 0-812-53306-2
CAN. ED.: 0-812-53307-0

Printed in the United States of America

0 9 8 7 6 5 4 3 2 1

For Jack Williamson,
who seems to have come up with the idea first
back in the dark ages of SF,
with love and respect.

1.

Spade & Marlowe, P.I.'s

It ain't often when a big case just up and walks into your office on a bright spring day, but being a private dick is all danger and adventure and you never can take anything for sure.

The dame looked exotic, like she was just off the boat, but her movements and particularly her eyes said she was here with a definite purpose in mind, one I might not like. She was covering a lot up, that was for sure. Her hair had more black dye than a licorice factory and she reeked of cheap perfume like a whore out for her first trick, but I knew right away that she wasn't no woman of the evening. Her big brown eyes met mine and her mouth turned up in a nasty curl, as if she wasn't real pleased with what she was seeing. This was a dame with a will of her own, one that wouldn't be easily turned from anything she had in mind to do.

I felt like a kitten caught raiding the garbage pail; she had that effect on you even before she said anything at all. Somewhere in the back of my mind I had the feeling we'd met before, like when you remember dreaming the winning horse in the fifth but only after the race was run and you bet on the nag that was still trying to find the track. And now she spoke, the words in accented English striking my heart like machine gun bullets at the Jersey marshes.

"Hey! Horowitz! You want I should clean this pigsty, and maybe the pig with it?"

I sighed, my lovely fantasy shattered. "Mrs. Kybanski, have you ever heard that a little politeness will get you a long way?"

"No. Sing a few lines. Besides, if I wanted to work with people, I would've taken the waitress job at Denny's. You're the only one left in this dump, and since it ain't been condemned as a public danger yet, I got to clean it. Bad enough I got to walk these streets after dark. I don't have to do it so late except for you. Why don't you go home? You ain't gonna miss no clients. They don't even come *here* in the daytime!"

Unfortunately, that was close to the truth, but her stock appeal for pity had a flaw in it. "Mrs. Kybanski—there are twelve offices in this run-down excuse for an office building, and eleven of them are empty. You just came in five minutes ago. Clean them first. I'll probably be long gone by then."

"Yeah, sure. Use *your* routine, *your* schedule, *your* convenience. Why not just go home to your *shikse* and get a good meal for a change? Not that you don't look like you been getting a good meal once too much."

That was why I tolerated, even liked, Mrs. Kybanski in spite of her wonderful manners and disposition. No matter what her other flaws, she was the only one I'd met in the seven years I've been married who thought of Brandy as a *shikse* and nothing else. That was why she could work this neighborhood. As for being in the neighborhood after dark, *I* might get a little nervous, sometimes, but anybody who dared to attack Mrs. Kybanski deserved what he would get.

"That's who I'm waiting for, Mrs. K.," I replied. "She's been out all afternoon on a case, and she's overdue getting back." The truth was, I was worried. I always worried when she went out alone on one of these things, even though it was just tracking down the address of a guy who owed about ninety years' worth of child-support and alimony payments. We were on a contingency fee, as usual, which made it all the more important. The wife had thought the guy had skipped to parts unknown, but a few days ago somebody who knew him swore to her he was running a 7-Eleven over in south Philly. Trouble was, she couldn't remember *which* 7-Eleven store, and there were like fifty over there. Those damned stores multiply faster than coat hangers and grocery bags.

So all I could do was sit around the dingy little office with its cracked door-glass and its cardboard-and-tape patch on the window and try and occupy my mind. We had a drawerful of unpaid bills, a bunch of collection notices, and very little else. The only reason they let us stay in the office was that nobody else would be idiot enough to rent it, but even that had its limits. The fact was, we were sinking fast, and were only really keeping going by handouts from Brandy's large family and from old friends of her dad who'd started this agency long ago. Me, I had no family to speak of and no real friends, not since I got married, anyway. Of course, they weren't real friends at all if that was gonna put them off. The closest relative I had was Uncle Max in Harrisburg, who owned a number of car dealerships, but he hadn't even sent me a birthday card since I got married. Worse, I hate most police and detective work; it's boring and you get no respect at all. Trouble is, I don't know how to do anything else and I never saw anything else any better. I often think I was just born wrong. I was intended for one of those rich multimillionaire Jewish families that have twin BMWs and get wings named after them at Mount Sinai Hospital because they needed a tax loss that year.

God got the religion right, but He must have been having an off day that time—something I'm accustomed to (off days, that is)—and dropped me in the family of a shoe salesman in Baltimore, with no rich relatives except Uncle Max (and he wasn't rich then), who worked six days a week to feed and clothe and house us and to try to save enough money to get me a good education and not have to go through this. Instead he only got ulcers, then a heart attack of the kind you never go back to work from and where the medicines cost a hundred bucks a month, and Mom had arthritis so bad there was no way she was gonna make it, either. I managed high school—public, not the fancy prep school with the old-boy network they wanted for me—but I knew right off that if I was gonna make it in the world, it had to be Uncle Max style. He started selling cars for others while living like a dog, putting all the money in investments, becoming salesman of the year repeatedly and doing a lot of politicking. He even switched to a synagogue miles away because its members had better business connections.

So, he finally finds this daughter of a rich lawyer and marries her, although she's a hundred-percent Jewish American princess, a loudmouth nag, and to me she always bore a strong family resemblance to Lassie. But her daddy bankrolled the car business and now Max has nine dealerships, a couple of million bucks, his-and-hers Cadillacs (he doesn't sell German cars), and, last I heard, a mistress or two on the side to console him. Me, I just couldn't play that game, so as soon as I graduated I joined the Air Force.

Now, that's not all that dumb. You actually have to volunteer for flying duty, and I never much liked airplanes, so if you check "nonflying status" you get an office job or a mechanic's job and you go home at night. In fact, the only potentially dangerous nonflying job the Air Force has is Security Police, its own cops. So, naturally, they made me a cop.

I had thought about letting the Air Force send me to college, but when I found out how much time you owed them for it, I kept putting it off; so I didn't go. Traffic detail at Otis Air Force Base on Cape Cod wasn't exactly bad duty, and neither was security patrolling at Homestead just south of Miami, but trying to keep a bunch of crazy anti-American protesters out of Clark in the Philippines when you're ordered not to use a weapon is something else. After I got out of the hospital, I started looking somewhere else for a career.

Now, there is a sort of old-boy network among service cops, and I found a job as a patrolman up in Bristol, New Jersey, that was close enough to home and quiet enough generally to be comfortable, although they didn't pay beans. They did, however, underwrite getting a degree, along with my service benefits, but the degree they wanted was in either criminology or police science—the liberal arts of the crime-busting world. That got me bumped up to detective and almost sixteen grand a year. It might not sound like a great salary now, but it was a lousy salary *then*. How I'd settle for it now, though. . . .

Anyway, junior detectives always get stuck on Vice, which even in the best of towns is like working in a human sewer half the day and doing paperwork the other half. Almost all the officers were on somebody's pad, which is how they made out on that salary, but the first time you bust a thirteen-year-old hooker, or try and find the source of a fifteen-year-old with more needle marks in him than a pincushion, you find it hard to protect the scum behind them. You know, the guys with the big houses and the twin BMWs. . . .

Not that I'm so morally against corruption that I would never take anything under the table. I just couldn't bring myself to do it in that world, even though I knew that world would grow and thrive with or without me. The big trouble was that if you weren't on the take, your fellow officers couldn't trust you. I drew the out-of-town leads, the dead-end stakeouts, and the cases involving competitors to the entrepreneurs who supplied central Jersey who they wouldn't mind getting taken down a peg or two. I admit I wasn't very diligent at it; they also would hand you the kind of stuff that could get you killed real quick. It wasn't real comfortable, but it was more of an education than Temple ever gave me.

So there I was, as usual, the outsider, the loner, the misfit. I guess I should have taken up religion again or something, but while I'm proud of my heritage I just couldn't take all the social stuff, the insularity, the class divisions, that came along with it. Besides, I always had to work weekends. I'm no beauty and I never went in much for the social graces; and the Levittown princesses didn't want a cop, they wanted a doctor at least. I'm moon-faced, hawk-nosed, with a potbelly, and I started balding at twenty-five (Thanks, Dad). So long as I stayed in Bristol I was stuck anyway, and the trouble was, I just had no place to go. Uncle Max offered me a job selling cars in Harrisburg, but if I wanted to do that kind of work, it was easier—and paid better—to just go on the pad.

So, anyway, they stuck me on this kiddie-porn case that involved liaison with the Camden police, a bunch of guys with bigger payoffs and an even more jaded outlook on life than my own sweet department. I was trying to track down a couple of long-missing local kids whose faces had shown up in a kiddie-porn magazine in Denmark, some of which had gotten imported back here, and they were recognized. The importer was in Camden, and clearly was far more than just an importer, and we were all on him. Even bad cops draw the line someplace. Most of 'em, anyway. With some relief they assigned me to temporary duty in Camden because they needed more men for stakeout duty than Camden could spare, and that's what first brought me to this neighborhood and how I met Brandy.

The neighborhood looked older than England and not nearly as well kept up. Blocks and blocks of narrow streets and rowhouses and smashed windows and sour smells and garbage all over the place. There was this one little office building stuck in the middle, so run-down-looking that to this day I believe that if they took away the boarded-up and condemned row homes on either side, the place would collapse. It kind of bends in the middle, somehow. The windows are all barred but rusty, and they're all cracked or have holes through them filled with tape or cardboard. The neighborhood itself was mostly black here, although there were some Asians now, mostly Koreans and Vietnamese who couldn't afford even the slums of Philadelphia just across the river. A couple of blocks away were a few small white enclaves, mostly old folks and those too poor to move to a higher-class slum. Eighty percent of the place were on permanent welfare; the other twenty percent were burglars, dope dealers, pimps and whores, and folks whose businesses needed this kind of anonymity.

There was no way I could stake out a neighborhood like this; I'd stick out like a sore thumb, but I needed a place staked out, preferably by somebody familiar with the place. I needed a good source of information, too, since it was clear that Camden Vice leaked like a sieve even on kiddie-porn scum. A source had recommended a private detective agency actually in the district; shady, the source said, and on a shoestring, but they did anything for a buck and kept their prices within an investigation's contingency fund. You went in this building and walked up two flights and it was the second door on the left.

SPADE & MARLOWE, Private Investigations, it said on the door in faded and peeling letters. The glass was frosted, but it was also cracked, and was held together with masking tape. Inside, it was full of file cabinets and a week or two of half-eaten lunches; and roaches had the right of way in the small outer office, which contained no desk and only one chair, an ancient overstuffed thing like you'd see in my grandmother's living room in the old days but cracked and torn, with stuffing coming out this way and that, and springs that had surrendered when Grant had commanded the Army. The door to the inner office looked open—I soon discovered it was nonexistent—and I walked to it and looked in.

There was a single old oak desk piled high with crap, a thirty-year-old manual typewriter on the floor, an old black dial phone from the fifties at least, and heaps of papers and other residue. It looked like my apartment. At first I thought nobody was there, but then I heard noises coming from behind the desk and then a head popped up and looked at me.

She was chocolate brown, with a full oval face, the biggest brown eyes I ever saw, and Afro-style hair so huge and bushy I thought at first it had to be a wig. "Oh, sorry, didn't know anybody was here," she said in a very low, throaty voice. Then she stood up, all five foot five of her, and stared at me. "You a cop?"

"Yeah, I'm a cop. Sam Horowitz—out of Bristol, so don't get upset. I need some help, and I was told this agency was handy for the kind of help I have in mind."

She was chubby, almost fat, but it was as if weight gained after a certain point had gone entirely to her breasts and hips. She wore a faded tee shirt with a marijuana plant on it and the words BUY AMERICAN!, and faded and patched jeans that seemed far too tight. "What kind of work?"

"Uh—excuse me—but the place is called Spade and Marlowe. Are you one of them?"

"Marlowe's dead," she responded matter-of-factly. "I'm the Spade."

I was always uncomfortable with that kind of humor, but it was too good a line not to appreciate. It was soon clear that she wasn't the secretary or a partner, but the whole damned agency. She picked up a creaky old wooden chair that had been overturned behind the desk and pushed it out and to the side. "Take a seat," she invited. "That's the only chair, but I don't use it much anyway."

"Thanks, I'll stand. Now, then, Ms. . . . ?"

"Brandy Parker. This job pay?"

"Some. A lot if we can get some results. The families involved have big rewards out."

"How big?"

"A few grand. The rewards, anyway."

"Take the chair," she invited, perching on the desk. "I'm suddenly very interested."

I told her about the case so far, the missing kids, the kiddie-porn pictures, the tracing to the distributor who worked out of a building in this area, all of it. She listened attentively, asking a few very good questions when she needed clarification, and seemed to get increasingly interested when I showed her the magazine and the pictures of the two kids before they were snatched. I liked the fact that the more we talked, the less money seemed important and the more her own anger grew. She was used to all the shit that went on around these neighborhoods, but this was particularly dirty, and the faces—and the contrast in the pictures—made it very real.

The cops had been right; she was very good when working in her element, and turned up a number of solid leads within forty-eight hours. The Camden cops would have to make the official bust, but we needed to feed them place, time, and the rest. Brandy's car was broken and she hadn't had the money to fix it, so we used my unmarked one, which for anything requiring traveling meant we saw a lot of each other. The word finally came down that a pedophile ring was working a seedy hotel in the low-rent district, and we staked it out for very long periods. A week of all-night stakeouts will let you get to know somebody pretty well.

Maybe it was because we were both lonely, both generally depressed, or maybe that we just had the same idea of right, wrong, and maybe, but we just sort of clicked in spite of our ingrained prejudices. No, it's not the way you think. She had more prejudices about Jews than I ever had about blacks. Hell, three fine, upstanding white guys had stood around while I lay bleeding on the ground back at Clark while two black SPs had finally braved the stones and dragged me back, saving my ass. Even though we'd been poor, my parents had always marched in civil-rights campaigns—they were old enough to remember "restricted" neighborhoods against Jews—and I never thought of blacks as being any different than Poles, Germans, Spaniards, or Chinese for that matter. In my family's world there were only two kinds of people, Jews and *goys*.

Brandy Alexandra Parker. Her father, the colonel, had always liked that drink, and it made a cute and appropriate name for his only child. Except for the fact that Harold Parker had been a career soldier and career MP, he and I had a lot in common. I think I would have really liked him. He'd joined the Army as an enlisted man at age eighteen, and worked his way up. He was a "consultant" to the Navy at the Philadelphia Navy Yard when he realized he'd never get any higher than lieutenant colonel—when you're an Army career man and they post you to the Navy, they're trying to tell you something—and he'd retired. He was a proud man who felt a keen obligation to excel just to prove that a black man could be ten times the soldier of those white smartasses, and considered prejudice not a barrier but a challenge. He was too old and too overqualified to get civilian police work, and the places where he could sign on offered him low and insulting positions, so he decided to try it on his own.

He also was caught up in the romance of the thing, to a degree. Spade & Marlowe. Sam Spade and Philip Marlowe. Only the best of company for Harold Parker. He didn't have much savings but he had a pretty fair pension, so he went out, got a license, rented a cheap office that looked right, and even hired a neighborhood girl just out of secretarial school as a secretary. A year later, at age forty-six, he married her. She was already six months pregnant at the time. Brandy wasn't his biological child, something she was kept ignorant of until she was in her late teens and he was trying to keep everything together and keep her from quitting school to help him. Her mother wasn't there to help; she had suffered from rip-roaring high blood pressure, and after Branday's birth, was warned not to try again. She worshipped the colonel, though, and became pregnant. The combination of that and being sloppy with her high-blood-pressure pills proved fatal. Brandy had been only ten when her mother had dropped dead of a stroke. She hadn't even gotten to thirty.

The colonel had set up the agency in the Camden ghetto at a time when it was rare to have a black private eye. He saw a need and filled it in the good old American tradition, arguing that black folks got divorces and skipped support payments and fooled around almost as much as white folks did. For a while it paid. Not handsomely, but when added to his retirement it was adequate—of course, his clientele then was of a higher class. When the ghetto became a place for the very poor, the paying clients went to large agencies with fancy offices and set rates, some black-owned and -operated, others the same ones that before hadn't wanted their business. He found himself working longer and harder for a diminishing client base, and he was no youngster anymore—but he had a youngster. The paying jobs often required him to be out late, and she wound up more and more in the care of her mother's relatives, mostly cousins and the like, who really considered it an obligation and weren't very good at the guardian job.

Brandy understood, but she developed a crushing case of private-eye-itus, caused by having a father who was a P.I., and by too many television shows, and she had little interest in school. She was a fat girl with no real family life and was a class wallflower, kind of like me except for the fat

business—that came only from Bristol. She went a
little wild as a teen. The only way to get boys to
pay attention was to proposition them; the rest was
taken care of by readily available drugs. She
spent the rest of the time watching black-female-
avenger pictures and reading lurid novels. She
was a good reader because her father always was,
but she got lousy grades and didn't really care.
Her father, increasingly trying to hold the business together and with his health beginning to
fail, finally couldn't help but notice and did a
little personal detective work. The first thing he
found out was that the report cards he'd seen had
been stolen blanks. She had more absences than
days present, and although he thought at sixteen
she was in high school, the fact was that she was
still in the ninth grade.

Just as bad, her closest girlfriend had been
dead on arrival from an overdose of drugs and
pills, and never mind the two abortions. The guilt
hit him like a lead weight. I kind of feel sorry for
him at that point, torn between trying to force
her to the straight and narrow and his guilt at
letting her go off in the first place.

I'll never know what that scene was like, but
somehow a compromise was reached. She didn't
want school and he wanted her out of that crowd,
that was for sure. She dropped out and went to
work for him at the agency as his secretary,
receptionist, and assistant. She had promised him
she'd get away from the bad crowd, stop fooling
around, and in a year or so get her GED high
school equivalency and even go to college. She
never did, though. Of course, she was a good
reader, a fast typist, and she knew the basics of

math, and she was smart and could learn whatever she needed to learn. The fact was, her reading alone made her better educated than half the people I know who are college graduates, but her lack of formal schooling did have an unfortunate side effect in that she has the same inferiority streak in her that a lot of folks who never finish school have, and had an inordinate respect for anybody with a lot of education, even if they don't deserve it and know less than she does. If she ever runs into an ax murderer who is also a college professor, we're in deep trouble.

The cure, at least, worked. She loved the work, had his files straightened out in no time, found out how little money they really had, but the cases he got she worked on, too, and became good at stakeouts and at making endless phone calls for data. She also went on a diet and took judo and karate lessons at the "Y" and from one of those Korean karate mills that have popped up all over. She got to brown belt, which makes her formidable and gives her confidence in the streets, anyway. All those black-female-avenger films, I guess. She's also a very good shot, although even now she's only licensed to carry a pistol when performing a task for a client, and then only when hired as essentially a guard.

She saw herself in much the same way her father had seen himself and the business. He had spent his life battling prejudice and doing the best job possible, and she saw herself as showing that not just a black but a black woman was as good in this profession as any man.

Then, one day, the case of a lifetime walked in the door in the form of a chief aide to the Reverend Billy Thomas. Thomas was one of those

superman types—young, personable, golden-voiced
degrees in divinity and law, a family whose
power in the black community came from
decades of fighting for equal rights and justice. . . . Well, you know the sort. He was in
Philadelphia, and he was about to run for city
council in a district that was about fifty-fifty in
racial makeup but had always been represented
by an Italian. He was convinced that his oppo-
nent had organized-crime ties, and that to break
him loose from his sixteen-year seat they'd have
to get something on him they could use in the
papers. They could have hired a bunch of big
shots, but they wanted to use somebody who was
black and totally independent of any larger companies. If the colonel came up with something
really useful, it was worth twenty-five thousand
dollars to the campaign, and he got a grand as
up-front expense money.

The colonel was good at his job. If he hadn't
clung so desperately to his failing independent
company and had gone with one of the big
Philadelphia concerns, he could have made it big.
This one, however, was different; a last miracle
from heaven. It not only paid well, but if he could
bring this off, the resulting publicity from his
success—where bigger and better companies had
failed—would bring him so much business he'd
have to hire assistants and get good office space.

For the first couple of days, he was very excited
about what he was finding, but he used Brandy
only as chauffeur on occasion and for random
checks from cop and lawyer sources. She couldn't
follow the thrust of his investigation from that,
and he was pretty close-mouthed. It wasn't that
he was trying to exclude her; it was just that this

case was everything he'd gotten into the business to do, and for a right moral cause. Soon, though, his elation turned to frowns and gloom; he was finding information on the councilman's ties far too easily and there were disturbing undercurrents. Telling her he'd know once and for all after a night's work, he'd left.

They found his body, with five bullets in it, floating in the Schuylkill River the next day. The cops said it was an obvious mob hit, but could not tie the councilman into it. Brandy buried her father, then went to work. She dug, probed, traced, deciphered her father's notes; and because she knew his sources and knew how he thought, she began to reconstruct his movements and learn what he had learned. Eventually she came to the same conclusions her father had: there were clear trails to mob money on the part of the councilman—too clear. So clear you needed only a legislative aide and not a private dick to find them. The fact was, most Italian big shots, like Jewish big shots and Methodist big shots, had inevitably crossed paths again and again with bad elements. It was almost as if somebody had already traced out all those paths for the councilman and then filled in the blanks showing sinister motives when, say, the councilman met a mob godfather at a Columbus Day dinner, or belonged to the same Knights of Columbus lodge as a couple of mob men.

The fact was, the old Italian wasn't clean, but he was as clean as a city hack politician can get. There was, however, a mob connection in the race. The Reverend Billy Thomas looked very much like a wholly owned and operated subsidiary. When it was clear to them that her father knew this and only needed confirmation, they had acted, setting up an informant's meet late that night, one that was to turn over incriminating documents. The colonel had his own sense of moral outrage, and was even more upset that this would be pulled by his own people and others he admired and trusted. He also was smart enough to know that the headlines from busting the Reverend Billy would be every bit as good as the ones from busting an Italian. They knew it, too. They hadn't taken any chances.

With single-minded determination and solid detective work she broke the case, and proved to the Philadelphia cops how the incriminating evidence on the councilman was manufactured. They were delighted and pulled out all the stops to do the rest. They never got the actual triggerman, but when they began to get the real goods on the Reverend Billy, he began to get the sweats. Somebody behind him didn't trust him, either. While this was still unfolding, an armed band of intruders broke into his home and killed him— during a robbery, of course. It was only a surprising coincidence that he was to meet the next day with federal prosecutors to cut a deal.

The results were not, however, what Brandy would have expected. She had proved herself to both herself and the world, but the only mention of even the agency in the papers was that her father had been killed by mobsters linked to the reverend. The Philadelphia cops were highly impressed with her, but it wouldn't do to admit that a twenty-one-year-old black female high-school dropout had broken a case they couldn't. Her own family and circle of friends, however, almost completely cut her off. She was a "traitor" to the black race; her old man deserved what he got for trying to bring down a black leader. So what if the rev was crooked? They all were. At least he was *our* crook. Business fell to zero. Even those who didn't know a thing about it were not about to hire a girl like her working alone.

Interestingly, the only people who seemed to have no ax to grind with her were the crooks. She sold the house in west Philadelphia and moved into a studio apartment in an old section of Camden near the office. She paid off a lot of bills and lived on the rest for a while. And, although it was sparse and didn't pay very well, she actually got a few clients—all from the wrong side of the law. Loan sharks out looking for deadbeats and not able to run them down; guard jobs at illicit gambling dens; finding goods on cops who arrested the wrong people. Not big money, but it helped. The cops, too, used her on occasion, which is what had brought me there. She had deep sources among the small potatoes of the underworld, and while she was not about to squeal on them she was occasionally useful in digging for major crimes in places the cops just couldn't look.

When I met her, she was pulling in just enough money to keep in business, but she'd have made more by closing it and going on welfare, in real cash terms. She was her father's daughter; she couldn't give up the dream no matter how impossible it was, and she'd managed to make herself just useful enough to both cops and crooks that she was reasonably safe, and the local junkies knew that she didn't have anything anyway and was a bit too dangerous to tangle with. The only thing was, the cops and crooks both knew they didn't have to give her much; just barely enough to keep going. What kept her going was her dream, her felt obligation to her father, and the fact that she was good at the job and she knew it.

The grimness of reality had made her withdraw into something of a fantasy shell, though. She didn't date. She had contacts, not friends. That's when I met her.

Of course, it was timing on my part, too. My dad had finally died after years of inactivity, and my mother lasted only six months after that. I could have made use of the old-boy network through the synagogues and social organizations, but I hadn't been to *shul* or belonged to any of those things since I was eighteen. There was nobody, really, but Uncle Max, and I already told you about him.

So, anyway, two people who really needed somebody and were in the same line of work, more or less, but were socially unlikely to ever come together had, through the Fates, done so. I kind of got a taste of things just hitting a bar or restaurant with her and seeing the kinds of funny reactions and sideways looks. It didn't matter if it was a black place or a white place, it was all the same.

Oh, yeah—about that kiddie-porn and kidnap case. Well, we firmed up that the old hotel was the place where pedophiles of all races, creeds, and colors met in the area, and we linked our distributor to not only the hotel but also to, would you believe, a professional baby photographer in Cherry Hill. An undercover cop then made the connections and infiltrated the network.

He chose the easy way, setting up a kiddie-prostitution meet and then picking one of the two we were looking for out of photos kept in a nice family album. The kid—the girl—was all fancied up and brought to the hotel, but they smelled a rat, somehow, at the last minute, and we could sense it. There were squad cars around ready to make a move on the undercover man's signal, but it just didn't happen.

I was pretending to doze in the lobby, dressed like a bum and smelling of cheap booze, and Brandy was all dressed up like a hooker, all made-up and really underdressed, cigarette dangling from her lips, and perched sexily on the edge of an end table leafing through a magazine. Both of us looked totally natural in that cesspool. We saw them bring in the kid and I was shocked at how they'd made her up, and even more by her glassy eyes and automatic behavior. The undercover guy came in a half-hour later and went straight up to the room, but a lot of time passed. Too much. Finally Brandy read my mind and sauntered over.

"You take the desk clerk and call in the Marines," she whispered, as if coming on to me. "I'm going up and see what's wrong."

I didn't like that. "Let me go up."

She gave me a kiss—the first time she'd ever done that. "You just go do what I say. I'll be all right."

Yeah. *All right* is not the word for it. She swished and swayed on too-high heels over to the old elevator and I made my way over to the desk. I hate guns, but lives were at stake. I didn't want to risk identifying myself first; some of these places have floor buttons for warning signals.

The clerk was sitting back in a chair next to the old-fashioned switchboard reading the racing news. I checked my back, pulled my .38, and said, "Real quiet now, you be a statue. Police." He started to make a move and I was behind there and cracking him in the face with the gun in no time. I had been right—there were three buttons to the right of the switchboard, out of view of the desk area. He hadn't gotten a chance to push any of them. I picked up his phone and dialed a special number. "Come on in. It's going down wrong," I said, and that was that. I then looked around. A half a dozen hookers, bums, and junkies were around that place and not one of them even deigned to notice what I was doing.

The trouble was, after five minutes the cops didn't seem to be noticing, either. I decided we'd been had and ran up the stairs. When the desk bastard woke up he could push all the buttons he wanted.

Brandy had been listening at doors on the third floor, but just as I saw her there was the unmistakable sound of a shot from one of them and she ran to it, reaching in her purse and taking out the biggest damned handgun I ever saw. She blew the lock off, then kicked open the door but kept her back to the wall, very professionally. There were screams and shrieks inside the room, and when Brandy saw me she whirled and plunged right into that mess.

The bastards had gone down the fire escape probably before she'd blown the lock off, leaving the kid screaming there and one very badly wounded detective. I got to him and he opened his eyes, saw me, and groaned. "Setup," he

managed. "They knew. . . . They wanted *me*. . . .
Where the hell's the backup?"

That's what I wanted to know.

By now the hotel resembled a cemetery, and
not from the bodies. At the first shot the place
had erupted like Mount Saint Helens, spewing its
human garbage all to hell and gone before the
real cops got there. Not even the deskman was
there. I got down there, called for an ambulance,
then called the Vice tactical number. The sergeant seemed very surprised to hear from me.

"What the fuck you doing there *tonight?*" he
roared. "We got it set up for *tomorrow* night!"

"Like hell! Your man was here and now he's
bleeding his guts out on the floor upstairs. We
were here, and so were the bastards and the girl.
I called the ambulance—I can hear it coming
now. We were set up, you son of a bitch!"

"Hey, man, take it easy! Yeah, it was on for
tonight, but we got orders at roll call direct from
on high that it was off until tomorrow."

"Then you got a high leak who might just have
gotten your man blown away. Patrol units are
just coming in the door now, along with the
ambulance." I told the floor and room number to
them and they didn't wait, they went right up.
"You want a bad cop who's a cop killer, you find
out who was on the other end of that tactical
phone number I called when this went down. You
call Internal Affairs and get them moving *now!*
Either that or you retire before you find a hole in
you!"

They got the undercover man to the hospital,
and he made it, minus one lung and the use of his
legs. They took the kid into Juvenile, and after a
lot of questioning got much in the way of where

the kids were being held and how it all worked, but in spite of fast raids they came up short. The word was out and everything had moved and dug in.

Internal Affairs finally traced the leak to a desk sergeant and his girlfriend in Communications. I don't envy them their stay in New Jersey's less-than-luxurious prison system, surrounded by folks who just *love* cops. At the price of one good cop's lung and legs we got one of the kids back, and state police finally nailed a bunch of small-fry and the photographer, but that was that. The distributor's still in business, still living in a fancy Cherry Hill home with the twin BMWs and the ideal American family, and somewhere the other kids are still in hell. That's the way the business goes, and why I was more than ready to quit it.

I found myself, at the end of that wild night, just sitting there on that creaky couch in the lobby and trying not to think. Brandy came up behind me and began massaging my shoulders. "Want to go get a drink?" she asked.

"Yeah. Any distilleries nearby?"

I still looked like a bum and she looked like a hooker, but there were several diners with bars attached in Camden where even that wouldn't attract attention if you showed money, and she picked one.

"Who did you think you were up there?" I grumbled. "The Ebony Avenger or maybe Supergirl? They pay *cops* to do that, and train them."

"I'm just now getting the shakes over it," she admitted. "Still, those cops they pay weren't there, and that little girl and that undercover cop were. It just sorta clicked and I didn't even do no thinking about it. The truth is, even though I'm scared about it now, I really *enjoyed* it. I mean, I—we—saved two lives tonight. That's more than I done in this job in all those years. I don't know. Maybe I should just get my diploma and be a cop."

"It's just as boring as what you're doing, only it pays regular," I told her. "For the pay and perks, though, you spend ninety percent of your time playing politics or getting stepped on." I paused. "You did good tonight, kid, even if you did scare me out of a year's growth and make the bald spot bigger."

"Huh? I *did*? Scare you, I mean? Why?"

" 'Cause you're one of the good guys in a world full of garbage," I responded. "Maybe because you're making about thirty cents an hour out of my payoff fund for this and you still put those lives over your own." The booze was getting to me a little, and I was bolder than usual. "Maybe it's because in that outfit you're the cutest, sexiest black bombshell I ever seen."

Well, you can figure the rest. We went back to her place, and went at it all through the night. I had to. She pointed out that her conscience wouldn't allow her to throw any white man out in that neighborhood at that hour.

Even though the case was wrapped, I only lived and worked an hour or less away, and we kept seeing each other. It was amazing how well we meshed, considering just how different our backgrounds had been. Oh, sure, she loved to dance and I couldn't dance a step, but that was minor. She liked the Phillies and hated basketball, same as me. Neither of us could ever get worked up

over which dumb millionaires with glandular
conditions could put a ball in a basket without
jumping. My taste for jazz was matched by her
fondness for blues music. We both liked spicy
ethnic foods and neither of us could get excited
over a fried chicken. We even liked the same kind
of books—murder mysteries and detective novels,
I admit, both old and new, where detectives did
the kinds of things real detectives only dream
about.

The truth was, I couldn't think of much but her
when I wasn't with her, and she was getting the
same way about me, as it turned out. She couldn't
move in with me, though, because she couldn't be
a long-distance call from her office and her
contacts and stay in business at all, so we found
an old but serviceable one-bedroom apartment
in the old suburbs of Camden and moved in
together; but my hours plus the commute and her
erratic schedule didn't leave us much time together. I tried to get her to quit, since with her
overhead, small as it was, she wasn't bringing in
much money anyway, take the high school equivalency exam, and maybe go to college, but she
would have none of that. And that's how I wound
up quitting the Bristol police and becoming a full
partner, such as it was, in Spade & Marlowe.

We got married shortly after that in the courthouse, and honeymooned as fancy as we could
afford—Atlantic City. The moment they discovered that I'd married a *shvartse*, my old friends
always had something else to do and never
called. Her few friends weren't much different,
particularly the men. Uncle Max never returned
another phone call. Even the Associated Jewish
Charities stopped sending form letters asking me

to contribute. She also took my last name; something that pleased my ego, although it wasn't anything I was hung up about or even expected. She just loved the idea of somebody who looked like her being Brandy Horowitz.

We did get some new friends, though. Every time we came across another salt-and-pepper couple there seemed a kind of instant bond, although the nature of the bond was never mentioned. The fact is, though, that in the five years we've been married I've never been unfaithful to her and never really wanted anybody else. We were like two kids and we didn't give a damn. Even the looks don't bother me anymore. Knowing just how hand-to-mouth life would be, and how insecure it would be, I'd still do it all over again with no regrets.

The funny thing is, after I came on with the agency, business picked up. Not great; maybe we cleared fourteen grand a year the best year after expenses, but it picked up. I don't know what it is, but poor black people want a white when they have trouble with the authorities. I guess it's just because the system is run by whites and they figure (wrongly) that a white guy can talk their language and cut through the bullshit, but it picked up. The usual stuff of real P.I. work— divorces, money transfers, security analysis for the little businesses, that kind of thing. Noting that you can reduce holdups by half by just painting the curb in front of a store yellow, for example. The city never knows if it's legit or not, but while it doesn't help crooks fleeing on foot, or local burglars, it sure as hell makes holdup men uneasy to park in a yellow zone waiting for a getaway. *That* cops notice. So, instead of taking a risk, you hold up the drugstore down the street without a yellow curb.

That kind of stuff is readily available to franchises and chains, but little mom-and-pop stores never think that way and it's cheap to pay a fee to somebody like me to show it to them. They save more than my small fee in the first holdup they don't have.

So now Brandy's out in the twelve-year-old rustbucket that's all the transportation we have, looking over clerks at 7-Elevens, and I'm sitting there getting worried. It wasn't that she was out alone; she was pretty well equipped to take care of that. The fact was, she had really poor vision for somebody that young, poor enough that I wouldn't let her drive me to the hospital if I were dying, and certainly poor enough that the next time she had to take a driver's eye test she'd flunk, and I just knew that sooner or later she was going to crack up the car and herself with it. She has a pair of glasses but won't wear them, and they're out of date anyway.

Finally, the phone rings, and I pick it up, thinking by now it's the cops or the morgue.

"Hey! I got him!" she said excitedly. "That asshole who gave us the tip don't know a Seven Eleven from a Wawa Thrift Market, that's all!"

I was relieved, but I didn't want to show it. "So where are you now?"

"Down halfway to the airport. How much cash money you got?"

I checked. "About twelve bucks. Why?"

" 'Cause I'm blowin' my last nine on gas and I'm starving. Pick you up in, oh, forty minutes and we'll hit a drive-through or something. Guess that's all we can afford on that money. All the Jews in the world and I got to pick the one with twelve bucks. Gotta go or I won't be able to pay for this call and get 'nuff gas to get there. Bye."

I sat back and sighed. Two days of combing those stores, and after expenses we might get a hundred bucks out of it. Worse, there wasn't anything else ongoing at the moment. Things had been slow, real slow, for months now and we were up to our necks in debt, and behind in almost everything. We needed to clear about two grand a month to keep up and still survive at the poverty level; the past four months we'd made a *total* of about three. We'd had slack times before, but we always had a little money from my withdrawn pension funds or something to cover things, but they were all gone now. There was nothing wrong with us as detectives, but things were so low-class now that it'd take a big chunk of dough to pump new life into the agency. One of us would eventually have to take a job outside the business; we couldn't even afford to get sick at this rate. Brandy had looked around, but found offers only for menial jobs, cleaning and fast food and that kind of thing, all minimum wage and no benefits. Me, I was more than ten years her senior, and there wasn't much of a job market these days for a guy my age whose only qualifications were being an ex-cop and a failed P.I. Somehow I felt I'd go on welfare before I'd get a job selling shoes.

The time was coming, though, when we'd have to grow up and be adults. It might already have come. Being good wasn't enough. It had never been enough. It was who you knew and what you

had that counted. More than once I wished the
Air Force had decided to make me an accountant
or a medic or something. Right now I could
forget the twin BMWs and the big house in the
suburbs. I wasn't ambitious and material things
had never much mattered to me; still, I'd settle
for being lower middle class.

I figured we'd talk it out tonight. It wouldn't be
the first time, but we'd never been this far down
and this behind before. We were approaching the
point where we could never catch up, and fast.

2.

Something Big

Sitting around a little apartment-building laundry room in your underwear on a hot, muggy night at about three in the morning feeding quarters into a Korean War vintage washer and dryer and watching the moths dive-bomb the lone light bulb was not exactly the most romantic of situations, but it increased my already deep depression.

One of the craziest curses of being poor is that you get fat. That's because the kind of stuff that's cheapest to buy is full of fat and starches. Most of me stayed automatically thin, so it all went to the gut. I had three rolls of fat there, which I named Goodyear, Firestone, and Michelin. Brandy was five five and admitted to weighing two-twenty, all of it in her breasts, hips, and thighs. I didn't mind—she was still sexy to me—but neither of us had any clothes that really fit or any money to get new ones. My shirts were on their third set of buttons and still opened themselves when I sat down, and I split my pants so much there's nothing in the seats but repairs. I wasn't sure I could even get into my one old suit if I had to. Brandy's whole wardrobe consisted of jeans she could barely get into and tee shirts so faded you couldn't tell what color they started out being, and that old hooker's outfit she'd used way back when (but since, only over my dead body). It wasn't that we were so poor we couldn't spring for new clothes, it was just that at twenty bucks a shirt, thirty bucks for pants, never mind her wardrobe, we'd be up around five hundred bucks, and when you start thinking that way the money goes elsewhere.

I sighed. "Babe, we got to talk."

"You got that surrender look in your eyes," she said accusingly.

"Yeah, but a good general knows when. We owe Corbone Properties seventeen hundred bucks for back rent and utilities on the office. We owe this dump about seven hundred more. The car's so bad, if we take it to the mechanic's he'll pronounce it dead—that is, if we paid him what we owed him so he'd even look at it. We got another two, three thousand bucks in other bills, and we got eight hundred and fifty-two dollars in the bank. And none of that counts what we owe the IRS. It's over, babe. I got the word today. End of the month, pay up or out at the office. End of the month, pay up or out here. Peter Pan time's over. They're ordering us to grow up."

She sat down and put her arms around me. "I know. I didn't know 'bout the landlord, but I knew the rest. Can't run even what we have, with no phone and no office. I guess I knew it was comin' all along. I just kept *hopin'*, somehow, that something would walk in. Something *big*, you know? It ain't gonna walk in, though, is it?"

I shook my head. "No, something big wouldn't even find the address. I got a call from Joe Wilkins down in Cape May County the other day." Joe was one of the salt-and-pepper brotherhood; he was black, his wife was white. The difference was that Joe was an accountant and had a real-estate license. "He knows what shape we're in, and he remembered us. They're opening one of those fancy beachfront condo developments down on the Delaware shore, and they're looking for a resident security supervisor. It only pays about fifteen grand a year, but it comes with a furnished two-bedroom apartment, medical plan, all that. It was designed with an older couple in mind, but he thought of us. It isn't bad. On the water, and the only expenses would be food and clothing."

She thought about it. "Where'd you say it was?"

"Just north of Rehoboth Beach. South Delaware shore."

"I never been down there, but I guess it's like Wildwood or something. Pretty seasonal."

"Yeah, five months of intensive activity and seven months of presiding over a pretty morgue, although there'll be a few permanent residents— well-heeled retirees and the like—and some sailor nuts will be there on the weekends even in lousy weather."

She sighed. "Not much for me down there, though. Funny—I never thought of myself as a housewife. Not 'til recently, anyway. Still, I been doin' a lot of thinkin' lately, and maybe it ain't so bad. I look around that old neighborhood and this dump and I ask what I been clinging to all this time and what do I got to show for it? I shoulda dropped it all six years ago, when we first moved in together. We'd have a nice apartment, maybe a couple of kids, and you'd still be a steady cop. Who am I kiddin'? You ain't my daddy, and I ain't, neither. His dream was worse than dead before he was. It was worse than that. It was out of date, like Sam Spade and Philip Marlowe and the Continental Op. Like Shaft and Magnum and all them others. All I did was drag you down here with me."

I hugged and kissed her. "You didn't drag *anybody*. I came because I met the prettiest, sexiest, smartest lady I ever knew who had the same crazy dreams I did and I fell in love with her. I still am." I kissed her, and we got real passionate for a while.

We took the clothes back up to the apartment and flopped down on the bed. "You're taking this better than I thought you would," I noted.

"I—I been doin' a lot of thinking lately. I saw the bills, I saw the bank account, and I know what business we don't have. I been tryin' to sort things out in my mind, you know. There's some that can be Supergirl, but maybe I'm just not one of 'em. Just goin' through Philadelphia suburbia, I got to lookin' at nice houses and apartments, seein' families in the stores, like that. I got a great husband I'm in love with, and I never really saw how *important* that was to me. You gave it up for me, now I'll give it up for you. Ain't no big sacrifice anymore, anyway. This don't sound like much work. We'll be together most of the time, nice apartment near the ocean."

I looked her in her big brown eyes. "What do you *really* want me to do, babe? I'll do whatever you say."

"I want to be with you. I want to be your wife

and have a whole passel of black Horowitzes that'll confuse the living shit out of people. I think I always really knew that. I just wanted to make a *go* of it, just for a while, to see if I could really do it. Ever since I nailed Daddy's killers, I been really *scared* to be anything else. I—I never told you this, but I got that hooker outfit one time because I was down this low, and I thought that might have to be what I'd do. Johnny Redlegs—you remember him—he was workin' on me when you showed up, and I was almost desperate enough to take him up on it. You and that case were the only things that kept me out of it."

I remembered Redlegs. He was a pimp who gave new meaning to the word *stereotypical*. Pink Cadillac, fur coat, floppy hat, and a fairly big stable. About the only thing that set him apart from his competitors was that he had a reputation for not being violent with the girls and depending on heroin to keep them loyal subjects. I tried to imagine Brandy out there now, age twenty-seven, turning two or three tricks a night for her daily fix, and the trouble was, I *could* imagine it.

I could also, for the first time, really understand her almost instant attraction to me. I was a savior whose background and tastes reminded her of her father, and I was there in the nick of time.

"I'll call Joe," I told her. "Then we'll spend the rest of the month packing up and cleaning up the few loose ends of the business, and put the agency in bankruptcy, where at least we'll get out from under those debts. We'll get some new clothes and pay up on this dump if they let us out of the lease, and then that will be that."

"Yeah," she agreed. "That will be that."

It was about nine days later and we were well along. There wasn't much salvageable in the office, but there were old client files to either destroy or put in a safe place—we decided to give them to those we could find and to burn the rest—and a few other details to go through. The place in Delaware wasn't finished yet, but we were welcome to come down the first of the month and they'd put us up in a motel until the first units were ready, about twenty days after that. It had originally been scheduled to open in the early spring, but somebody had forgotten what the sea does to beaches in winter storms.

Brandy actually seemed more cheerful than she had in a long time. She was almost a changed woman, but that wasn't a big surprise. She might brood and worry and think everything through a hundred times, but once she decided something, that was *it*, and she'd decided she was going to be Mrs. Horowitz by the seashore. For the first time, she was cutting loose from the burdens of her father's dreams, and it didn't seem so painful. I wasn't overjoyed—I still would have preferred a marginal business of my own in the city to something like this—but the agency wasn't even close to the margin.

And then, almost at the last minute, Something Big walked through the door.

Something Big was actually a skunk everybody called Little Jimmy Nkrumah. He was actually built like a fullback for the Eagles and had a face that looked like it'd played one too many games.

I'm not sure about the *Jimmy*, but the *Nkrumah* wasn't the truth, either. He wasn't a Muslim—he wasn't anything, I don't think—but he'd changed his name to something African sounding because it helped his image and his business.

Little Jimmy was a loan shark, or at least that was the part of him everybody knew about. He ran the Star of Africa Finance Company, a little hole-in-the-wall that made legitimate loans— few—by financing some of the little black-owned furniture and appliance stores in Camden, but his real business was with the folks who couldn't get credit on a bet. When those folks borrowed from friendly and understanding Little Jimmy, they got a rate around ten percent per month and the collateral was their legs, arms, eyes, spouses, and children. We knew that he was connected up with organized crime—even loan sharking in *this* part of town didn't get you a fifty-thousand-dollar Mercedes sports car and a house in the exclusive suburb where *he* lived—and probably was into more, but we didn't have much to do with him. Brandy knew that it was Little Jimmy who'd sugggested her dad to the Reverend Billy.

Little Jimmy dressed fairly conservatively, but the suits were hand tailored and only of the best material. I think he had three people on the staff just to get rid of scuffs on his shoes. His voice was abnormally high and silky, but very cultured, sort of as if Stepin Fetchit had gone to Harvard. We just stared at him, surprised he'd even walk into a dump like the office without sending ahead a squad of cleaners and shampooers.

"I hear you're closing down," he oozed, sounding for all the world like a black Don Corleone.

"Too bad. I mean, the little lady's daddy's last legacy and all that."

"Yeah, well thanks for the sympathy, Nkrumah," she responded, bitterness now in her tone. "You sure tried to help things along."

"If you're referring to the unfortunate outcome of your father's case, I can only say, as I always said, that I was really trying to do him a favor. I owed him one, but that's another story. I was truly distressed at how it all came out, but who would have thought that *anybody* could be that much of a straight arrow? Meaning no disrespect, but your daddy was handed a golden opportunity late in life on a silver platter. All he had to do was take it, and money, fame, and political connections would be his."

"He was too good for the con," Brandy shot back. "He really *believed* in the Reverend Billy."

"To be so naive at his age and experience was the cause of his downfall. I offered him the golden platter; he chose his own fate. It was no doing of mine that he did so."

Brandy was losing her temper fast. "Some folks would rather be dead than turn into house niggers like you!"

The insult stung, but only briefly. Little Jimmy wasn't paying a social call.

"What do you want here, Nkrumah?" I asked him. "If you're gonna offer to bankroll us to keep us afloat, forget it. You got your own boys to do your dirty work, and we couldn't afford your interest."

"It isn't the interest I'm worried about, it's the principles," the loan shark replied. "Are you like your daddy, or are you interested in some real gold, no strings attached, if you don't mind getting a little dirty in the process."

I looked at Brandy and she looked back at me, and both of us had identical frowns and shrugs. "Go on," she said to him. "It don't cost nothin' to listen."

Little Jimmy smiled, which was not a reassuring gesture. When Little Jimmy smiled, you felt like the worm just about to be dropped in the river.

"Would the potential of two hundred and twenty-five thousand dollars and no con job like the one they pulled on your daddy make you interested?"

It was my turn to gulp. Considering the pay at Ocean Estates, he was talking fifteen years' wages at least. "Keep going. You can kill half of Camden and part of Philadelphia with that kind of money, even now," I noted.

"Someone has absconded with two and a quarter million dollars of money that I was responsible for," Little Jimmy told us. "The finder's fee on the money is ten percent."

I sat down on the floor and found Brandy already there.

"How'd *you* get that much bread?" she asked him suspiciously.

He sighed. "What I tell you is death to repeat," he warned. "Still, I said I'd tell it all, and I see I *do* have your interest and maybe your principles, too. Money's like that, sometimes. The money is not mine. It belongs to a large multinational corporation that often makes the papers and is devoted to supplying the public with all the goods and services that people want but which they like to pretend are evil and so outlaw them. You know the company, I'm sure."

We did. It used to be a mostly Italian holding company with some Jewish members, but now it was strictly equal opportunity.

"The narcotics business in this area runs to billions a year," Nkrumah continued. "There's a heavy demand to meet. The dealings with the suppliers are strictly cash, now that even Switzerland and the Bahamas aren't totally safe anymore, and sometimes that amount is very large. Many big banks are involved, of course, but lately there's been a lot of heat on. A bunch of banks have been exposed, and it has been very costly. Lately we've gone to a system of small and intermediate suppliers, middlemen, between the big and small banks. This time it was my turn to help out with confusing the source and the destination, as it were. I took out a business loan for expansion at a major bank, and I was to invest the money, as it were, in a number of places. The loan would later be repaid, with interest—all aboveboard. Never mind where it went from me; you know what it came back as, and where the interest came from."

Yeah. Maybe a thousand percent interest over a short period from everybody from suburban middle-class junkies to Johnny Redlegs's girls. It was a pretty clear picture, and told us for the first time just where all that money Little Jimmy made really came from. It was kind of clever. Everybody, including the cops, knew Little Jimmy was a shark, but a little shark. Using a little crime to cover a big deal was subtle. It was probably worked out by computers or something.

The plan was deceptively simple. Little Jimmy was small potatoes, but he really could deal in millions without raising any red flags. Even a little outfit like his had several million in capital. He would take the loan for "investment" purposes and invest it, ostensibly in real estate and other ventures that looked solid but were actually fronts. They, in turn, would pay the suppliers through other dummy companies, and by paying large sums to companies for, say, excavations or engineering work that never actually was done or needed to be done. In return, the junk would come on up—or over or wherever it came from— and hit the streets in a movement that would be totally unconnected to Little Jimmy. The profits would be paid back through a totally different network that reached the same dummy sources, which would then repay Little Jimmy's investments with interest, and he'd repay the bank. In the meantime, the dummy companies would go on the block and be absorbed or bought out by holding companies, getting the rest of the money in the process, all neatly laundered and pressed and even on the tax books, although with that kind of money you could always find enough breaks to avoid the bulk of the taxes.

The weakness was that if you knew both ends, you might intercept things. This was known, but, considering the risks involved in bilking *that* corporation out of fifty bucks, let alone millions, it was considered acceptable, just as the loans Little Jimmy took out were really paid back since otherwise he'd be out of the loan-shark business in a hurry.

The loan had come in, from Tri-State Savings Fund, one of the bigger banks in the region and one of the first to get into interstate banking in a big way when they dropped the barriers to it, and Little Jimmy had then made his "investments,"

prudently investing no more than ten percent in
any one firm on a list of up-and-coming small
companies. The trouble was, the list was given to
him by the loan officer at Tri-State; it turned out
to be a very different list than the one Little
Jimmy was supposed to get. When the real
companies started contacting him about not getting their investments, Little Jimmy hit the roof
and quickly discovered what had happened. His
next problem was to keep his own bosses from
finding this out; they would take a dim view of
his blind obedience to the system and his failure
to verify everything. He quickly advanced two
and a quarter million of his own money, but he
was only really worth about three million—
only!—and much of that wasn't really liquid.

In other words, Little Jimmy had to take out a
real loan to cover the loan. By tax time, there
would be much interest in why he'd borrowed
five million—partly by mortgaging his house, his
cars, and his business—all to sink into specula-
tive companies with short lifespans.

Of course, when his share came back he'd still
have to repay the bank, and that would leave him
up to his eyeballs in hock. His godfather or chief
corporate officer or whatever might very well not
give him more than a scolding since the deal
went through anyway; but Little Jimmy knew a
lot of names and routings and the like, and would
be in a very tight squeeze later on, a squeeze his
bosses might just expect him to get out of by
making a deal. Little Jimmy remembered what
was the ultimate fate of the Reverend Billy. He
decided that it might be best if this . . . mistake
. . . was not reported or revealed to anyone else,
and to see if he could get at least some of his

money back, not to mention the fellow who was behind all those *other* dummy companies. He had, of course, put the word out that this fellow was no longer "reliable," but he wanted some of his own working on this. He couldn't trust his own people with the real story—somebody would blab across the river just for brownie points—and so he came to us. Not us alone, almost certainly, but here we were.

"So what's the name of this guy?" I asked him. "And why can't you find him?"

Little Jimmy sighed. "His name is Martin J. Whitlock the Fourth, and he is—*was*—chief operating officer at Tri-State. We're pretty certain that the business-loan officer who set me up was innocent. Just following the boss's orders. He didn't even know it wasn't a straightforward deal. Since then, Whitlock has disappeared, and nobody but me even seems to have noticed."

Brandy was still suspicious. "Why us? You got resources. You probably got all sorts of folks on this all over."

"It *is* a contest, I grant you that, but there's more to it. I think I owe you a shot at it simply because of our unfortunate past associations. Also, Whitlock has certain unsavory avocations in low sections where you two operate so well. And, of course, there's the fact that your cousin, Minnie Slusher, is the Whitlocks' live-in housekeeper."

"Ten to one he's not even in the country by now," I noted. "This is a cold trail from the start."

"Indeed, yes, it is somewhat cold, although all this has happened in just the last few days. The moment I learned of it was but three days ago, and Whitlock went to work that morning and did not return that evening. Trace him. Track him down. I don't care if he's in Brazil. You don't even personally have to recover the money. Just give me where he is, and we will do the recovering and you will get your finder's fee. Ten percent of everything we get back."

"A banker can really hide that kind of stuff easily," Brandy noted. "He's an expert at it, and that's small change to a dude like him."

"True, but a banker can also tell me where he hid it and how. Just give him to me."

"This will take real money to get anywhere," I noted. "You know how much we have."

"Yes, you must have a retainer," Little Jimmy agreed, and reached into his coat pocket. He brought out a wallet so overstuffed he lost ten pounds just taking it out, and he opened it and counted out a wad. "Five thousand dollars," he told us. "A retainer. Not a loan. All cash, no taxes, no reporting unless you want to. That—and these." He pulled out, so help me, two MasterCards and handed them over. One had my name on it, one had Brandy's. We kind of stared at them in wonder. Both were on the Tri-State Savings Fund.

"They're real, and they'll work," assured Nkrumah. "They are billed to a business I own. They're not approved for cash advances—you already have that—but they're good for purchases such as clothes and airline tickets. At a hundred dollars a day, I've hired you for the next fifty days. If you bring me a name sooner, the cards will be invalidated, but the retainer is yours. Naturally, though, the retainer and whatever is charged will come out of your percentage of whatever is recovered."

I stared at the money and the cards. "Yeah, but what if we don't turn him up? Or what if you don't recover before he croaks? What if one of the big boys finds him first? What happens then?"

"Then you cover the charges with whatever is left of the retainer and you keep the rest, if any. If there is a deficit, the balance still will not go below zero. You'll have nothing, but that's exactly what you have now."

He had a point, but the trail was growing colder by the hour.

"We have to talk this over," Brandy told him. "Leave this. If we take the case, time will be important. If we don't, we'll drop them by your office today."

Little Jimmy smiled again. "Oh, I know you will," he responded. "Good day." And, with that, he walked out, leaving that pile of bills and those two cards that were better than bills sitting on a box in front of us.

I looked at Brandy. "Well?"

"You think we really got a crack at this Whitlock dude?"

"No, but we'd always wonder if we didn't try. Ocean Estates isn't open yet; Joe was just doing us a favor. I can call him and tell him we'll be down later. That'd give us a month. I can't see any reason *not* to take it. Why? What's bothering you?"

"This. All this. Nobody with his underworld connections just waltzes in and hands over this kind of bread to two washed-up dicks on their way to the poorhouse. Remember, that same bad dude set up my father with a twisted scheme."

"You think he's using us in a setup, too? I dunno. This isn't the same kind of case. This is 'find a man.' Classic P.I. work. I don't know if his story is true or not, but the odds are Whitlock's into him or somebody anyway and skipped just ahead of them. What they do to him, or why, or even if there's no pot of gold at the end of this rainbow, it could make for a real challenging thirty days."

"Yeah, maybe, but Daddy thought his was a safe Something Big, too. If we're gonna go with this, you call Joe, but I'm gonna at least run down and unhock Daddy's gun."

A lot could be determined just on the phone, which hadn't yet been disconnected. Whitlock, Martin J., IV. Age: forty-seven. One of the blue bloods of Philadelphia society. Ancestors came on Penn's boat. Inherited a couple of million bucks. Harvard Business School, MBA, all the right clubs. Married Roberta Armbruster, of the came-over-on-the-Mayflower Armbrusters, added another million. Two kids: a son, Martin the Fifth, now in his freshman year at Harvard, and a daughter, Virginia, now at an exclusive prep school for future wives of aristocratic millionaires. The right blood, the right clubs, and several million in his own right. Why the hell would a guy like that stiff Little Jimmy in a con for two-plus million and split?

More to the point, why would a guy like that be a chief launderer for the hard-drug division of organized crime?

Part of the answer came in a listing of his holdings. It's amazing what you can do on a phone if you know what you're doing and have a decent acting voice. Give me four hours and somebody's name and address, and I'll tell you what perfume his wife wears, where he buys his clothes, who holds his mortgage, and his favorite restaurants—just for openers. It's incredible to me how porous the credit-card listings, check records, and credit-bureau files are to anybody who knows the right language and the right approach.

The motive for stiffing Little Jimmy was simple enough. When you think of the very rich, you think of them rolling in dough and lighting cigars with hundred-dollar bills. The truth is, most of the very rich don't have enough spare change for a Big Mac at McDonald's. The magic word is *liquidity*. His money was invested in stocks, bonds, certificates, real estate, you name it. His money didn't even go to him; he had a money-management firm that collected his interest and clipped his coupons and paid all his bills for him. The only real liquid asset he had was a Super NOW checking account with about ten grand in it for petty cash. The rich have the most valuable thing for living rich while their money works: almost unlimited credit. They just charge everything and the bills are sent to the business or the money managers or whatever. Must be nice.

He must not have figured on Little Jimmy wising up so fast. He *did* have reservations on a flight to San Francisco for next Sunday, but he hadn't even picked up the tickets yet. So now he's got over two million bucks in very liquid cash and convertibles, but he wasn't able to make good on his planned getaway. He couldn't use credit cards; that's the easiest way to be traced. This guy wasn't used to paying real cash, let alone using money to hide out from the mob. Still, he wasn't dumb. Even the richest don't get nearly straight *A*'s at Harvard, they just use their money and connections to get hired over the poor slobs that do. But this guy was smart, real smart.

A check with the Philadelphia courthouse showed that he was real popular, too. One of my old contacts who still worked there told me that there were a bunch of federal examiners and marshals in town, and that Tri-State was already getting a going-over. That explained even more. If he thought the connection with the mob was about to be exposed and himself implicated, he'd have vanished right off. In fact, that may have saved him, although it made my life more complicated. The odds were that he might *not* know Little Jimmy was onto him yet; he might just have smelled the feds and bolted early. That saved his life, but it meant that the feds, at least, were looking for him right now. Worse, he was still an amateur at disappearing acts, and he'd had to panic, bolt, and run. That meant it would be messy and leave trails even an idiot or a fed could follow, and they had the lead.

That still left the question of why he was in this mess in the first place. Not that guys like him were honest; it was just that they generally let the underlings do the dirty work and take the big falls.

It took about three hours to get the file together on him, and that was just about the time Brandy returned with a whole mess of packages. These proved to be some shirts and pants for me and a small wardrobe for her, all off-the-rack stuff. She'd tried on only a couple of hers, and guessed at my sizes, but she was dead on. The sleeves on the sport coat were a little long, but it was a damn sight better than what I had at home.

I was a little surprised when she stayed with her old jeans and sandals and faded shirt. "I called Minnie," she explained, "and she's expecting me. Any black folks in *that* neighborhood don't look like Aunt Jemima are arrested for suspicion of burglary. You still got that old cop ID with the fake shield?"

I nodded. "Uh huh."

"Then you take the missus and I'll take Minnie."

We walked down to the street, and I was startled to see a new-looking Ford parked there behind ours. Brandy handed me the keys.

"You didn't charge *this!*"

She laughed. "Sure I did. At Avis. Looks a lot like the cars the detectives drive. You take the front and it; I'll take our car and the servants' entrance. We'll meet back at the Midway Diner and compare notes while we buy each other dinner."

Whitlock's place was a simple one-story brick rancher off a long driveway in Ardmore, one of the richer suburbs of Philadelphia. The fact is, the place didn't look all that big from the front, but if you started walking around you found out it went back a ways. Like maybe Pittsburgh.

There was only a single Mercedes wagon in the driveway, but even Little Jimmy could tell me that Whitlock's two-door sports Mercedes coupe was still parked in his marked space in the Tri-State lot downtown. I put on my glasses, which I normally use only for reading, and was just going to the door when I saw our two-tone Chevy come up and pull around to the side and Brandy get out and walk on back. I rang the bell and stood there awhile, wondering whether it was that nobody was home or only that with the housekeeper occupied, it was beneath the dignity of a Whitlock to open her own door.

It wasn't. I guess even blue bloods get caught in the john.

She was tall and very slender, with a conservative hairdo, with makeup even in the late afternoon with no place to go. "Yes?"

"Mrs. Whitlock? I'm Sam Horowitz, with the Department of the Treasury. Is your husband at home?"

"You know he isn't. Your people were here earlier today."

I harrumphed apologetically. "Well, there are two separate agencies involved in this, and I guess you understand the bureaucracy." She finally invited me in, and we had a pleasant if inconsequential talk. I did finally get to see a photo of him; a distinguished-looking man, much younger in appearance than his years would indicate, with short, peppery hair, light complexion, blue or gray eyes, clean shaven, no moustache, beard, or even sideburns, which look a bit out of date these days. I have bushy sideburns myself, but that was overcompensation for what was missing on top. I know what I look like with a beard, though, and forget it.

I didn't expect to ever get back here—or be able to, once the feds found out I was here at all—so I decided to play a chance card or two and see if I passed Go.

"Mrs. Whitlock, I know how hard this must be for you, but we have some evidence that your husband was involved with organized crime. Laundering drug money, to be precise. That's what this is all about, and why we think he left. We think he stole some mob money and skipped."

She was not completely surprised by this, but some of it was new. "Oh, my. They said something about the Mafia or something, but I find that hard to accept. *Drug* money, you say! He—he was on the Mayor's Council for Stamping Out Drug Abuse. He always *hated* drugs. Wouldn't permit a smoker in the house, and had to be ready for the hospital before he'd even take an aspirin."

"If that's true, then it makes even less sense," I told her honestly. "I mean, he had a nice family, money, position. . . . Why do it? He wasn't a thrill seeker, was he? Somebody who might do it just out of boredom?"

"Oh, my, no! He never even drove the speed limit in spite of his sports car!"

"Then they had something on him. Some kind of blackmail. Do you have any idea what they had that they could blackmail him with?"

"Certainly not! His life was an open book!" But I could tell by her eyes that she was hiding something.

There wasn't much more I could press, and I kept seeing the real feds coming back any minute now, so I made my apologies and my sympathies, palmed a cameo portrait of him from an end table, and bid her good-bye. Our car was still in the driveway, but I wasn't going to wait for Brandy.

The tail wasn't hard to spot; they *wanted* to be noticed, and on the winding little road leading back down to the expressway at Conshohocken, there wasn't much chance of shaking or evading them if I wanted to. I knew who it was, and when we got to the bottom just before the entrance to the Schuylkill, the flashing light went up on top and he pulled me over into the parking lot of a rustic-looking restaurant or catering joint.

I got out and leaned easily against the car, waiting for them. There were two there, but one was on the radio while the other glared at me, then finally got out and came up. "Can I see your driver's license and registration, please?"

"Can I see your ID first?" I responded. "I want to know who I'm dealing with and I got a right."

He reached into a breast pocket and did a quick flip of a case too fast for me to read, so I reached in and did the same damned thing. He reached for it and I said, "Uh uh. You show me yours open and I'll show you mine."

He took it back out, looking pissed, and held it open. Marshall Kennedy. Neat first name. I wondered if it had influenced his eventual line of work. He wasn't a marshal, though; it was Drug Enforcement Administration.

I nodded. "Sam Horowitz, and I'm private, licensed in New Jersey," I told him truthfully.

He frowned. "So what was that shield you flashed?"

"My old ID with a regular shield. I use it like you do, to get into places easily. It's part of the job."

"You're looking for Whitlock." It wasn't a question, it was a statement. "Why?"

"I was hired to."

"By who?"

"You know I can't tell you that. I suspect, though, that it was by somebody who wanted to bring the whole weight of the feds and local cops down on me so they could free their own people to look for him."

He considered that. "I still want the name.

P.I.'s don't mean shit to me, and don't give me any shield-law crap. There's no federal law covering you. Besides, might be interesting to find out just who you told the little lady there you worked for. Impersonating an officer's good for a yanked license and maybe a year."

"Better a year than getting my brains blown out," I told him. "Be reasonable. I'll tell you what I know, short of violating my ethics and my right to life, and you see if you're happy. You know I'm the patsy in this. I knew it from the start, only the money was too good and I was flat broke."

"I'm listening."

I told him about Whitlock stealing mob money and putting the squeeze on the middleman. I also told him about what I'd learned so far, and that I hadn't yet figured out how he'd gotten sucked in in the first place.

He wasn't communicative in return, but I got the very distinct feeling that he didn't know, either. They were at the same point we were, in spite of their head start. He did, however, offer one *very* interesting new fact.

"He didn't leave the country. He called his wife this morning. Didn't talk long, so we couldn't get a trace, but it was definitely a local call. You wouldn't by any chance be carrying something he wants or needs, would you? If you are, you're aiding and abetting a federal fugitive and I'll slam you *real* hard if you don't come clean."

"I'm as clean as they come. Search away if you want."

He did, starting with me. "There's still a price tag in this jacket," he noted. "What'd you do? Raid Sears today?"

The car was given a good but not complete

going-over, since they'd had me in sight from leaving the front door and I sure hadn't had time to do much more than stuff something between the seats or like that. While they were still searching, night fell, and Brandy drove by in the car. I pretended not to notice, but I sure hoped she had.

The fed finally was as satisfied as he was going to get. "Okay, Horowitz. You're on my list now. You be where I want you when I want you, and you report anything you learn to me even before you tell your client. I'm letting you run only because I think you're what you say you are—a stalking horse. I have to say, though, that I don't like you very much. I don't give a damn about P.I.'s one way or the other as long as they stay out of my way, but if you're working for the ones he stiffed you're no better than they are. You're free only so long as you're useful, but to me you smell like an accessory, and that's the way it'll read if your client finds out something from you before I do. Get it?"

"I got it. Now I'm telling you to back off and give me some room. All you'll do is spook everything if you come along with your heavy boots like you did here. I don't care who gets him, but I want a crack."

Kennedy shrugged. "We'll keep a safe distance, don't worry. I'll even give you one lead, if you don't have it already. Not much, but it's a brick wall. He had a second life someplace. He'd be gone sometimes from home for weeks at a stretch, supposedly out of town on business, but the bank has no record of those trips or expenses for them. His marriage has been mostly name only for years."

I raised my eyebrows. "Mistress on the side?"

"If so, we can't find any trace of her. It's weird. He'd be at the bank sometimes but never leave the parking lot to go home. That's why nobody was surprised that his car stayed there overnight. Sometimes he'd take a leave of absence for a while, often up to a week every month, but nobody knows where. He sure didn't use any family funds, or bank funds, either."

"Nice puzzle. Let me see what I can do."

I drove off then, feeling very lucky, but I was now paranoid about every pair of headlights. Now, at least, I knew why we were worth the bucks. We'd trod the well-worn trails with the feds knowing us and breathing hard on us while Little Jimmy's big agency, probably an out-of-towner, poked and probed in anonymity. Was it worth fifty gees—maybe a hundred, the way Brandy was using that card—to somebody to do that? When this much was at stake, maybe it was.

Brandy was waiting at the diner, and I told her about the feds and what I'd learned. Come to think of it, except for the picture, I'd learned more from Kennedy than I had from Mrs. Whitlock. Brandy, however, had far more.

"He's pretty kinky and she knows it," she told me. "There's three closets up there in the master bedroom. His, hers, and hers."

"Two wives? He keeps his mistress's clothing at his *house?*"

"Uh uh. The other hers is also a his. He's a transvestite. He likes dressing up in women's clothing and pretending to be one. Minnie says there's an old album she found once in a closet that shows him in drag back from his teenage days. She says he's better looking than his wife."

"Hmmm. . . . That explains a lot, including how he was able to vanish so completely even in a panic, and maybe why his marriage is a name-only affair. So he *is* a thrill seeker after all. Probably not gay, though. Few of them are."

"He might swing both ways. That's Minnie's feeling, anyway. But most of the stuff at the house hasn't been touched in months, and the bulk of it was donated to the Goodwill long ago."

It was beginning to come together. If he had photos, so did others, and somebody on the wrong side, maybe even an old classmate from Harvard who was graduating Magna Cosa Nostra, knew about it and filed it away. He had another place somewhere, and that place was probably downtown. He had periods when he came to work normally, yet didn't go home at night. He wouldn't want to risk going even by taxi or public transportation, for fear of being recognized by some bank employee or other and finally being traced. That meant walking distance.

"Sansom Street," we both said together. "Now, who do we know in that area?" I added, trying to think.

Sansom was a tiny little street right downtown that was the focus for the local gay community, but also had been a refuge for the social misfits from other areas. It had those kinds of shops that sold incense and handmade leather goods, and had others that sold bean curd by the pound. It was more picturesque and quaint than raunchy, which is why it survived. The raunchy areas weren't far away, but Sansom was safe.

These blue bloods sure had more interesting lives than the folks *I* hung out with.

The trouble was, while this narrowed down the area and gave us someplace to look, it also vastly complicated matters. We didn't really know what he looked like dressed as a woman, and Minnie had said that the album had vanished and was never seen again after that one time. Hell, he could be wearing a wig in any style, made-up, wearing a padded bra under a dress, high heels, and come right up to us and ask us to buy him a drink. Worse, he'd walk right past the feds at the airport or train station, laughing all the way out, carrying the money in checked luggage.

Maybe Little Jimmy *did* simply need all the help he could get.

3.

The Path to G.O.D.

I have to admit that I'd really underestimated
Martin Whitlock, just like the feds and the mob
had. It took some kind of brains to steal two and
a quarter million bucks from the mob, get exposed in a drug-laundry scheme, and vanish for
three days without a trace while not moving
more than six blocks from his office. The only
amateur's slip he made was calling his wife. That
was the crazy thing. I think they still loved each
other, in a way. She wasn't just protecting him
for image's sake; this stuff was bound to hit the
papers in a big way sooner or later—his disap-
pearance already had, and the reporters had no
problems tying it to federal bank examiners
moving in at Tri-State. Hell, Minnie might well
sell the sordid stuff for the right price if nothing
else happened. No, his wife was protecting him
because, in spite of everything, she still loved
him. And he had risked a farewell phone call to
her, too. And I thought *we* had problems! Just
goes to show that millions of bucks and two
Mercedes mean less than you think.

Of course, I'll still take his money and my marriage any day.

The trouble was, this new situation had made me fall back on resources I really didn't like to use. I called Little Jimmy and briefed him on the case to date, and he seemed really excited about it. I also told him about Agent Kennedy, something he took in stride, and his taking it in stride made me very upset.

"Listen, Nkrumah, I'm not doing any stretch because I was hung out to dry for a measly few grand and a charge account. You want me to lead them away, you tell me, and I'll lead them away instead of pressing this. No more games, though, huh?"

"Why, Samuel! I wouldn't *dream* of hanging you out to dry on this! In fact, those people are why I cannot move through normal channels. They have everything sewed up tight. I can't *breathe* without them noticing and in their ham-handed way notifying certain parties of my, ah, problem. In fact, if it makes you feel any better, give this Kennedy a call and brief him from time to time. Just be certain it's the *second* call you make."

"That won't give you much breathing room," I noted.

"Oh, that's all right. I have resources in high places."

"Seems to me you're thinking that your own bosses are mighty dumb," I couldn't help but point out. "I mean, this guy's vanishing act hasn't hit the front pages yet, but it will sooner or later."

"Oh, they won't care about *him*. I don't mind if they *do* think he took a powder just ahead of the bank examiners and the narcs. It's my money, not theirs, that is at stake, and they are getting things exactly as they expect. Don't worry. I can keep things under control—if you can on your end. It might be best if we arranged a different number to use. I really don't mind them discovering who you're working for—they probably already know—but I really would mind if they overheard something and queered it. Don't call again. I'll be in touch with alternatives."

"Okay, but I need a guide through these local sewers. Somebody with clout whose information will be reliable and who won't go squealing to Kennedy all the time."

"I have an idea. Go home. Get some sleep. I'll see what I can do."

And he was as good as his word. Believe it or not, the next morning the man from Federal Express came by with one of those overnight letters and it was from somebody I never heard of in Sacramento, California. Still, when I opened it, there was a note that I could only assume originated with Little Jimmy a couple of miles across town.

There will be somebody at a phone booth at seven AM and again at seven PM at each of the numbers below. Call them, in order, at the indicated times with your reports and needs. Ask for Sandalwood. If the person on the other end is not responsive, hang up and try the next number. Do not reuse a number. When the last one is dead I will get you a new list. As for your trusty guide, try Sgt. Albert Paoli, Central District Vice. You and he will just hit it off perfectly.

I knew Paoli—or, at least, I knew *of* him. He was wholly owned and operated by the mob, although which branch I never really knew. Still, with his years on the pad and who-knew-what skeletons in his vast closets, he wasn't the kind of guy to betray anybody—and he was too low a fish to get complete immunity if he got a sudden case of nerves or conscience. The last thing any cop wants is to do time in the pen.

Paoli was an all-right sort of guy with some people, but he had certain strong dislikes that you might call hatred. He hated Jews, for example, even more than he hated blacks, and he hated the idea of mixed marriages even more than both of those groups. These paled only in comparison to his total and complete hatred of all private investigators. The word to cooperate might have originated with Little Jimmy, but I'd bet my life it was delivered in Italian.

Brandy and I stopped by a shopping mall before going into Philadelphia, and spent some time there, and a fair amount of Little Jimmy's dough. In fact, I was beginning to think that if we recovered all two and a quarter million, we'd still owe the big weasel money. Still, with me there to try things on, I had clothes now that looked decent and fit me, and Brandy had almost a wardrobe. It was the first time she'd done much with cosmetics and jewelry since she played that hooker, and even though this was understated and looked real good, it still didn't seem natural looking to me after all this time. After a nice, expensive charged lunch, we drove over to see Sergeant Paoli.

He was a thin, dour-looking man of maybe forty-five going on sixty, with less hair than I had, all gray, and one of the biggest noses this side of the ocean. Had a desk out in the middle of a combined office, but ushered us back immediately to a small private office obviously used in interrogations. The look of total disgust on his face was undeniable. Shoot somebody, yeah. Frame 'em, sure. Take bribes, screw your fellow officers, fine. But *we* were garbage.

"I need some reliables in the Sansom Street district," I told him. "Ones who might know the transvestites and the queens equally well, and know where they hide out in the daytime."

"Thinking of coming out of the closet?" he shot back like he meant it. "That's a pretty closed society in there, even harder because it's quite small. Most of that sort aren't downtown, they're down in south Philly."

"Either who I'm looking for is there, or he goes through there to make his changes," I responded. "He's real good at covering his tracks and he's now on the lam from You-Know-Who, and maybe the law as well."

"You want to give me a name?"

"You sure you want to know?"

"Yeah, I'm sure."

"Whitlock. Martin Whitlock."

"The banker? Well, I'll be damned. . . . He's hotter than the Fourth of July right now. The feds are in. I can't do nothing about the feds."

"Screw the feds. I want him, and when I'm through they can have what's left. I've already got a deal with them, so don't think of getting into this thing yourself. I guarantee it'll just give you a choice between a bullet or ten years' hard time."

"It's your funeral," he replied, making it sound

more like a wish than a warning. "All right, I'll give you a couple of names and places. You'll have to track them down yourself. You can use my name to open the door, but after that, you don't *ever* use it again."

That was fair enough. I was fascinated by the fact that although we both sat there, he had refused not only to addresss Brandy but to even acknowledge her existence. We didn't like to stay where we weren't wanted, and we got out of there as quickly as we could.

"He don't like us much," Brandy noted. "I guess he likes the old days when everybody was named Capone, or Banana-nose, or something or other. Well, Lone Ranger, what we do now?"

"We park the horses, Faithful Indian Companion, and we leg it."

Joey Teasdale, Paoli's first suggestion, wasn't hard to find if you were patient, had a lot of twenty-dollar bills, and didn't seem to be cops. We were all three, although we must have walked three miles and spent a couple of C-notes before we found him sitting at a table in the first joint we'd covered. He was almost your stereotypical queen, with loud clothes, high-heeled boots, earrings, and more perfume than Brandy had worn in a lifetime. At least you felt reasonably safe with him; he sure wasn't any threat to Brandy, and I sure as hell wasn't his type. He was, however, extraordinarily courteous to Brandy, which was more than Paoli had been.

How long you been off the gooseberry lay, son?

"Paoli sent us. We're looking for somebody," I told him.

"You cops?"

"Private. The man lifted something of value

from somebody you should never, never steal from, and split. He's hot and we need him before the good guys get him.''

Teasdale whistled. "That hot, huh? Who?"

"Whitlock. Martin Whitlock, the banker."

"*Him?* What makes you think *he* would come through *here?*"

"Look, we got no time for games," Brandy put in. "We got money 'cause the Man got ripped and he don't care what it takes to get even. You got it? Now, those who make themselves useful earn big brownie points with the Man. Those who don't, well, that goes in the report, too."

That hit home. "Yeah, okay, he comes through here regularly," Teasdale said with resignation. "Been coming down here for years. Not the usual kind, though. I mean, I'm a *man*, wouldn't be anything else. No offense, dear lady. We get a lot of those kind of guys who have a wife and kids and position because that's *important* to them, and then they come down here sneaking around to make little liaisons, if you know what I mean. He's not that kind. When *he's* down here, it's total. Looks, acts, sounds all girl, if you know what I mean. Even gets the voice soft and sultry. The drag queens, they just like the *pretending*. They're good, but they're acting and they always know they're acting. Not him. It's like they were two different people, one male, one all female. I sometimes had the idea he'd gotten the operation. Become a she, if you know what I mean, and that the man part was the acting."

I exchanged glances with Brandy and knew that we were both thinking the same thing. Suppose Joey Teasdale was right? It would explain a lot about why he and his wife hadn't had a real marriage in a long time but might still care for one another. It would also explain some of the long absences and why a guy like that would need enough money to be into the mob. If so, there might be nothing short of fingerprints that would nail him.

"You got any line on him?"

"Not immediate, but he never played around. Oh, he'd come into a place now and then, but mostly he didn't stick around here. He had a regular thing with somebody up in northeast Philly, I'm pretty sure. Only saw the guy once, when he came down to Honey's to get some of her—Whitlock's—things and they wouldn't let him in the door. I happened to be passing by and played kind of Sir Galahad; got somebody who could go get what he wanted."

"What'd he look like?" Brandy asked.

"I dunno. Average height and build, I guess. The only thing I remember clearly is he had long, flowing blond hair and a bushy blond walrus moustache and really *gorgeous* blue eyes. Looked kind of like an overage drummer from some rock band. Dressed that way, too. He was *quite* attractive, but it was kind of funny."

"Yes?"

"You sometimes get a sixth sense about these things. It can't be, of course, but I'd *swear* he wasn't the least bit gay."

I nodded. "When was this?"

"Just day before yesterday. That's why I remember him."

That was about all we could get from Joey, but it was both valuable and puzzling. Now we had at least one other player in Martin Whitlock's bizarre double life, and that player was a total unknown.

Honey Rodriguez was the second and last name on our list, and was also the one referred to by Joey Teasdale. This was strictly Brandy's to handle now, for the same reason that our mysterious blond man couldn't get in to get Martin Whitlock's things, although it was frustrating to me. They just didn't let men in the Center City Lesbian Center and Coffee House without a warrant.

She was in there about forty minutes while I guzzled black coffee on the corner across from the dump, wishing I'd taken up smoking again when the money came back. Brandy had, unfortunately, which only made it worse. Neither of us needed to smoke at all, and poverty had been a real good excuse to give it up, but deep down it was the *only* reason we'd given it up. It's bad for you, and antisocial these days to boot, but, damn it, we'd only ballooned out to our weights when we quit, and while I might be healthier now I sure didn't feel any better. Maybe not cigarettes, but in self-defense maybe an occasional cheap cigar or one of those curved Sherlock Holmes–type pipes. On Little Jimmy's card, naturally.

She finally came out and gave me a smile and crossed over and we walked over to a small cafe off Chestnut. "Well? Did she convert you?" I asked her.

Brandy laughed. "There were some mighty-good-lookin' broads in there, but when you got down to it they all lacked an essential ingredient, and since it's the only thing we keep you men around for anyway, why spoil it?"

"Got anything?"

"Some real interesting stuff, but it only gets crazier and crazier. This kind of shit ain't for small-time P.I.'s, honey, or big-shot feds, either. It's booby-hatch time."

"Shoot."

"Whitlock took a bunch of pills and shots and stuff, all right. Hormones, almost certainly. Kept a whole medical kit in a private locker in the back of the center, there. Whitlock money's been supportin' that place, almost. Thousands of bucks' worth. They all swear that Whitlock's a she passin' as a he, not the other way 'round, but several were there when she or he or whatever changed, and they swear there's not a scar or stretch mark on that body, and that it had all the right curves and moves, including average boobs that were strapped down in a kind of corset that also filled out the upper body, made it look muscular. I don't know much about transsexuals, but the people over there seem to know a lot, and they swear that Whitlock was as natural-born a woman as they know. What do you think of *that?*"

"I don't think. Not at this stage, anyway. So if that's true, then who fathered those two kids of his? Besides, they aren't *that* old. I think Mrs. W. would have noticed a lot sooner, at least by the honeymoon. Besides, I got on the phone that he was a member of the Triangle Health Club, and that's rich men only. If he went through that kind of operation, it'd take months and cost a fortune. He couldn't cover it up that long and keep his regular schedule. Those things take months before all those hormones kick in."

"Where'd you learn so much?"

"The *National Enquirer*. So I'd bet my booties that old Martin was a man until just recently and would still be more castrated man than full-figured gal."

"They said this started more than two years ago, and they saw her then."

I nodded. "So this leads me to a deduction, Watson."

"We don't make enough to pay taxes now."

"Quiet. Us geniuses need clear heads. The only way I can figure that we have the Marty Whitlock everybody knows *and* the female Marty down here is if there isn't much kinky going on at all. You get an estimate of height and weight?"

"Hard to tell. She wore heels there, and dear old Honey noted that she wore real finely made elevator shoes as a man. They all thought it was a great scam, and they didn't look much closer because of the money."

"Few do. But the height?"

"Honey said, with heels, they were about the same height. Call it five ten."

I nodded. "Uh huh. And Marty was five ten as well. Now, if we assume that the *real* Marty Whitlock didn't wear elevators, let alone heels, we can account for maybe three inches."

"Brother and sister, maybe? Real close look-alikes?"

"Have to be real close. The trouble is, he *does* have two sisters, both accounted for and neither one likely to be able to pass for him even with Hollywood special effects working on his side."

"He could have just passed her once and seen the resemblance and got her on the payroll. He'd have a hell of a good payroll. It'd beat workin'."

I considered it. "Maybe, but it's unlikely. The clue here is that she looked enough like him to convince everybody down here that there *was* a masquerade. Remember what Joey told us? As a woman, he looked like somebody totally different, a real woman. Except for one thing, we've been led down a garden path. Not only does he vanish into this sexual anywhere, but he leads us to a point where it appears he's either a drag queen or a transsexual. Now, why?"

She shrugged. "Maybe it's because he knew he'd have to disappear someday, and he figured this was a real neat dead end. Everybody would now be looking for a drag queen or a transsexual, not for him."

"And left it in place for a couple of years?" I thought about it. "It's almost too clever. You wonder how somebody with his background would even know about these places, let alone work them out that neatly. It explains the call to his wife, though, even though it's one of only two mistakes he made. She knows what's going on. Most of it, anyway. *Damn!* This is frustrating! You don't hire somebody to go through this kind of elaborate shit for *two years* just as a blind alley, and even if you have this kind of shit going you can't buy much more time than if you got a fake passport, went up to Canada, and took the plane to Rio or whatever. No, this smells. This stinks. He did this for a reason other than to cover his tracks. This was something ongoing, something he maybe needed to develop so he could get out from under the Little Jimmys of the world one step ahead of the feds. Why stick around here at all? He could just as easily and untraceably have called her changing planes in Chicago."

"Unfinished business. He had to move in a hurry, faster than he figured. You said two mistakes, though."

"Uh huh. Get another description of that guy who came by to pick up her gear?"

"Yeah, it was pretty much as Joey told us. About five ten, blue eyes, long blond hair and moustache. . . ."

"The operative stuff is at the start. Five ten, blue eyes. Probably a real good blond wig and a real professional matching fake moustache."

"The real Marty Whitlock," she sighed. "But why come at all? Testing out the disguise, or what?"

"Uh uh. Remember, he was spooked into moving a few days early. His girlfriend was told to stay away. Considering the trail he laid, they'd be more likely to be looking for her than him, or so he'd think. Those rich upper-class types really believe the cops are that good and that fast. But *she* needs some stuff from there, or something in the locker was traceable. So he puts on an old pair of jeans and a tee shirt, maybe old tennis shoes, and with some difficulty gets the stuff. We can forget the blond shit, though. He knows he was conspicuous, so he'll ditch 'em or at least stick 'em in the trunk and use something else. Big beard, shaved head, maybe tinted contact lenses, and he's off. Dead end, babe. We don't even know the name he was using in northeast Philly—if that was where he was doing whatever he was doing—and there's only three quarters of a million people out there. It'd take us years to canvass enough to find this pair."

Brandy grinned. "You won't have to. See, they thought she was one of *them,* and they smelled somethin' real odd about this dude even if he *did* have the handwriting and all. After all, Whitlock was their sugar daddy or mama or whatever. So when he left, they tailed him. I have the address."

I almost jumped across the table to kiss her. Naturally, this spilled my coffee and her Coke, but I didn't care. Finally I said, as the waitress and several patrons stared at us in disgust, "I think we go out there—after I make two phone calls."

"Little Jimmy and who else?"

"Agent Kennedy. I'm gonna give 'em both everything up to the sex change. If they're any good, they might get further, but maybe not. In the meantime, I'm in good with them and we'll be the first there."

There were still several hours of setup and work involved. The place was one of those older middle-class apartment houses with sixteen apartments in the place, and there was only so much you could expect even from Divine Providence. You could use a hundred scams to talk to the neighbors, but I once tried the insurance-agent ploy and half the people wanted to talk policies. It was easier just to fall back on the old reliable and flash the badge while Brandy cased the joint. It wasn't too hard to find their apartment; it was the one couple nobody knew much about and everybody thought a little nuts.

That left getting into apartment 2–09. I wasn't much good at petty burglary, but when it was clear that the place was dark and unoccupied, I turned things over to Brandy. She had that nice, big safety lock picked in about two and a half minutes of sweat. I did the sweating, of course.

At this stage, our pair had been pretty casual. They never expected to be coming back, and they never expected anybody to be able to find the place. At the end of the lease, which was prepaid only to the end of the month, the landlord would use his master, open the place up, get a cleaning crew in, and rent it out again.

These weren't furnished apartments, but it's

tough to make a smooth getaway in a moving van. Most of it appeared to be rental furniture, with the stickers still on, pretty much like I figured. It wasn't terribly full of stuff, though; a couch and a couple of chairs in the otherwise barren living room, a queen-sized mattress and box spring in the bedroom, and a dresser. Most of the clothes and some of the toiletries were gone, but the small fridge was still reasonably full— fortified skim milk, Perrier, some never-to-be fondue, and even a couple of bottles of sixty-buck-a-fifth champagne. Overchilled, but not bad. Brandy took care of the small tin of beluga caviar; I never could see the appeal of solid-salt fish eggs that cost ten cents a pinhead-sized egg. Just your average lower-middle-class apartment dweller's emergency rations.

Then we started looking under mattresses and behind furniture. It didn't take very long, considering the underfurnished nature of the apartment, but we came up with a whole bunch of junk. It's amazing what falls in back of dressers, and there is some sort of law that states that anything left for any period of time will migrate to spots where you will never see it or find it. Most of it was the ordinary debris—a plastic hair curler, a couple of combs, some loose change, a magazine sweep-stakes form, that kind of thing. One very crum-pled little piece of tissue-thin paper, however, stood out and Brandy carefully unwrapped it. "Aha! The master detectives strike!" she an-nounced with a flair and handed it to me.

It was a credit card slip.

The thing was hard to read and seemed to be fairly old, but I could read the name and the number and the expiration date, and it was still current. Amanda W. Curry, and a card good until the end of this year. Now, for the first time, we had a name and a way to track them. Whitlock just wasn't the type to go around packing suitcases full of cash, and he could hardly walk in and ask to buy two and a quarter million bucks in American Express traveler's checks without attracting a little attention. He would keep most of the money in dummy accounts probably spread all to hell and back, and contract with a money manager to pay the bills on this new set of credit cards. Little Jimmy had provided me with a sample of Whitlock's handwriting, and I took it out of my wallet and compared it. The charge slip was definitely signed in a woman's hand, yet there were certain similarities in the way the letters were formed, particularly the *W*. I handed them to Brandy. "If it's not the same, then they grew up together and learned from the same teacher," I noted.

She squinted, then said, "Yeah, that's right. I can't figure this out yet, but it sure is strange. Every time we figure we're dealin' with one person, we find two. Every time we figure two people, it looks like one. Don't make no sense at all."

I handed her the other prize from the junk trove, a crumpled and torn business card. She examined it carefully, but I had the strange feeling she wasn't reading it. "Just how bad *is* your vision?" I asked her.

"Good enough."

"Uh huh. Then read that card."

She sighed. "Okay, so I can't. So I'll blow some of this money on new glasses, all right?" She handed it back. "Now what's it say?"

"General Ordering and Development, Inc.," I told her. "McInerney, Oregon. Never heard of the place, but it sure doesn't sound very big. No address. Two phone numbers, though. One of 'em's been circled, sort of, in old pencil. Funny, too, there's no name on the card. Just 'Western Distribution Center.'"

She thought a moment. "Kind of crazy, but that name seems familiar, somehow."

I shrugged. "I wonder if they call it GOD, Inc., around the plant?"

She snapped her fingers. "Yeah! That's it! The Amazing Stork Knife!"

"Huh?"

She was rolling now. "And the Motorized Minnow, and Pet-er-cize, too!"

"Slow down. If you can't manage English, try it phonetically."

She looked excited. "You don't watch enough TV."

"We hocked the TV months ago," I noted.

"Hell, this has been around for *years!* You know all those ads for all those crazy junk things that come on in the middle of the late show, or are all over cable TV? Things like pocket fishing gear, steak knives, and exercisers, disposable telephones, stuff like that?"

I nodded. "As much as I tried to avoid them, yes."

"Well, right down at the bottom they got to say who's *really* selling them. Not the TV station you send the money to or the eight-hundred number you call, but the real company, down in fine print. They made 'em do that after there were so many phonies getting into the act. Well, General Ordering and Development is one of the biggest!"

This was beginning to get interesting. "So they sell a thousand products by buying cheap, late-night ads from Hong Kong distributors and junk makers. If this is one of the biggest, then it's a multimillion-dollar company at the very least. You say it's been around awhile?"

"Years, anyway. They came in with a roar and bought up a bunch of the smaller outfits who started this whole thing. Why?"

"Well, those companies borrow money to buy the junk in huge quantities, and those are short-term, high-interest business loans. The bigger you are, the more banks you need behind you, if only to guard against the inevitable turkeys you get stuck with and can't fool even the sleepy public into buying. Big banks. Banks like Tri-State."

Her eyebrows went up. "I *see*. . . . But why the western division? Why not the east?"

"It doesn't matter to a bank where it is, so long as it's a good risk, and some banks at some times have more money to lend at better terms than others that might be close-by. In these days of quick flights across country and instant mail delivery and electronic funds transfers it doesn't really matter. The trouble is, we don't know if this is anything or not. It might just be that Whitlock met with a guy the day he came over here, and lost this."

"That's probably it," she agreed, "but at least we have a name. Wonder what a check of the airlines for the past two days might show?"

The funny thing about that was that it was so simple to do. Guys like Whitlock have secretaries and agencies to make their plans, and they tend to have corporate deals that keep them to just a couple of airlines. Even if he was sneaking off, I had a hunch he'd still fly his favorite, and I knew from his abortive Sunday tickets west what airline he favored. His idea of a real fooler might be to fly coach, but I was even wrong there. Curry, Mr. and Mrs., first initials M. and A., were flying strictly first class.

"Still San Francisco," I noted. "Why?"

"Simple. You can get real lost in a city like that, and they would have connections with the underground set through their friends here. When did they leave?"

"They landed two hours ago," I told her. "Might as well be two days or two weeks."

Brandy thought for a moment. "Want to play a wild hunch? Maybe an expensive one?"

"What do you have in mind?"

"Well, I was just wonderin' how you get from San Francisco to a little burg like McInerney, Oregon, strictly first class."

"You know the odds of there being any connection between that business card and what's happening now?"

She stared at me with those big brown eyes. "I know what the odds are unless there *is* a connection. You wanna call Little Jimmy and turn the rest back in, or do you wanna see San Francisco, maybe a little of Oregon, too, all on him?"

I had to admit that she had a real point there. "All right; then, we'll spend a little time here this evening seeing if we can get some descriptions of them and some impressions, then we'll fly off after them tomorrow if we can figure a way to do it quiet."

"You gonna call Little Jimmy and the feds?"

"Yeah. Little Jimmy I'm gonna call from a phone booth in a few minutes with the whole thing.

The feds I'll call a little later. We'll give 'em the apartment and that's it. I think we'll keep this charge slip and business card for ourselves."

She thought a moment. "You got to figure the feds have been doggin' our trail all along, maybe Little Jimmy, too. How we gonna explain San Francisco if you don't give 'em the name? Or stop 'em from keepin' on following us?"

"I been thinking about that. We'll have to come up with something, and fast."

I saw that evil smile on her face. "Maybe we just gotta take a leaf from old Marty Whitlock."

"Forget it," I told her. "I'm not shaving my legs and I'm not wearing any dress."

There weren't many people to canvass by the time we left, but we found a few. They knew little about the occupant—singular—of that apartment, but they knew what she looked like. Real butch, right down to the haircut, usually dressed real mannish, too. Kept to herself, had a few visitors and no close friends, and was away a lot. One couple thought she *was* a guy, although they'd never talked to her or seen her close-up. It was more of the same androgynous pattern, only this time from the other end.

The major asset Brandy had during that period when she tried to keep the agency afloat after her father had died, and even in tracking down his killer, was the number of relatives her mother had all over the metropolitan creation. Cousin Minnie had been just one of these; there were many more, and while she was close to none of them, it was true that blood was thicker than water. We didn't have a whole hell of a lot of time, and we had an awful lot to do.

My old bum disguise was out; not only was it pretty well known, but it's kind of conspicuous for a bum to buy an airline ticket at all, let alone with either cash or a credit card. Instead, I dyed gray the hair I still had, and added a matching false moustache and my reading glasses, although they actually limited my vision for all but reading, and I usually just carried them in my pocket. In fact, just looking in the mirror I *felt* old, and I didn't like it. I had the uncomfortable feeling that I was staring at the not-too-distant future. Adding a small and worn hat and a very rumpled blue suit, and walking a little bent over and carrying a drugstore cane, I was pretty sure that nobody who didn't come straight up to me and examine me would recognize me.

Brandy slipped out of the apartment while it was still dark. She had a more extensive makeover to do, and we agreed to meet later, having set up a system with her cousin Lavonia, who happened to be a cabbie. Lavonia was perhaps more distant than any of the other cousins, but it was amazing how sweet and loyal she could be when presented with unregistered cash. Still, we could take no real luggage with us. All that nice stuff we'd bought had to be abandoned for now. We'd have to buy what we needed when we got there.

I left the apartment house at nine in the morning on a bright, sunny day, after spending an hour making sure that I looked and acted correctly and consistently. About a block down I finally spotted the feds' tail, sitting there in his car sipping coffee and reading the newspaper. He gave me half a glance when I walked by directly across the street from him, but nothing more. I couldn't spot Little Jimmy's tail, if it existed, but

I was reasonably confident that if the feds ignored me when they knew I'd had a reputation for disguises as a vice cop, Little Jimmy's cretins would be even more easily fooled.

Lavonia was sitting in her cab where she was supposed to be, and I walked up and opened the back door.

"Fuck off, geezer! I'm off duty!" she shouted at me with the usual tact and diplomacy of a cabbie.

"Take it easy, Lavonia; I'm the one you're waiting for," I responded, and got in and shut the door.

She turned and stared at me suspiciously for a moment through the bulletproof glass partition separating her from her fares. She looked nothing like Brandy; light-complected, skinny, and with a face that was born hard and mean. "That really you, Horowitz?"

"Yeah. Let's get going. There's a fed just around the corner, and who-knows-who-else looking around."

She switched on the ignition and pulled out into traffic with the usual disregard for traffic, pedestrians, and stationary obstacles. I often think that there is a factory someplace that makes all the world's cabbies. They all look different, have different accents, but deep down they're all the same person.

She dropped me at one of those motels on the north side of the city that rents rooms by the hour and asks no questions. I would have to stay pretty much on ice for a few hours until Brandy was ready. We had decided to fly out of Newark rather than Philly because 'there wasn't any use in taking chances on people stationed there, and also because Newark had a couple of cheap airlines flying cross-country where you basically bought your seat on the plane. That made it damned difficult to get an advanced passenger list, and by the time they found out the reservations were in assumed names, it would be too late. The trouble was, it took extra time. It would take maybe ninety minutes to get up there, add an hour to make sure you got there in time to keep them from giving away your seat, and the earliest you could figure on was a flight at six-thirty in the evening.

I got lunch at a diner down the street, keeping in character—though having a tough time when the waitress kept calling me "Pops"—but it wasn't until after two, when my nerves and patience were really thin, that somebody knocked at the door. It was Lavonia.

We drove over to a row-house area that had a number of small businesses in the basements, stopping in front of one that looked older and in worse condition than our building and had a weathered sign that read, New You Salon and Beauty Parlor. They sure as hell lived up to their name. I wouldn't have recognized Brandy, just passing her in the street, and that's saying something. Only when she approached and then got into the cab was she unmistakably my Brandy.

Most dramatically, they had given her a very short haircut, then fitted her with an enormous and very natural looking wig of slightly curly reddish-brown hair. Cosmetics had been neatly applied that subtly changed the way her face looked, topped off by crimson lipstick and long and complicated golden earrings. She was also wearing a fancy-looking sleeveless top with a leatherlike dark-red vest and a skirt of the same material, slit a bit up the sides, as well as matching boots with the highest heels I'd ever seen. It couldn't disguise the fact that she was chubby, but the whole thing used that to minimize it, or actually make it something of an asset. I was stunned. "You look absolutely beautiful," I told her.

"Yeah, and you look like hell," she returned. "In a way, it ain't fair. I got to suffer with this damned girdle and you get to look like an old slob."

We went over to the turnpike and headed north. There were no evident tails, but you could never be sure. We wanted to cover all the bases, though, so this would be our only opportunity together until we got to San Francisco. I would be dropped a block from the place in East Brunswick where you got the airport van, and Brandy would do the same from Union. From that point we wouldn't know or acknowledge each other until we got outside the airport terminal at the other end. Nobody was going to get the chance to remember a salt-and-pepper couple, or think it odd that a young comer would take an inordinate interest in an old white geezer.

"You found the place and got some contact names?" she asked me.

I nodded. "McInerney is in the mountains east of Bend, so if they would fly up, they'd go there. That means either a commuter line out of San Francisco or Oakland, or a hop to Portland and then a line over to Bend for a pickup. It's one of those old logging towns that almost blew away, and I'm told that this company more or less bought the whole place. It was always a company town; just now it's a different company and different business. It's a small town, but we'll stand out as much or more than they would. There's not much anybody else could tell me from here, except that this General Ordering and Development corporation is big but no Fortune Five Hundred affair. It never lacks for money or credit, though, so there's somebody big behind it. I didn't have time to run down the corporate officers—it's officially a Delaware corporation, although that's just a mail drop—but there was nothing immediately dirty or suspicious about them. The home office is actually in Iowa, with branches for the west, central, east, and south. They sell a lot of stuff, but they make most of their money with their regional phone hookups. They take orders for just about everything from just about everybody."

She sighed. "Yeah, I know it's a long shot that they would run there. There's no reason for them to run there, I guess. Still, it's the only thing we got. What about contacts?"

"A few phone numbers of people out there, mostly in California. Nobody had much for Oregon. I had to use pay phones for all of this, so we'll have to do most of our follow-up once we're there. A P.I. in Oakland and a couple of contacts who were associated with our friends down on Sansom." Those were long shots, of course, just in case this Oregon thing was as blind as it seemed to be.

I had called the feds from our apartment the night before, and they'd gone to the north Philly address and done their thorough job. Kennedy, in fact, had actually called back, quite pleased with what he was getting from me, and given me another of those crazy facts. They had found only three clear sets of fingerprints in the apartment among, of course, the thousands of smudges and useless partials. One set was mine, one was Brandy's, and the third was undeniably Whitlock's. That satisfied them, but left us with even more of a problem.

"Did she wear *gloves* all the time or something?" Brandy wondered aloud. "I mean, if *his* prints were there, and he was only there some of the time, then hers just *had* to be there, too. I could take it more if they'd found hers but not his."

It bothered me, too. I was dead certain now that we were after two people, Whitlock and this Curry woman or whatever her real name was. There were enough signs in the background information we'd developed and the witnesses we'd interviewed and even in the apartment itself, not to mention that two people had taken that San Francisco flight. Everything pointed to there being two, and to an incredible scheme to make it seem like there was only one, a scheme totally out of character for Martin Whitlock IV, and not one he was likely to have come up with on his own. Yet, too, there was that closet of women's clothes in his house that Minnie had seen, and that album showing him dressed as a girl through a fair portion of his life. None of it made sense, and the prints made even less sense. They expected to be long gone and buried in new identities and locales by the time anybody discovered that apartment, if anyone ever did. Why weren't her fingerprints all over, more so than his, in fact?

The flight out wasn't much fun, either. These discount carriers were more like cattle cars with

wings than real airlines, to begin with, and that
was only the start of it. I sat up forward in
nonsmoking, while Brandy sat near the back
smoking away again, and every time I'd look
back she was surrounded by guys, mostly young,
black, and handsome and full of muscles, and she
seemed to be having a wonderful time.

Okay, okay, so call me jealous. I guess it's more
a deep-down insecurity. She's young and cute;
I'm a decade older, white, balding, and paunchy.
Everybody was real solicitous to the old guy,
meaning me, but I mostly growled and sulked.

We took off late and we landed later, but at
least neither of us had to wait for luggage. I
walked past baggage claim and noted that she
was having some problems getting rid of her
entourage. The lady had no bags, and everybody
wanted to carry them for her. She finally took the
last refuge of choice and walked to the ladies'
room, and when she emerged she'd removed the
wig and some of the cosmetics, as well as the
vest, and stuffed them into her big purse. It
wasn't much, but the change was dramatic enough
that nobody waylaid her as she walked outside
and stood next to me. Without the wig, though,
she didn't look at all terrific. In order to allow
her to use any sort of wig with minimum problems, they'd cut her hair so short you had to look
close to see any hair there at all.

We caught a cab over to an airport motel that
was next to a rental-car place. The firm was
closed, at close to ten o'clock, for walk-in rentals,
but I was in no condition to drive all over a
strange town that night, anyway. They had twenty-
four hours plus on us; either we knew where they
were going or we didn't, and only a lot of time

on the phone would tell that. I checked us in and we went up to the room.

Brandy flopped down on the bed with a sigh and then started undressing. It really *was* a hell of a tight girdle; it made impressions in her that looked more like what you'd do in modeling clay than in human skin, and I wasn't sure if she'd ever be able to get that thing on again. She was quickly my old Brandy again, except for that haircut. She got up and walked into the bathroom and looked at herself in the mirror, then sighed. "Maybe I should just shave it. It's gonna take a year before it's lookin' decent again." She came back out and looked at me. I'd gotten out of those lousy clothes and tossed the false moustache in the ashtray. "What do you think?" she asked me.

"Might make you fit in real well around here," I responded grumpily.

"What's with *you?* Awww.... Don't worry. We'll buy some black hair dye for you first thing tomorrow."

"It's not that. It's just . . . Aw, skip it."

She seemed more amused than upset, and sat there and started a back and neck massage on me. It's one of my few real weaknesses, and one I can't deny. I'd let Norman Bates's mother massage there, if she was any good at it, and I wouldn't even check for knives.

"Yesssss . . . ?"

"Well, you seem to have had a pretty good time flying out here."

She laughed. "Not bad, for my first long plane trip. Oh, you mean the *boys!* Hell, honey, after all this time I kinda *needed* that just for my own sake. It's hard to explain—but I'm here, with you, not shacked up with one of them. I seem to remember that this was the place where coed showers were invented. Want to memorialize the occasion?"

"Maybe, but they sure weren't invented here. I think they were probably invented about ten minutes after they invented the shower."

Okay, okay, so I should have been down at a pay phone calling around, and I knew it, but there are some things a man needs more at a given time than duty. Besides, I never believed we'd get anywhere with all this, anyway.

Bright and early the next morning, though, I *did* make the calls, first finding out the recommended way to get to this nowhere in Oregon, and then being told that Bend was it. After that, you drove or took a local bus. There were more ways to fly to Bend from here than I figured, though—I never knew it was that big a place, although for me anything under a two-million metro is a small town. Still, using standard P.I. phone gimmicks, I had 'em in about two hours in spite of a real officious clerk at one of the airlines. I'd been afraid that they might have used general aviation, which would have been really tricky, but fortunately they took the quick route. In fact, they flew up there only that very morning, about the time I started my calls. I cursed myself for letting lust get ahead of business. If I hadn't needed cheering up and lots of romantic reassurances, I could have been there at the ticket counter when they showed up.

The fact is, nobody flies to Bend, Oregon, while on the run, so the million-to-one shot had been right. They were going to visit G.O.D.'s mountain, no question about that. I wondered why they'd delayed in San Francisco, but then it hit me. They needed time to set this up—this was a run, not a planned escape, after all—and maybe they wanted to see San Francisco. At any rate, they wouldn't risk any calls from Philly to McInerney, simply because it would stand out, and because if Whitlock handled that account it would be monitored by the feds. They'd wait until they were here, with no way in hell to monitor their calls.

Brandy was watching TV when I got back up to the room—I didn't want those calls recorded by any motel operator, after all—and she turned and pointed. "Look!" I looked.

"... *This miracle space-age device remembers up to a hundred phone numbers, including area codes, up to thirty-two digits. You just put it to the mouth of any touch-tone phone and press the coded buttons like this!*"

"What?" I managed, but she held up a hand. Soon the Superdialer number card was on the screen, with toll-free number and all the credit cards it took, so you could rush to your phone and buy one for only $39.95 plus $3 shipping and handling.

"There. Right at the bottom. See?"

Sure enough, in real tiny print right at the bottom it said, GENERAL ORDERING AND DEVELOPMENT, INC., DAVENPORT, IOWA. That was the home office.

I had always meant to ask Brandy about Pet-er-cize, but now I didn't think I wanted to know.

"So, what's the story?" she asked me.

"The story is that we were within a mile of 'em two hours ago, and they are probably still somewhere in the Bend airport this minute," I told her. "We sure blew it last night."

"You mean *I* did. But who'd have thought they'd still be around? They sure ain't movin' fast for folks with all creation after 'em. I guess we get dressed as we are and grab a bite at the airport, huh?"

"You know we don't have to," I pointed out. "We did the job. We actually completed the commission. All I have to do is call Little Jimmy, and tell him that Whitlock's in McInerney and has contacts or confederates in this company, and that's it. That's all he asked us to do."

"You know—you're right. I hadn't really thought about it." She gave a big grin. "So the super-detectives did the job and proved it all! We beat the feds, the mob, *everybody!*" She paused a moment, thinking. "Still, can you really give it up now? I mean, never know who the hell she was, or what all this was about?"

I didn't have to think much about it. "For a percentage of two and a quarter million, most likely ninety percent recoverable by Little Jimmy's friends; yeah, I could forget about it. It might drive me nuts, but I'd be *rich* and nuts, which beats poor and knowing any day of the week."

"*Sheeitt,*" she responded. "Let's call him from the Bend airport. It won't take much risk to us. I mean, where the hell could they go in a few hours from Nowheres, Oregon? How long you figure it'd take to drive up there from Bend, anyway?"

"Three hours, maybe. Depends on the roads."

"So they'll just be gettin' into town when we get to Bend. What they gonna do—run off to Mars in a Handy Dandy Super Flying Saucer, only One Million Dollars from our toll-free-number line, MasterCard and Visa accepted?"

She had a point, and I had to admit I was not only curious, but also a little mad at myself. The fact was, I'd like to see these bastards, more her than him. *Okay, doll, now let's see why you don't leave no fingerprints. . . .*

There weren't exactly flights to Bend every hour; in fact, you couldn't fly there directly at all, but with a change in Portland, as the pair had done, it wasn't that much of a problem. Once we decided to keep going, though, I couldn't resist a double check. I placed a call to the airline they were using in Bend and tried to have them paged. It was a long shot, but you figure they might be figuring on getting picked up by somebody with the company, and it wouldn't be that unnatural. The plane, in fact, had been late getting in, and had only been in for a few minutes, but nobody answered the page and I finally gave up and called the airline people to see if they were still at baggage claim. "A man and a woman who almost look like twins," I told the baggage office.

"Oh, yeah, they just left," said the guy. "Hold on and I'll see if I can spot 'em." He kept me hanging for about five minutes, then came back. "Sorry. I think they rented a car at Hertz, though. You might check them."

I did and they had, but they were gone now. The best I could get, even with my phony-cop approach, was that they were driving a new Oldsmobile, and she remembered them particularly, not only because they looked so much alike, but because they'd requested a Cadillac. Still, having the make, model, and license number wasn't bad, particularly since I knew damned well where they were going. What was most interesting was that they had rented the car for a week.

Now, that might not seem like much, but nobody rents a car for a week when they're only going to need it for a couple of days—unless it's fantastically cheaper to do so, and it certainly wasn't—and they particularly wouldn't if somebody else, say their friend in the company, was going to return it. That certainly implied that they expected to be around the place for a while and needed wheels for the whole period. They were pretty confident, I had to say that, still using the Curry name, which had to be in the federal files by now, and still using a credit card in that name. Given a couple of more days for the bureaucracy and procedures, even Kennedy or Little Jimmy could have tracked them here, at least to Bend. Without that business card, though, they might not figure on McInerney, not unless it was in fact a big Whitlock account.

I called Little Jimmy from the airport in Bend, while Brandy was filling out the car-rental form. It was four in the afternoon, but I'd almost forgotten the time difference and it was seven back at that phone booth.

"I got him," I told the contact. "Ready to deliver."

"Call the number I'm gonna give ya," the punk replied, sounding not at all impressed. "The man said to tell you to call it no matter when you called or why. Do it now."

I took down the number, puzzled, and called it, and was very surprised to hear Little Jimmy's voice on the other end of the line. He listened while I told him everything to date.

"Well, drop it," he responded. "Keep the dough, keep the cards until the end of the month if you want, but that's it."

"Uh uh. No welching. We did this for a percentage."

"Horowitz—I'm telling you to back off. Let it go. Let *him* go."

"You telling me there never was any money?"

"The son of a bitch stole every dime I said. He can keep it. There's no way I want anything more to do with him, ever. Even this distance is too close. If you know what's good for you, you'll go back to San Francisco, have a nice vacation, maybe find a job there if you like it. You want some references? You're good. Damned good. I think I could get both of you a nice position with some solid firm out there."

"Listen, Nkrumah, what in hell is this?" I growled. The fact was, Little Jimmy wasn't sounding like himself at all. He was sounding very, very scared. "The feds nail you?"

"No, no." He sighed. "All right, if you must know—I was set up all along. It was a scam. They busted Big Tony Guliano this morning, and at almost the same time they hit almost every cog in the smuggling game through which the merchandise passed. *Every* one! They have tied me to both Tri-State and Guliano, and I am about to visit the Cayman Islands for a while. Perhaps a *long* while."

"On what?" I asked him, not quite believing all this. If this pair was part of a federal scam, why this crazy scene with the transvestism and the rest of it? I was *sure* Kennedy hadn't known about that apartment until I told him. I'd still bet what I had left of Little Jimmy's money on it. "They stole your poke."

"That is none of your affair. My loans are being bought out if I am outside the country by tomor-

row night. I still have a future, but not for a little
while. Now it is time to take a much overdue
vacation. I will make certain your references are
on file in the right places, and will send you a list
care of the main post office general-delivery
window in San Francisco. This is it, Horowitz.
I'm sorry, but it is *over*. I truly am impressed
with your work, though. Truly impressed."

"Thanks for very little," I grumbled. This was
smelling as bad as Marty Whitlock's girlfriend.
"Don't write if you set up again."

"Horowitz—I want to emphasize only one thing,
and then I am *gone*. Don't take it upon yourselves
to follow them any further, and do *not* get near
that town or that company. You are ignorant of
what you are dealing with, as I was. I know more
than I wish now, but I want nothing more to do
with them. Be smart. Take that lovely lady of yours
and enjoy. Forget that couple and that company.
If you don't, you will either be dead or you will
pray to God that you die. That is all I will say.
None of my numbers will work from now on.
Farewell."

And, before I could say another word, the
weasel hung up on me, leaving me standing
there, stunned, with the phone still in my hand.

Now what the hell was *this?* There was no way
around it but to find Brandy, brief her, and then
call Agent Kennedy.

Brandy was even more intrigued by this than I
was. While up to now I had been willing to rest on
my laurels, and take the money and run, now
there was no more money, only a ton of questions.

I figured I might have some trouble getting
through to Kennedy if all this was going down,
but he was right there.

"Yeah, it's true, they busted a bunch of them today including Big Tony, but it wasn't us," he told me, sounding more than a little irritated at that fact. "Turns out the FBI was running a parallel operation and we almost queered it with this Whitlock business. Seems they found out about him and his kinky double life, and used him to go up and down the chain. A few of the middle fish haven't been rounded up yet, but the organization's broken but good. This one, anyway. There's always ten more to replace it, unfortunately."

"What about Little Jimmy Nkrumah? He on the list? He was the guy who hired us—and just fired us."

"Huh? Nkrumah? Nope. Don't see that name here anywhere. You're sure this guy was involved?"

"Positive. He was the middleman in the money tree, and it was his money that Whitlock skipped out with."

"*Hmph!* That's funny. Maybe they're just leaving him out to dry or something, since they say they traced the money all the way, or maybe they've turned him as one of their boys. I don't know, Horowitz. We're all one big happy federal family, right? Only we don't tell each other anything at all. Well, what's the difference? You did as good as could be expected, so there's nothing more between us, and you've lost a client and our quarry turns out to be the Bureau's man, so it's over."

"Uh—Kennedy? If it's over, what's Whitlock doing in Oregon with a woman who looks enough like him to be him in drag? Who is she, and what the hell are they doing out here leaving his wife and kids hanging?"

"Who knows? Witness protection, maybe. We got an order to lay off him, and you do, too, if you don't want to get back in trouble with us again. I admit there's a lot of funny, unexplained stuff with this, but I don't know it all; it's not my case anymore. I got a thousand more in the active file, so that's it. By next week some rival mob will move in and cover Big Tony's whole network, and nobody using stuff on the streets will even notice the difference. Just let it go, Horowitz—for your own good."

That was almost as unsatisfying as the call to Little Jimmy. All of a sudden everybody from the mob to the DEA was telling me that Whitlock was an untouchable, all the questions were better left unanswered, and all we needed to do to find the land of milk and honey was take the next plane out to anywhere at all but here. It stunk.

"So what do you want to do?" Brandy asked me.

"What *can* we do? I mean, right now our boy's gone from being the most wanted by everybody to being a total untouchable for all sides. For all we know, he's up in Hicksburg negotiating a new bank loan."

"But you don't believe that, and neither do I."

"No, but Little Jimmy wasn't scared of the feds; and one good reason was that the feds didn't know about Little Jimmy. They also think Whitlock passed the whole two and a quarter million down the line as per plan, but *we* know he skipped; and Little Jimmy did the passing of his own money and wanted Whitlock tracked down without his own boss, Big Tony, knowing he got skimmed. Little Jimmy would rather risk prison than write off almost his whole fortune, so either whatever scared him is worse than prison or somebody covered his losses. Who the hell would spend that kind of bread to buy out and protect a shark like Nkrumah?"

"Maybe it's the hand of G.O.D., Inc. Wanna go find out?"

"No, but I won't be able to sleep nights ever again if I don't anyway. Not when we're only three hours away from the answer. I just hate being my own client, that's all. The client's a cheapskate who'll stiff us."

"Maybe, but I'm game. I want to see these whackos, anyway. Move out of the booth. I got to call San Francisco."

"Huh? Who do you have to call *there*?"

"Overnite Courier. They got a box of mine I got to get forwarded up here somehow."

"A box? What? Clothes?"

"Nope. If these cards are still good, we'll take care of that next, and in style. But I ain't goin' up in those redneck mountains without Daddy's magnum."

"You sent your *gun* by overnight parcel?"

She shrugged. "Couldn't take it on the plane, you know."

4.

Shots in the Dark

I was getting used to this charge-and-never-pay business; I would be sorry to see the gravy train end in a couple of weeks. I wondered just who was now paying the bills that came in. Still, we had something of a wardrobe now, including a couple of suitcases, plus toiletries and the like, and we were both feeling a little more human. Brandy had reverted to her jeans-and-tee-shirt routine for now, although they were new, and some sandals, although she kept that professional-looking wig. She also had even found a couple of other wigs of varying colors and styles, and she'd picked up some better clothes in case the occasion warranted. Me, I'd gotten another off-the-rack suit, although right now I was in jeans and a plaid sport shirt, and I just hadn't been able to resist a pair of ranch-style boots and a black felt cowboy hat.

Brandy should have been excited about this part as much as or more than before, since she was the one who wanted to see this out anyway, but I found her somewhat moody. "What's the trouble, babe?" I asked her. "All this finally getting to you?"

She shook her head and stared out the rental-car window at the passing scenery. "Uh uh. I just—don't feel *comfortable* around here. We been through the airport back there, to a bunch of stores, and now on the road, and there wasn't a single black person anyplace we been. I never *been* in a place where there were no black people before except me."

The truth was, I hadn't really noticed, but now that she mentioned it I couldn't recall any. Oregon had the reputation for being real liberal near the coast, around Portland and Salem in particular, and as rock-ribbed reactionary in much of the rest of the state. "Anybody give you trouble back in the stores?"

"No, it's not that. Not exactly. They just sort of treated me like I was some kind of exotic animal or something. Funny comments—you know, like whether or not one of the wigs was *right* for my, er, well. . . ."

"Uh huh. Well, it's a price to be paid if you want to see this through. I can still turn around, get a room near the airport, and we can fly back tomorrow morning, all the way to Philadelphia and home if you want."

"No, no. I want to see this through. Specially after what that rental-car girl said."

It had been just another piece in this crazy puzzle that didn't add up at all. The couple had borne a striking likeness to one another, but *he* in his business suit had seemed somewhat smaller and younger than she, with a high-pitched tenor—and *she* had said virtually nothing, but seemed bigger, almost mannish. It had been almost as if the man and woman had been wearing each other's clothes and aping each other's mannerisms.

The town itself was on a main drag, as those things went, but it was no four-lane expressway. It was a winding, two-lane stretch that went up into the wooded mountains and became the main street of a bunch of little towns.

McINERNEY, the sign announced just before you got to the turn and saw it, POP. 1349. It was two blocks long and maybe had houses going back a block or two on either side, with the small business district using diagonal parking. There was a drugstore, a couple of small cafes, a post office, a sheriff's office, a little town municipal building, a small food market, a service station, four places selling redwood burl to tourists who wandered by, and a small branch bank. There wasn't even a McDonald's. It all had wooden fronts and twin boardwalks for sidewalks, and not much else. The only reason it didn't look odd was that we'd gone through a dozen nearly identical places on the drive up here.

The reason why G.O.D. picked the spot, though, seemed to have to do not only with the depressed area, but also with the railroad tracks we crossed just the other side of town that then turned and paralleled the main drag. We passed a small motel, then saw the complex through the trees although it was well hidden from the road. The whole roadside was bracketed by a chain-link fence that was high and imposing, although partially hidden by the trees through which it snaked; but when you looked back through, in a couple of spots you could see some mighty large buildings up there.

There were two entrances; one just north of

town near the railroad tracks, and the other a main entrance about a mile further up that looked like the entrance to a military base. It was wide and paved, although it took a strategic turn away from visibility as soon as you cleared the gate, and it had a gatehouse in the center with railroad-style crossing gates blocking entry or exit without the man in the gatehouse pushing a button. A sign there indicated that Truck Entrance and General Receiving was the road near the tracks, but nowhere was there a sign indicating what sort of company this was.

By the time we'd arrived, it was well after seven, so there was little traffic around. You couldn't help wondering, though, how a place like that could be supported by a town this small. Commuting wasn't the answer, either; you'd have to go a couple of hours in either direction over a road like this to round up enough people to staff it. There wasn't much more we could do now; it was approaching darkness. I turned the car around and we headed back for the small motel, which was also, as far as I could see, the only motel or hotel in or near the town. If Whitlock was coming here, and wasn't staying with friends or associates at or inside the plant, the odds were that he was using the same place. I hadn't noticed a red Olds in the lot, but that might not mean much.

The desk clerk, a grandmotherly little old lady, stared at the registration card. "Philadelphia. We don't get many folks from back east in here. You with General?"

"Not exactly," I responded. "But we do business with them now and again. They sell a product for us now, but only in the east and midwest, and we're seeing if we want to expand to the coast and if it's worth the cost."

"Oh, really? What sort of product?"

"Women's wigs, actually. Natural-hair wigs at reasonable prices, and a new way to clean and restore them at home without costly treatments."

She nodded and completed the registration, no longer caring or even very curious about us. Even so, if we didn't wrap this up in a day or so, I knew everybody in town would know about us and why we were allegedly there, and that would include the powers that be, over at the company. I was counting on the fact that places like that have a complicated bureaucracy and that the left vice president usually didn't know what the right vice president was doing.

The room was surprisingly nice for a little motel in the middle of nowhere run by Grandma Moses. They had a color TV with cable so we could make sure not to miss any General product ad, and the usual amenities, and the beds were clean and firm.

Brandy had arranged for her box to be sent up to the Bend airport office of Overnite while we went shopping, and now she unpacked it. It did in fact contain the pistol and a box of bullets, but it also contained an assortment of other stuff, including a can of mace and a set of brass knuckles.

"You ask about the Currys?" she asked me. She was really feeling self-conscious in these parts, and hadn't come in with me to register.

"No, I figure this is a company town from the word go. If I asked her, then it might just tip them, even if they just dropped into the office for something and she mentioned we were asking about them. This is a small place, and if you think you're out of place here, they are, too. I—"

At that moment there was a tremendous roar of an engine and the whole place started to shake, and did so for several minutes. I went outside and walked around back of the unit with Brandy. The damned train tracks ran maybe ten yards in back of the motel, and this was one hell of a train going by. It seemed to go on forever, not just boxcars, but covered gondolas full of stuff, and tank cars, as well as flatbeds on which truck trailers were attached. After a while, the train stopped, still not ended, and there was a long pause when it just sat there. Then it lurched, backed up slowly, lurched again, then went forward a bit more.

"They're switching off a lot of cars, that's for sure," I told her. "I guess they must have their own little switchyard in there. I hope nobody wants to go into or out of town for a while."

She stared at the train, deep in thought. "You know, these cars seem to be loaded up with stuff. Those open ones have covered loads, and the freight cars are sunk down on their springs."

"Yeah? So? Before they can send the junk out, they have to have it in."

"Maybe. But did you see any railroad cars with mail or United Parcel signs on 'em? I couldn't make 'em out too well in the dark, but this outfit sends almost everything either UPS or mail."

"No, I didn't notice any, but that doesn't mean much. They probably just ship it out in special boxcars to the parcel terminals," I responded. "It'd be the only easy way in or out of here. That post office in town wasn't big enough to serve our block in Camden. Maybe they got their own post office up on the hill, or their own private UPS station. Some big places have that."

"I dunno. Maybe. It just don't seem right, somehow."

I shrugged. "Maybe this is just delivery from the hundreds of makers and importers of stuff. Maybe a different train ships 'em out once a day."

We left the train to its dancing, and walked back around, and Brandy looked up and then almost pushed me against the building.

"Hey! What . . . ?"

"*Shhhh!* My eyes may be goin' bad, but I swear there's a big red car pulling into the motel!"

I peered around the end unit and, sure enough, here it came. It couldn't have been coming from town, though, not with the train blocking the way, and it was unlikely to have been coming from the north. They had been over at the plant, that was clear.

We were in number twelve, and they pulled into the space for number sixteen, only four doors down from us. "Stay here for a moment," I told Brandy. "I'm gonna walk down and get a Coke." The soft-drink machine was at the end of the unit, just past number twenty-four.

They parked the car and got out just as I approached, paying me no attention at all. So here they were at last, I couldn't help thinking. We'd played all the long shots and we'd won.

What everybody had been telling us about them was definitely true. They didn't look just enough alike to be brother and sister, they looked nearly identical. Well, not quite. Amanda Curry looked like Whitlock perhaps ten or more years younger; there was a smooth and youthful look to the face, and a slighter build. Both were dressed casually in jeans and work shirts and boots, pretty much as I was. There was no real sexual confusion in the two dressed like this, but her hair was cut almost in a crew-cut fashion, as short as Brandy's, in its own way. Removed from the three-piece suit and cultural background, Whitlock's face was strikingly androgynous. It, too, was smoother and softer than you'd expect, and his hair was cut in much the same short fashion as hers.

She had been described as butch, and she was certainly that. Her mannerisms, her way of walking and moving, were culturally quite male, and she was clearly aggressive and in charge. They locked the car, and then she went to the door and opened it, and he followed. The door closed.

I wandered slowly past their room with my drink and there was a small gap where the two curtains hadn't completely closed, but I couldn't see much without standing there, and I thought better of that.

Brandy met me at our door and we went in. She took the Coke and drank a fair amount, then put it down. "Well? What do you think?" she asked me.

"I think everything we heard is true. The real question is what we do now. There are several possibilities, including going up and introducing ourselves, or trying to bluff our way past that gatehouse. The trouble is, that place looked *huge*, and there's no way to know if there's anything up there worth looking for, let alone what it might be."

"Little Jimmy thought there was something crazy goin' on up there, something dangerous."

"There's only one thing it can be. This corporation's some kind of blind or legitimate front for some rival in organized crime. Whitlock was into this bunch, and they forced him to double-cross the old bunch. Now that old bunch is busted, there's two-million-plus profit from the deal, and Whitlock's under their protection since the eastern mob doesn't forget and loves to make examples."

"And this dyke twin of his? What about her?"

I shrugged. "I don't know. I sure can't figure where she came from and why she looks so much like him, but it's clear she was in it because of that striking resemblance. Some part of the scam involved him being in two places at once, maybe leading Kennedy's crew away, or maybe Little Jimmy's boys. I'm sure the resemblance is natural. If it was some kind of plastic surgery, they'd have used a man with the same general build. Now she's got to get away as well, to keep the old mob guessing as to how the thing was worked, that's all. Face it, babe—it's over. It was one hell of a case, but in the end it was just an ordinary, ugly war between two rival mob factions. I don't know if old Marty likes to wear his wife's panty hose or not, but it's either true or something cooked up to ease the sense of doubt when the male and female Marty switched long-range identities. It doesn't matter. There's no more case."

She sighed. "I guess you're right. They're bound to figure that anybody still chasing them has a contract with the old mob. So what happens now?"

"Nothing. We stay here tonight, check out tomorrow, and very visibly go back to the airport and then back to Frisco. Then we call somebody back home, get our mail sent out, and see if Little Jimmy really came through with the referrals. If

he did, we'll see if we might want to relocate and
work for somebody else. If he didn't, well, I think
we got about two grand in cash left. After that—
the Delaware shore, as before."

"I guess," she sighed. "Still, I—"

Her words were broken by the sound of a loud
shot from one big gun and the immediate crash-
ing sound of a broken window. Since it wasn't
our window, Brandy grabbed the magnum and I
instinctively dove for and hit the lights, then we
both peered out the window from the side of the
curtains.

It was dark out there; someody had extin-
guished all the lights along the parking area, and
the red neon MOTEL sign gave little light. "You see
anybody?" she whispered.

"Uh uh."

"I got some cover with the car. I'm goin' out
there."

"What! Why?"

"They might just have got the wrong room the
first time, and in case you never noticed, lover,
these places ain't got no back doors."

She crouched down, and I slowly and quietly
opened the door enough for her to crawl out on
her hands and knees. She made it to the car grille,
but I could see someone lying prone further up,
someone who just might have been either Whitlock
or Curry. I not only couldn't tell if it was dead or
alive, with the light this poor, I could hardly tell
which way the body had fallen. Clearly, though,
nobody, not even Brandy, could safely move
against an unknown potential assassin out there
someplace, maybe with a sniperscope, unless
there was a diversion. I crouched down low to the
floor and opened the door a bit wider.

"Hey!" I shouted at the top of my lungs through thé cracked door. "What the hell is going on out there?"

A shot came right through the middle part of the door, about where I would have been standing had I not been born cautious. Brandy, however, had taken the opportunity to move down, since if the bastard was shooting at me he wasn't looking four doors down. I risked another peek and saw she'd reached the downed figure. A third shot roared and struck the pavement, sending sparks flying, but it was a good several inches from her. Whoever it was hadn't moved fast enough.

I wondered where in hell the cops were. Surely some of the other guests, or at least the manager, had called them by now. It wasn't too clear, though, if maybe our man had cut the lines, and in back I heard loud noises and the shifting of heavy cargo. That damned train was still blocking access to town!

I heard Brandy whispering frantically to someone, but I couldn't make out the words. There was another shot, and I heard somebody say, "I see him now! Other side of the road. Too far to hit with that cannon."

"Maybe not, but I can make it hot for him," Brandy responded. "Sam! You okay?"

"I'm in one piece, if that's what you mean." It suddenly occurred to me that the woman with the gun had such lousy vision she couldn't have hit the damned motel, let alone a guy a hundred yards away. Well, she could shoot in the general direction, and *he* wouldn't know that.

"The man's hit! It's not bad, but we're sure as hell pinned down here. That shooter's got a clear field of fire and—oh *shit!*" I heard her suddenly squeeze off three shots with the magnum, and I heard a scream from further down the walk. *"Got him!"*

Just great, I thought. Two of them. And how many more? Just what we needed at the end of the trail. No big payoff, and caught in the crossfire of a hit squad. Brandy had been lucky, too. The guy had missed with his shot, and she had only to brace and sight along the motel's front wall to nail him. I bet she still couldn't see the Coke machine.

"How many bullets you got?" I called to her.

"Just used three. That leaves five left in the clip."

"All right." I went back, found her box of cartridges, and went back to the door. "I'm coming out low to the car and bringing the bullets. Give me cover if I need it."

I didn't need it, because just then the lights of two cars illuminated the area in front of the motel, coming in toward town from the north. They both illuminated and somewhat blinded the shooter, and I took advantage of them to make it out and to toss the box to Brandy before dropping down to the far side of our car. I had no idea if the shooter saw me at all, but if he didn't, I had an idea. I made it around to the car door, figuring that it would be out of the shooter's line of sight, providing he hadn't taken the opportunity to move. I opened the car door carefully, keeping down, and eased inside, then fumbled for my keys. The shooter had a rifle and a good night scope at a range of maybe a hundred yards. Child's play for anybody with any skill at all.

"Give him a full clip!" I called to Brandy. "I don't want him to hear the car starting up!"

She fired off the remaining five and I started the car. He returned fire, three shots in their direction, one busting the back windshield of their Olds. Hertz, I decided, wasn't going to like any of us one bit.

There was no way I could use the car for cover, and a getaway for any of us was unlikely, but there was one way to buy a fair amount of time if they were ready to move. The end of the rear unit was only eight rooms from where they now were, and that would give them cover and two exits. The trick was to make it that far. I only hoped that, in fact, the bastard *was* using a sniperscope.

"As soon as I stop, you move!" I told them. "Don't stop for *anything!* Now—you reloaded?"

"Yeah!"

"Give me all you got, slow, one at a time!"

I put the car into reverse and gunned it backward at her first shot, then whirled it around as a shot came right through the windshield. I hit the brights, full, threw it into park, and dove for the couple of yards I needed to get in back of the motel office.

Sure, I knew he'd eventually shoot out the headlights, but with a sniperscope those brights blinded him almost instantly, and now they illuminated the whole stretch of parking lot, road, and tree-filled embankment on the other side where he was. Those damned lights were full in his face, and until he got them out, everything in the darkened motel in back was invisible to him except maybe the Coke machine.

When you mount a sniperscope, it's for a specific purpose. It takes time to shut it off, then remove it (since it's a big sucker) so you can use the standard pin sights. The guy was good; he'd just finished shooting out the last of the four headlights in less than thirty seconds with a couple in the grille for good measure, but now it was going to take him almost that long to remount and recalibrate his scope again. I looked back, trying to adjust my own eyes for the dark, and I didn't see a soul in the back units.

I did, however, hear the unmistakable sounds that the train was now moving, not just rumbling back and forth as cars were switched and disconnected up front. That meant traffic would soon be clear, and there'd be an open run from town to here and back again. This had already gone on longer than the shooter figured, I thought with confidence. He counted on maybe nabbing one clear, then keeping them pinned down until his partner could get to the room and finish the other off, counting on the train to block both traffic and loud shots. Clearly they hadn't expected third-party intervention, and particularly not third-party-with-a-big-peashooter-of-their-own. At this point, our boy would either have to run for it or come to us.

He was determined, that was for sure. I saw him now run down along the road, carrying the rifle as bold as you please, and then run across to the nearest block of units. He was pretty good, really; Uncle Sam had apparently shown him the proper way to do things with a rifle and against hostile fire. Clearly he was going to come up in back of that block of motel units, maybe all the way back to the tracks, then try and stalk them— and here I was without a weapon to my name.

I went forward, worried about Brandy but also having enough common sense to realize that I had to act independently with what I had. I made my way around to the motel office and found the door ajar. Inside, there was nobody, but the switchboard phone had been ripped out and all the connector cords had their plugs cut off. It was still connected, though; the thing buzzed like a hornet's nest and there were four lights flashing.

Under the reception counter, however, I thought I found what I was hoping for. Two buttons; one red, one white. If the phone *lines* were still connected, the odds were that these were, too. I pushed them both, and bells and alarms started going on all over the place. God bless Oregon for a strict fire code. About thirty seconds later I heard a loud siren from off toward town; clearly the fire alarm had triggered the volunteer signal, something I hadn't figured on at all but didn't mind in the least.

Two cars with flashing red lights arrived within a minute, but they weren't who I expected. Both were white cars with SECURITY on them in big black letters. These weren't from town; they were from the corporation. I didn't care who they were. They had on plant-blue uniforms and they wore .38s. I went up to the nearest of them.

"Two guys started opening up on the middle unit," I told them. "One from over there, one from the end. The one at the end's been taken out, but the sniper is moving up in back there and he has a scope!"

"Who're they after?" the private cop asked, drawing his weapon.

"Two guests and my wife are back there someplace, with one gun."

There was a sudden sharp exchange of fire from in back of the motel. I heard the rifle go twice, and Brandy's magnum go three times, but it was hard to tell the order and impossible to say who got who. They didn't wait, though. One car went to each end of our middle unit and they got out, using the doors as shields, acting like real pros.

Red and blue lights from a sheriff's car appeared, and it too roared up, followed by a very large fire engine. I shouted for the firemen to get down—it was a sniper, not a fire—then threw caution to the winds and ran back up to the middle unit. Both rent-a-cop teams had moved in back, while the deputies split to cover the rear of the two end units. I wasn't worried about myself, but I was terrified as to what those shots might mean for Brandy. I suddenly realized just how much I needed her.

It had been over, however, before the reinforcements arrived. As I went around in back of the rental cops, I heard Brandy shout and then saw the cops move in back and switch on their flashlights. I followed, and found the trio in the culvert between the back of the motel and the tracks, with two of the company cops now putting away their weapons and leaning down to help the wounded. Two others were examining a form about twenty feet away.

Whitlock looked messy, but he really was pretty lucky. Most of the damage was nothing but superficial cuts from the motel window shattering. He'd been nicked in the side but it wasn't much; he'd simply tried to make it out to the car, and gotten trapped in the crossfire, playing dead because he was too scared to move.

Brandy hadn't gotten the shooter; Amanda had a rifle, too, which I'd mistaken for the hit man's shots. It just had a small, cheap, regular scope on it, though, useless from inside the room at that distance and in the dark. Braced here, though, with the hitter walking full-body toward her, she couldn't miss.

"We better get you up to the plant infirmary," one of the rental cops said to Whitlock. "You all right for the car or should I call for the town ambulance?"

"I—I can manage," he said weakly, and I was startled to hear his voice, which was low, soft, but almost—if not all the way—into the female register. Close up he looked smoother, more—I don't know, certainly not an ex-Marine, if you know what I mean. In point of fact, seeing the pair now, close and off their guard and not moving about, they *did* look damned near identical, but not in the way I figured. It wasn't a case of her trying to look like him; rather, it was he who was looking and sounding very much like her.

I went to Brandy. "You all right?"

"Yeah, I think so," she managed, breathing a little hard. "It was pretty hairy there, though, wasn't it? If you hadn't pulled that bit with the car lights, we'd all been dead ducks."

We walked over to the dead hit man, and even Brandy's eyes weren't so bad that she didn't give a little gasp and cry. This one was a real bloody mess, but the face was pretty much unmarked. That face, those eyes, were very familiar to me.

"What the *hell* is going on here?" I managed.

Lying on the ground, dead from three shots in the torso, was unmistakably the form of Martin Whitlock IV, looking very male and very ex-Marine and just like his picture.

I turned, ready to demand an explanation of this as an earned right, and came face to face

with the sheriff of McInerney. Or, rather, face to
chest. He was about six five, three hundred
pounds, all muscle, including the head. He was
the biggest, meanest-looking sucker I'd ever seen.

Brandy stared at him, equally openmouthed. I
think we both felt he was either somebody on a
break from a circus sideshow or he was going to
say, *Marlowe, I want you to find my Velma.*
Instead, he looked down at Brandy's magnum.
"Ma'am, you'll have to give me that," he said in a
very deep and commanding voice, the kind that
you would have obeyed if he'd said you had to
get down on all fours and bark like a dog. She
handed him the pistol, butt first. "What is your
name, ma'am?"

"Horowitz. Mrs. Brandy Horowitz."

The big man was certainly startled. "Horowitz?" He turned to me. "And I suppose your
name is Uncle Remus?"

"That's uncalled for, Sheriff," I responded, getting my nerve back. That kind of stuff never went
over with me whether in Camden or in the wilds.
"I'm Sam Horowitz and this is my wife. We're
private investigators."

"Oh, yeah? Then, I guess you have a license for
this artillery piece?"

The fact was, she didn't, but a good P.I. always
is ready. "Sure, but it's in Jersey," she responded.

"Well, we'll have to check that out. Will you
both come along with me, please?"

They were already taking the couple from the
east away, and I noticed that the private cops
were attending to the sniper's body exclusively. I
would have loved to have gotten a look at the
other hitter out front, but I was a little afraid
he'd look just like Martin Whitlock and I wasn't

sure I could take yet a fourth look-alike, particularly tonight. Still, I didn't like this treatment.

"Look, Sheriff, we just saved that couple's life," I pointed out. "I'm not saying we're owed an explanation, but at least I think we deserve some courtesy. Without us, you'd have two dead bodies."

"Yeah, well, we appreciate that, Mr. Horowitz, we really do, but that don't mean we don't follow procedures. We got two dead, and the one in front was killed with something other than a rifle—this pistol, I assume."

"He was shootin' at *us!*" she protested. "All I did was self-defense!"

"Well, ma'am, I'm sure an investigation will show that, but right now it's a shooting requiring justification. Just get into the car, please, both of you."

"So what's the charge on me?" I asked him. "I'd go anyway to get this ridiculous thing out of the way with my wife, but you're acting like I'm under arrest as well."

"Yes, sir, you are, and it's my duty to inform you that anything you say from this point can be taken down and used in evidence against you, and that you are entitled to a lawyer before any questioning begins. If you can not afford a lawyer, one will be appointed for you without charge. Do you understand that?"

"Yes. I want to know the charge on me."

"Well, sir, suspicion of vandalism, suspicion of breaking and entering, and turning in a false fire alarm, for starters."

"This is absurd!"

Absurd it was, but they took us in, booked us, and brought us up before a very-sleepy-looking magistrate. We waived the right to a lawyer right now, since in a company town there was no way in hell he'd do anything but cost us money, but we reserved the right to import one later. The judge looked over the charge sheet and also a list of what had been on our persons at the time of booking. Unfortunately, that included our last two grand and our credit cards.

"Samuel Horowitz, you are accused of three misdemeanor counts. Do you have counsel?"

"Not at this time, Your Honor, but I will."

"Very well. Trial is set for nine in the morning on the fourth of August. Bail is set at five hundred dollars, with a condition that you remain within this county until the trial date. To insure that, should you post bail, we will retain your wallet, cards, driver's license, and investigator's license. Meals may be taken at Malone's Cafe, and lodging at the motel, said charges to be deducted from your bond upon appearance. Next."

He looked down at Brandy and you could see on his face that he didn't much like her color or her attitude.

"Brandy Parker Horowitz, you are charged with willfully causing the death of another, identity to be determined. As the sheriff's report indicates that the victim himself possessed a weapon and it had been fired, the holding charge is manslaughter pending the outcome of a final investigation. As no holster was found, under the laws of the state of Oregon you are also charged with carrying a concealed and loaded weapon. As these are potentially serious charges, trial is not set, pending the outcome of a complete investigation. Bail is set at—ah—one thousand seven hundred forty-six dollars and twenty-seven cents. Condition of bail is that you not leave the jurisdiction of this court until trial." The other conditions were the same as mine.

In effect, the bastard yokel had taken every cent we had, including pocket change, as well as every single thing we had—those credit cards, driver's licenses, you name it. Ordinarily I'd have called the bar association all the way over in Salem and gotten a civil-liberties man here, while refusing to pay, but I didn't like the idea of Brandy being locked up in a redneck jail like this even for a few days. Frankly, from their attitude at the booking, I didn't think they'd be real nice to even a white guy if his name was Horowitz.

It was dawn before they had a deputy drive us back up to the motel, and when we got there, dead tired and pissed as hell, we found that they'd cleaned up most of the mess, although the window to Whitlock's room was still out and there were still two holes in our door. When we got inside, we discovered that we'd had visitors. The contents of our new suitcase and Brandy's box had been dumped and gone through carefully, and they'd taken anything that might have been a weapon. Also missing was my photo of Whitlock and all that pertained to the case.

"Well, Little Jimmy warned us," I sighed, undressing and flopping down on the bed. "Remind me next time to let anybody who wants to shoot and kill anybody else they want, if we aren't getting paid to save 'em."

"It really burns me," she agreed, flopping next to me and looking just as tired. "They took the help, but they didn't even say thanks."

I stared at her. "Still, just when you think you got it, something else pops up and sticks it back in the Twilight Zone or something. How many Martin Whitlocks *are* there?"

"I dunno," she responded, yawning. "But if they're gonna keep us on ice in this place, I think maybe we oughta get a look at that plant. What's one more charge, more or less, anyway?"

She had a point there.

"I'm dead," she said, "but I think maybe I'll go out for a moment and get something from a few doors down."

"Huh? What?"

"They took most of the stuff from the box, but the little fingerprint kit is still there. I just thought of something, if they haven't cleaned it up. I'll be right back."

She returned in less than a minute, triumphantly cradling something in a handkerchief, and she put it down and unwrapped it on the bed. It was a small flask, gold plated but unadorned with designs or symbols.

"When she crawled out to him, she brought this to ease his pain, thinkin' he was hurt worse than he was. He took it and drank some, then put it down. You got off in the car then and I was shootin', so I wasn't sure what happened to it. It was still there on the walk." She carefully removed the small brush and powder from her kit. They'd pushed their hands in to make sure nothing was hidden there, but that was all.

"What's the difference?" I asked her. "They even took the print samples I had of Whitlock."

"Yeah, but they both touched this in my presence, and neither of 'em were wearin' gloves. I just *got* to know."

There weren't many prints on the thing, although enough were smudged that you couldn't tell anything for sure, but there were four or five clear ones of thumbs and index fingers. "Yeah—

see? All three thumbs match and both index fingers match."

"So? It just means the smudges are the other one's."

"Uh uh. See here? One of those sets is slightly smaller than the other, and there's a difference in the grip." She showed me, and I was doubly impressed with her, sleepy as I was. You had to really look at them, but there wasn't much doubt in my mind that they were two different people's prints.

"You're telling me that Whitlock and Curry have the same fingerprints?"

"Nope—*that* says so." She carefully applied the fixative and then the paper, and peeled off the prints. "If only we coulda done this with the sniper. I wonder if the prints match?"

"If they do, then we've shot hell out of all police work," I pointed out. I was beginning to really feel like I'd fallen into the Twilight Zone now. "No wonder they only found one set of prints in that apartment."

"Sam—just what in hell are we dealin' with here?"

I shook my head. "I dunno, babe. I remember reading about clones a while back. Make a whole new you from one cell of your body. I knew they could do it with some plants and stuff, maybe worms, but not people. And why Whitlock?" I paused. "No, that won't work, either. In your genes you're either male or female. We're dealing with a male one—the shooter—a female one in Curry who even the lesbian locker room accepted, and our own target, who looked a little of each last night. Damn! They don't like Jews much around here, and they don't like blacks. Maybe it's some kind of neo-Nazi genetic experiment using the rich blue blood of the east."

"That would sure explain that sheriff. Nobody like him was ever born natural."

"Well, I'm gonna sleep on it, if I don't have nightmares," I told her. "Later on, when I'm awake and reasonably normal, we'll see about looking over that plant."

They had completely cleaned up the mess four rooms down by the time we awoke, and somebody had been by and towed away both our car, which was shot to pieces, and theirs, which was only slightly better. It looked deserted and lonely.

We walked the mile and a half down to the cafe, stopping at the railroad crossing and looking off into the woods where the tracks vanished. There were two sets of tracks, both with polished rails, telling me that this was no spur put in for the company's convenience but at least a backup main line that had some regular traffic on it. That meant that there was probably a spur just up from here, leading into the plant itself, that necessitated the long loading and unloading and the back-and-forth shifts of the train. It would be interesting to know just how much of the train was uncoupled and stored there. Possibly quite a lot, judging from the hour or so it blocked everything up.

I didn't wonder that they hadn't locked us up in town. The whole sheriff's office seemed to have just two cells, more like holding areas, and both of them were used for drunks and the like. Normal procedure, if they were serious about the charges against Brandy, would have been to hold her until she could be transferred to a county lockup, wherever that might be, and to process her and set bail at that time. The fact was, they didn't want us off with state authorities and real lawyers and judges outside the company's control. They just wanted us on ice until they—or the company—decided just what to do with us.

The cafe extended the friendliness we'd come to expect from the town. We entered and were told to wait, although there were only three tables with people at them, out of a total of maybe twenty tables and booths. The waitress went back, and brought out two large bags and two cans of Coke and handed them to us. I peered inside. It looked like a burger, fries, a small wilted-looking salad in a plastic dish with a cover on it, and a commercial brownie. We sighed and started to sit down at one of the tables, but the waitress stopped us. "I'm sorry, but you'll have to eat outside somewheres," she told us, not sounding the least bit sorry. She lowered her voice. "Some of our patrons object to eating in the same place as you."

We looked around. None of the patrons there now seemed more than mildly curious about us.

Brandy looked her straight in the eye. "You mean with black folks?"

The waitress shrugged. "We are sensitive to our customers' wishes. They're our bread and butter."

"You never heard of the Civil Rights Act? The Equal Accommodations Act?"

"No," responded the waitress, and it sounded like she meant it. "Look, you better go before there's trouble. Some folks here won't take kindly to you causing trouble, and it wouldn't do no good to yell for a cop. Besides, where else you gonna get food? You go or you starve."

We got the idea. I'd seen some of those guys in the logging outfits and big pickups around town already, and I just didn't think it was the best time to get into a real argument with them, not to mention the fact that we did indeed depend on this place for even the leftover shit they handed us. At least the Coke was fresh. There was a little park near the railroad tracks with a lone picnic table, and we ate the food there, such as it was.

"What do you think?" Brandy asked me.

"I think we're in deep shit," I responded honestly. "Look, there's a phone booth over there. If I had a quarter to activate it, I'd try a few collect calls or charges to our home number."

"This do?" she asked me, and reached into her purse and pulled out a small amount of change. Small, but at least a buck's worth. I stared at it. "How'd you manage *that?*"

"It all fell on the floor last night when I was cleanin' out the purse. Before any of that shit hit the fan, I mean. I got some of it, but most of it wound up in back of the bed. I thought of it this morning."

I took a quarter and walked to the booth, wondering if we finally hadn't had a break. This proved, however, to be a rather unique phone company. First of all, the operator apologetically said that it wasn't the policy of the phone company to permit charges to an out-of-state number. It wasn't a question of dealing with AT&T or GTE; she wouldn't give me a long-distance line. I tried a couple of collect calls to numbers at home, including Kennedy's DEA number, but each time that same operator told me that they refused to accept the call. When she refused to connect me to the Oregon state cops, I got the message.

At least I got the quarter back.

"No good," I told Brandy. "They got us cut off. They own either the phone company or the operators here, too. The only thing now would be to hitchhike up to the next town, where they might have a freer phone system, or hop a freight and scram. They don't seem to be watching us too closely."

She thought it over. "Maybe, but even if we could get out, then what? We got no money, no ID, no *nothin'*. We go to the state cops, they just turn us back over here—and you know it. We go to some lawyer, he ain't gonna believe a word of this, and it's our word against theirs and they got those charges. I ain't gonna spend a life in this wilderness washin' dishes and lookin' over my shoulder for no cops who want me on no murder rap and you for aidin' and abettin' a fugitive. Hell, this crew could probably get Hertz to give out interstate warrants on us for stealin' their car!"

And that, of course, was exactly why nobody was keeping close tabs on us. The fact was, they didn't much care if we escaped. Either we'd be ruined for life, and on the run, or we'd get picked up and trucked right back here. Brandy lit a cigarette and looked at it mournfully. "And I only got four more packs of *these!*"

"I told you not to start again. Come on, if you're done. I think I'm in the mood for a romantic walk in the woods."

We walked along the railroad tracks for a few hundred yards, then came to the switching point. The whole area cleared out fairly good just up along the single-track spur, and for the first time we could see the complex that was General

Ordering and Development, Inc. It was damned impressive.

There must have been thirty or forty railcars on sidings, eight per track, along with unloading areas for both bulk cargo and containers. A number of truck cabs and frames sat in a neat lot nearby, waiting for goods. Two warehouse-style buildings were visible, both of which seemed to go off into the distance. Because of a ten-foot fence topped with barbed wire and a solid and locked gate across the tracks, that was all that could be seen of the complex.

Brandy gave a low whistle. "They sure didn't get this big on Vegetrons," she noted. No people were visible, but when Brandy shook the fence, more in frustration than to do anything, there was a sudden, furious barking, and from the vicinity of the boxcars came a whole horde of very nasty-looking Dobermans. We didn't need any more hints; we started back before they started hurling themselves at the fence.

"You got to figure they use those to check the trains for visitors," she noted, disappointed.

"Yeah, probably, but it's still the weak link in their system. They have to keep those dogs locked up when the fence is open. You can bet on that. Ten to one they don't roam much during regular hours, either, or no employee there would be totally safe. If we rode in on a car and then managed to get up toward the buildings before they secured the place, I think we'd be safe."

"Yeah, then all we got to worry about is their own cops and alarms, with them all uptight to keep what happened last night from happenin' again."

"Then, we play it by ear. But if a train comes

through tonight and stops, then at least one of us is going up there. I can't see how anything short of execution is any worse than what we got now. If we can discover something, then maybe we can make a deal."

We weren't exactly equipped for burglary, but the bottle of black hair dye I'd bought during our Bend shopping spree had enough for my hair and also to dye one of her tee shirts black. I figured the plaid shirt and jeans would do for me.

I hadn't really expected another train the next evening. For one thing, it was Saturday, and any plant was likely to be closed the next day, particularly in this northwest version of the Bible Belt, but I was wrong. I wondered just where the hell they were going to park the new cars, since the sidings up there had looked pretty full.

We went out in back of the motel and began walking alongside the train. We didn't see anyone, but kept out of the light and close to the brush just to be sure. Finally we came to where the road curved to go into town and the tracks crossed the road, and there we saw flashing lights not only from the crossing signs but also from cars blocking the way. Both the sheriff's deputies on the town side and the company cops on our side were actively at the crossing and out of their cars. Up near the gate they were bound to have active security, and we clearly weren't the only ones to see this point as a weak spot.

"Can't ride the rods," I told Brandy. "They're sure to check there. And I don't see any open boxcars. The only crack we have at it might be that gondola just in back of that livestock car or whatever it is."

It was a tarp-covered load, and seemed to be

filled with a dark crushed rock. We crawled in and under the tarp, and both of us quickly wondered why the hell we'd bothered dying anything. You just sat in that stuff and you were covered with black soot. It was almost like fine coal dust, a whole railroad car full, but it definitely wasn't coal. I couldn't figure out just what it might be. The car in front, though, turned out to be chock-full of live and very agitated turkeys, very much awake in the middle of the night and protesting loudly. It covered any sounds we might make, but it worried me. This General Ordering wasn't likely to be doing TV ads for live turkeys, and that implied that we might be in a section that wasn't going in at all.

"If we don't, we don't," was Brandy's response. "The hell with this. Either we get in there tonight or we take this train to someplace where we can call home and get some help from somebody."

We waited several endless minutes and then the train lurched and started to move slowly forward. As we crossed the intersection, the law had lights shining under the cars and through the couplings, and men there to check 'em out. We kept real still and didn't watch much of the festivities.

We stopped in the woods short of the gate and there was another lurch. I risked a peek and saw a whole line of cars ahead of us being pulled off onto the siding. I couldn't see around the turkeys, but I could've sworn the main engine wasn't attached. That truck and rail yard was really lit up, though, and there was a bunch of people around, many coming this way from the gate and checking under and even up on the cars. I didn't like that.

I could hear a bunch of them close-by now, and for some reason all my mind could picture was a marching army of Martin Whitlocks.

"Hey, Al! What you doing up there?" somebody called. "You think somebody's gonna climb in there with them turkeys? Anybody does that deserves to get through. Those things peck like hell!"

There were some grumbles from ahead and some casual laughter from nearby on the side. If they were this thorough, the odds were that they were going to take the damned tarp off. There wasn't much to do but burrow down in this soft, sooty stuff and get as still as possible.

The tarp came off, although I knew it more by sound than by sight. I just held my breath and prayed I wouldn't sneeze, and I hoped Brandy was doing the same.

A couple of guards jumped up on either side and stuck their hands in the muck, one not too far from me. "*Yuk!* This stuff's really lousy!" one of them said, and the others seemed to agree. They put the tarp back on and jumped down. I was about to burst, but I gave them as much time as I could before slowly easing my head up and taking a breath—and then trying to stifle a coughing fit. Brandy, as a newly returned chain-smoker, was in worse shape than I was on this, but the train gave a noisy lurch and we were going forward again as she hacked the stuff out of her lungs, me not far behind her. I finally crawled up and peeked out, and saw we were through the gate and being pulled onto a siding. Off to the left, I could see a small switcher pushing a long line of railcars out the other side and back to the main track.

Well, at least that explained the storage and the back-and-forth jerks. They uncoupled the engine, drove it forward a ways past a second switch, then took a number of cars on a switcher out to be hooked up to the big one, while other, full cars were pulled into the newly vacated siding.

"I hear dogs barking," Brandy hissed to me. "Think maybe they do a check with them and a trainer?"

"Bet on it. We're gonna hafta get the hell off as soon as we stop, and get to cover up by the main buildings."

"*Anything* to get out of this shit bath," she said, and I could only agree with her on that one.

As soon as we stopped, I looked around, saw nobody, and got out, then gave her a quick hand down from a ledge to the ground. We went immediately under the next row of train cars and out the other side again, and none too soon. The dog barking was getting real loud, and just as we cleared the next set of standing cars they lurched. We had to keep going, under and across, as long as possible.

There was a short stretch of open track rows at the end of the last line of train cars, and it was well lit. Up top in a tower were two figures looking very busy as they surveyed it all. The switchman and the dispatcher for the yard, most likely. It was maybe thirty yards to any real darkness and cover, but it was only about thirty *feet* to the base of that tower. Under it, we couldn't be seen by the men above, and we'd have a little cover in the shadows while we waited for our best chance to run the rest of the way. We poked our heads out, and looked in both directions from under a boxcar. There were a few figures walking down at the far end, but nobody seemed close. The big danger would be if one of the two guys in the tower looked down, but we had to chance it.

"Now!" Brandy whispered. "Nobody close; one dude up there is gone and the other's lookin' through binoculars." Unthinking, I followed her to the tower shadows as fast as I could run, then braced myself against a support beam, breathing hard. I looked over at her and saw she wasn't breathing all too comfortable herself.

"Take your time," I said in a low, hushed tone. "We got twice as far to run the next leg and we don't want to collapse halfway." I stared over at her, concerned, and still a little disconcerted by her looks. Without her old hair or the wig she really looked different.

She looked at me and grinned. "In all this time, this is the first time you've ever been blacker'n me."

"Guess again. All it did was equalize us. *Sheesh!* I don't know what that stuff is, but ten to one it's cancer-causing at the very least."

"Smells like some kind of gasoline," she noted.

"Yeah. Must be some petroleum product, some plastic powder. It's probably easy to store and ship that way, then gets poured into little molds and heated to make plastic widgets for nineteen ninety-five. You ready?"

She nodded. "Ready as I'll ever be."

"Then, let's do it!" A quick check showed nobody in sight, and we headed straight back for the darkness at the edge of the tracks, which proved to mark a point about two thirds of the way up a hill or embankment toward the plant itself. The thing wasn't totally dark, but as black as we both were, it gave more than enough cover. We had experience from the night before how hard it was to spot somebody in a dark place.

We ran most of the way up that hill until we hit another high fence. It wasn't expected, and we both stopped and sat down against it and looked back at where we'd covered. It seemed an impossible distance.

Brandy pointed. "Rental-cop lights, up and down between those far cars. See 'em?"

"Yeah. Maybe the dogs smelled us. I guess we got to keep moving. Wonder if there's a break in this fence?"

"Got to be. Question is whether or not there's people at the gates."

She was right, of course. There were two large gates big enough for trucks to pass through, both open but both with people on them. There was a smaller gate further down, just people-sized, that was unguarded, but there was no way in hell we could get to it without getting past the truck gates, and if we could do that we could go through them.

There was only one guy on the closest gate, and he didn't look like a guard, more like a truck driver or factory worker. A truck cab came down and stopped, and he talked to the driver and pointed. Just a yard boss or traffic manager, I thought. "Well? Do we take him out or wait him out?" I asked her.

"Let's wait a couple minutes. Then we'll take him out if we have to. I don't like the lights down there, but there ain't much can be done 'bout it. We got to get through and I forgot my wire cutters tonight."

Sometimes, patience will give you a little break. Another truck came up and stopped, and this time the guy jumped up on the step and said something to the driver, and they drove down to the yard, the gate man hanging on. We didn't wait for an engraved invitation, but started crawling down to that open gate as fast as we could. I made it first, got up quickly and turned the corner, then flattened in the darkness on the other side. Brandy had more trouble than I did, but, then, she wasn't shaped right for it and she hadn't had the benefit of Uncle Sam's technique.

It was a nick-of-time thing, but we made it. No doubt about it—they had some holes in their security, whether we'd had luck or not. They knew it, too; about twenty seconds after Brandy had cleared the lighted area and had joined me prone on the grass on the warehouse side, a private cop car roared up to the gate, stopped, and radioed something. Within two or three minutes a guy, maybe the same one who was there before, came running up from the yards and started getting into a screaming match with the rent-a-cop. Finally they had the last words and the cop drove on up past us and back into the complex. I didn't know who won, but the guy on the gate gave a rising finger in the direction of the cop's taillights and at least had the satisfaction of the last word.

"Okay, sweetheart," I said in my best Bogie voice, "let's go case this joint."

5.

The Labyrinth

The place was *big*, bigger even than we'd thought from the outside. It went back, it seemed, almost forever, an endless series of gigantic warehouse structures with office-type fronts and loading-dock rears, interconnected with a network of roads. This was no television-junk joint, I don't care how much they make. This was many millions right here, and this was only a *branch* location. I hated to see what they had near Davenport.

Still, in a way, it was *less* than I expected, too. "This joint's as big as General Motors," I noted, "but where's the smokestacks?"

She frowned. "Yeah. I think we're gonna wear this gunk forever, but if it's some kind of raw plastic, then where's the place they make it into little plastic thingies? You're right!"

"I'm more than right. We haven't been over this whole place yet, having been here more like an hour than a week, but so far I haven't come across any big parking lots, either. Place this size must take hundreds, maybe thousands, of people to run. So far, outside of the rail yards, all I've seen are rent-a-cops and gate guards. Oh, that's a lot over there, but it's for what? Ten? Twelve cars, tops."

"Maybe they bus them in from town," Brandy suggested, thinking.

"That whole town would have to be here, and there's no sign of it. That town would be bigger than it is, just supporting the work force this place must take. I mean, two jail cells, two little cafes, one gas station, and a grocery store that was a real mom-and-pop operation? Come on. That town isn't real. The whole damned thing's a front, run for this operation by folks out of work for years with the logging bust, taking their money and being their whores. It's bought and paid for, so nobody looks too close and nobody notices things out of the ordinary. How they get up the tax assessor I don't know, but bigger fish than him have been bought and paid for. If I remember, this was the state where that Indian swami and his cult took over and ran a whole county for years."

"That doesn't answer your question," she pointed out. "Where are the people who work here? Who are they and where do they live?"

"Even better. Where in here do they process a couple hundred live turkeys?"

The rent-a-cops had been real active in patrols, but if they thought anybody was inside who shouldn't be, they didn't act like it. They were easy to dodge, even though the streetlights within the complex were well thought out. The real problem was the sheer size of the place, and the inability to really get a look inside those massive buildings. Many were lit; it appeared as if the biggest one in the back was active and at work, although there was no sign of life outside nor any crowd of cars or whatever anywhere around.

The buildings, too, were mostly wired with elaborate burglar alarms and remote sensors and switches. It wouldn't be easy to get into one that wasn't lit up and in operation.

We did eventually find a parking lot attached to a large one-story structure, but it looked more like the headquarters for the state police, with maybe a dozen plant-security cars parked there and spaces for at least as many more, along with spaces where regular cars were parked. At least the cops commuted.

Without a full tool kit, with jumper wires and pliers and glass cutters and the like, it was unlikely we were going to break into any of the buildings. Worse, sometime the next day we were sure to be missed by the folks down at the town, and while they might figure we scrammed, they would also be thinking of the plant and grounds here. I wasn't sure I wanted to spend much time around here like this. The black stuff smelled and itched like crazy, and there was no food, and no evident water, either. We'd spent so much time on getting in, we hadn't even thought about getting out.

"Let's get over by that big building that looks like it's open," Brandy suggested. "Maybe we can find some way to see in."

"Sounds like a good plan to me," I agreed, just wanting to get *something* out of this experience. We headed over that way, but then had to drop as a door leading inside the building opened and two people walked out, both dressed casually although not in any particularly recognizable fashion. One was a big man, fat but imposing, sort of the kind you expect to see either selling door to door or driving one of Oregon's ubiquitous pickup trucks; the other was a slender woman of medium height. They were engaged in an animated conversation, and I couldn't make out a word of it. It sure as hell wasn't English.

"Sounds like a record bein' played backwards," Brandy whispered, and the fact was, it sounded *just* like that, only very natural, very conversational.

They passed quite near us, oblivious to our presence, but we stared hard at them. The woman, for example, looked very young, yet she had shoulder-length hair that looked snow-white and a smooth, dark complexion that was hard to make out in the available light. The big man had a face that seemed dark and covered in hair; not just a beard, but more like a monkey's face, and his arms showing beyond his short-sleeve shirt were also the hairiest I'd ever seen. I resisted the impulse to check the moon to see if it was full, although I never really believed in werewolves.

They went to another building, and the big man took out some keys and opened a small box set in the door, and punched a combination that sounded like a push-button telephone being dialed. Then he opened the door and they both stepped in and switched on lights.

"Want to jump into the fire?" Brandy asked. "We'll probably get caught, but it's the only way."

"I don't want to do anything but get out of here," I answered truthfully, but I followed her as she approached the newly unlocked door and tried it. It opened, straight into a small reception

room with a desk, chair, and phone, but there
was no sign of the hairy man and the white-
haired woman anywhere. "They could leave and
lock us in here," I whispered.

"Uh uh. There's fire exits, and there's a phone I
bet don't go through town," Brandy responded.
"We're better off than we were and we get a
chance to look around. Come on."

There was a sudden sound of starting machinery, the lights dimmed for a moment, then
the whole building started to shake as whatever
it was that had been turned on got up to speed.
We cautiously approached the inner door, opened
it, and peered into a still-darkened warehouse. It
was hard to see anything on the floor of the
place, although there were catwalks high above
that had small lights on them, and far off along
one side was a glass picture window at catwalk
height that was lit up.

We went along the wall, hitting a stairway up
to the catwalks, and both of us got up on it a few
steps and tried to see into the darkness of the
warehouse floor.

"Sam," Brandy said uneasily, "I swear that the
whole bunch of dark there just *moved.*"

We went further on up the stairway to a metal
porch that seemed well above the floor and just
below the catwalk level. We were on the opposite
side from the picture window and couldn't even
really see it from where we were, so it was
unlikely we'd be spotted.

Whatever was happening, it took a tremendous
machine to do it; and that machine seemed to be
under the floor of the warehouse. I stared into the
blackness in the center of the place that should
be visible, at least in outline, to me at this point

but wasn't, and I saw what Brandy had talked about. The darkness seemed almost a solid mass, and it appeared to be shifting, moving, changing shape and form. It was weird, whether real or some kind of optical illusion.

Old Sam Spade and Phil Marlowe had never had to face anything like *this*.

There was another start-up-type whine, and suddenly the center of the warehouse wasn't dark anymore, although I'm not sure just what it could be called. In the center of the darkness, there appeared another, flatter darkness. Sorry, that's the only way I can describe it. It was shiny but nonreflective, like a mirror, and the only reason it could be discerned at all was because it was framed by a pencil-thin outline of blue light. The blue was quite clear, but gave off no radiant light, so the rest of the warehouse floor was still bathed in darkness. Every once in a while, across the surface of the mirrored blackness, small trails of blue light would shoot like stars on a summer night.

It scared the living shit out of me.

"It's invaders from Mars or something," Brandy breathed. "My God—did Little Jimmy know about this?"

"Not at the start, not when he hired us," I managed, unable to keep my eyes off the strange thing on the floor below. "I think maybe he found out more than was good for him before he canned us, though." What would make a weasel like Little Jimmy write off over two million? *This* might. The deal was clear. You call off your dogs and take a long vacation in the tropics, and we'll bail you out and keep you off the bust list.

The crazy thing was, I was ready to believe in

Martians or whatever with no real effort, even that they'd hole up in a place like this. Where else? They'd be kind of obvious in downtown Philadelphia. But the Martians involved in a drug deal and double-crossing a Mafioso? *That* I couldn't handle. Not yet.

The big mirror changed. It seemed to fold in on itself, like a file card being crimped in the middle, then go through itself, and when it finished there wasn't one mirror but two, the other intersecting the first at a clean ninety degrees. Now there were more folds, each section folding in, and the thing began to take on a crazy pattern, not regular at all. It reminded me almost of those pictures you see of those old English gardens with the hedges cut like a kid's maze. But this thing was in three dimensions right here on a warehouse floor, and it was turning.

"Let's get out of here," I told Brandy. "We don't know how big and complicated that thing's gonna get, and how safe is safe. That pair up there is up and beyond that floor behind glass. We're not. We don't know where safe is. Maybe it's just gonna take that plastic powder and instantly make forty million plastic Jesus statues, but I don't like to be this close to it until I know a lot more."

"Yeah, okay," she answered huskily.

I took her hand and together we went down the stairway. I could see the door only a few feet beyond the end of the stairs, since it not only showed light around the edges but even had a little red EXIT sign illuminated above it. That *thing* was still twisting and turning, faster and faster now, and I knew we were in a race. I had my eyes only on that door now, and, naturally, I

missed the bottom step and fell onto the cold
concrete floor of the place, Brandy falling on top
of me. I was hurt, but not enough to matter, and
Brandy got up and reached out to help me up,
taking my hand in the near darkness. I found it,
took it, and was just pulled to my feet when one
of the edges of that blue and black thing folded
and hit us like a revolving door.

Suddenly I could see Brandy, and she could see
me, very well. We both had glows of the blue
stuff all around our bodies, making us stand out,
but all around us were constantly changing walls
of blue-framed blackness. I gripped her hand
tight, fearful that we would never again see each
other if I let go, and looked for the door and the
sign. There was nothing, nothing but constantly
changing panes of black mirror framed in blue.
Only they weren't mirrors. They weren't *anything*.
One swung around on us before we knew it and
passed right through us. I braced, expecting to be
slapped down by a solid swinging door, but there
was no sensation at all. It just came, passed
through us, and went on its merry way.

I don't mind admitting that I was scared to
death—not only being trapped in that thing, but
scared, too, that I would lose Brandy's hand and
my only remaining touch to anything real. She
held my hand just as tight, and I could tell that
the same thoughts were going through her own
mind.

It did no good whether you stood still or
started walking; the endless series of blue-outlined
panels kept moving anyway, so I pulled on her
hand and started walking in the direction I was
certain was the exit door. With no physical
sensation, the light show lost some of its threat-

ening aspects. The effect of moving, though, was unnerving, since all of a sudden it seemed as if everything stopped shifting around but you were boxed in with a cube of blue-outlined squares. Stepping through brought you to another cube, then another, then another.

I tried to call to Brandy, but she seemed unable to hear me, and I saw her own mouth form words but bring no sound. In fact, there was no sound at all anymore, not even the sound of the big motors driving this, whatever it was.

There was no choice. Stay still, and you stood in a box, so you moved through them, panel after panel, side after side, trying to move out of the thing. I mean, the warehouse was big, but it didn't seem all *this* big.

Suddenly, we stepped into one and stopped, for beyond the panel to our left there was a solitary metal desk at which sat a man. He was wearing some sort of gray uniform, but he looked quite ordinary; an older man with a walrus moustache and, of all things, a monocle. The desk itself had some sort of device built into it that looked to me like some kind of sound-mixing console, with hundreds of little dials and levers. He looked up from the panel, stared at us for a moment, then moved a control. We started toward him, but he took the monocle from his eye and said, *"Frabish-snap!"* and threw a long lever. His voice sounded quite odd and amplified badly, like over a poor loudspeaker system.

Suddenly the whole cubic structure shifted, and now, even though we were stopped, the panels came at us faster and faster. Every once in a while one would blink on, for just a moment, then blink out before we could go to it.

A parched desert landscape with nothing alive under a blanket of eternal clouds. . . .

A jungle scene, thick and lush, with the remnants of some tropical monsoon washing down from the growth that blocked all views. . . .

A reddish-brown landscape, with tremendously high grass of some pink color stretching off into the hills as far as the eye could see under a blue but unnaturally light sky. . . .

There weren't too many of these, although I had the distinct impression that I was actually seeing far more than the few sunlit scenes. It was quite possible that most of what I was seeing was, in fact, the inside of dark buildings at night.

There was a sudden, disorienting shift in balance and point of view, and we both got dizzy and fell . . . onto wet grass. Sound hit me like a full orchestra, although it was only the basic sounds we all live with and the rustling of wind in the trees.

"Brandy?" I whispered. "You okay?"

"Yeah. Yeah. I *think* so. You?"

"I'm suddenly feeling it where I tripped on that last step. I have a hunch I'm gonna be bruised for a while, but I feel okay otherwise." I sat up and looked around. "Where in heaven's name *are* we, though? And how did we get here?"

"I—I don't know. Jesus, Sam! Are we on another planet or something? What the *hell* was that thing?"

I shook my head and looked around, then up. There, in the sky, was a very familiar-looking quarter-moon, the same moon you could see back east. "If it's another planet, it's one just like the one we left," I told her. "That's the moon, all right."

She looked. "Yeah. It is, isn't it? But—where's the warehouse? Where are all the buildings, Sam?"

That was a very good question. I sat there a moment nursing my wounds, and tried to think. "Hypnosis, maybe. Some kind of hypnotic machine. All that spinning and whirling in the dark. Who knows where they took us? As a matter of fact, they probably never knew we were there. We just kept walking in a trance or something, and now we're lost in those damned hills. I bet that's it." It made me feel a little better.

"I dunno, Sam. That funny dude with the eyepiece—did you see him, too?"

"Yeah, and heard him, for all the good it did. Looked like something out of comic opera, Gilbert and Sullivan or something. If you saw him, too, the odds are he was real, if nothing else was. That's bad. It means somebody knows we were there."

"Sam—maybe it wasn't hypnosis. Maybe—this is crazy, but I can't help thinkin' of that train yard and them two dudes up in the tower switchin' cars from one track to another. Suppose that thing was some kind of—railroad, I don't know, whatever people from outer space or somethin' might use. We kept goin' on a track, or something, and then we came to a switch place, that little man bein' in the same job as the train men. He sees us, knows we ain't supposed to be there, and so he kinda, well, *switches* us. Switches us onto a siding or something like that. Just like they do with the trains."

I thought about it, and didn't like the thought at all. "If they'd dumped us in a desert or under that pink sky or if we had two moons or something, maybe I could buy it," I told her, "but this is Earth. The odds of there being two moons just like that is pretty slim. No, I can't buy it."

She sighed. "Yeah, but if this is still the Oregon woods, then it's hotter and wetter than I remember it bein' not too long ago. You can cut this air with a knife. Sweet Jesus, Sam! What did we get ourselves into?"

She was right about the heat and humidity, but it was too subjective a call for me to admit anything right off. "We got into something we shouldn't have, babe. We shoulda cut and run when Little Jimmy gave us the ax, that's for sure."

She reached into her pocket and took out a crumpled pack of Kools and a small lighter.

"You better give 'em up again, babe. Might be a while 'til you see another pack," I warned her.

"Shit on that. Never in all my born days did I need a smoke more than now. Just too bad it's got to be *tobacco*." She lit it and sat back for a moment. "God, that crud we lay in itches!"

That it did. I looked around the horizon, but all I could see were trees in all directions, although we were sitting in a clearing of sorts. I had been around enough to know that when it's pretty dark, even a small town's lights show up as a glow on the horizon; but there were no lights to be seen at all except the stars and the quarter-moon.

Then, off in the distance, I saw a flash; then it was gone. I had hopes for just a moment, but then the sound of distant thunder came to us, and the horizon in that direction seemed to blacken very quickly.

"Storm coming," I noted. "Maybe our way. Just what we need."

"The hell with it. If it comes here and rains buckets, I'm gonna strip out of these clothes and let it give me a shower, and maybe the clothes, too. *Anything* to get this crap off." She took off her boots and stuffed the remaining cigarettes and the lighter deep in the toe, then set that boot on its side, away from the storm. That was one of the reasons I loved her. She was always thinking and always practical, even in the strangest situations.

The clouds rolled in like tar spread across the sky, blacking out the moon and stars. The wind picked up tremendously, and it wasn't too long until I felt the first drops. Brandy was already stripping, I could see from the lightning's illumination, and I finally decided that she had the right idea. If anybody came up and caught us now, I'd just as soon be nude and washed than covered with foul-smelling grime.

I didn't like thunderstorms much—lightning always scared me, and I was always sure I was going to get hit no matter where I was—but the nearest shelter was the tall trees, and I knew damned well you didn't go next to trees in a thunderstorm.

The next ten minutes or so was the longest ten minutes of my life. It was one *hell* of a storm; the rain came down like I'd never seen it before, and all around there was a thunder-and-lightning show that was both scary and awesome. I never knew that much water could fall over such an area; it was as high-volume as if you were under a fire hose turned on full. It was more like being in a swimming pool than a shower or rainstorm, but it sure as hell got rid of that black, smelly powder.

It tapered off as quickly as it had come, and off in the direction from which we'd first seen it, the stars actually began appearing once more, while the area behind us was getting the treatment. That sucker was some storm.

I had mostly stood, frozen with fear, through the thing, and I found myself damned near unable to move now. The grass was high, thick, and very wet, and although the soft wind was drying me out, it wasn't doing anything for the surroundings. I could hear running water everywhere, and to take a step was to *squish*. At least Brandy had guessed right about taking off our clothes; on us or off us, they'd have been just as soaked, only now we were reasonably clean underneath.

The clothes, however, were definitely not wearable for some time. We picked them up and tried to wring them out, but no matter how much you twisted, there seemed to be more and more water, and that was just the shirts. Twisting out fairly new jeans wasn't easy, either. I always thought they were sort of water-repellent, but they just seemed to absorb more than the shirts.

Brandy had prepared for the washing as much as possible, while I hadn't thought much about it, so like a fool I'd left my boots straight up to the sky. One had fallen down, but toward the storm, and the other was filled to the brim with water.

"Well, what do we do now?" I mused aloud, not really talking to Brandy.

"I think we head for the trees and find someplace to hang this all up to dry," she replied. "Then we settle down and see if we can get any sleep or what out here in the wilds. Don't seem no use to try and find out where we are 'til mornin'. Daylight comes, maybe we can find a road or something."

There seemed like nothing else we could do. We didn't know one direction from the other and wouldn't until the sun came up, but with the clearing, we figured the clothes would get some kind of breeze and *some* sun no matter where we hung them, so long as they were exposed. All we could do, of course, was find some low bushes and drape them across the tops. Neither of us had remembered to pack clothespins.

There wasn't anyplace really dry to settle down, but we found a spot behind a big tree that was grassy and had escaped the full force of the rain. Somehow, though, with the dripping-down, I didn't think we'd get much sleep that night. We lay close together, and put our arms around each other.

"Well," I sighed, "back a couple of weeks ago I figured we were about as low as we could go, and now here we are, stark naked in the woods in which live who knows what, with nothing but some drying clothes, a partial pack of cigarettes, and a pocket lighter, stuck in the middle of nowhere. We got nothing, not even answers to any of this."

She sighed and kissed me. "I know. Maybe we're jumping bail to boot, too. No matter what, I keep draggin' us down more and more. Now it's Adam and Eve and no fruit trees. At least I got no trouble with bugs. Nothin' that lives 'round here can be as scary as the cockroaches of Camden. It's like a punishment, somehow. Everything I ever did, I screwed up. School, business, Daddy's dreams, everything, including you."

"I was wrong," I told her. "I said we got nothing and I was wrong. I'm like the guy on the news whose house burns down, and he's standing there, crying about how he's lost everything, with his wife and kids all standing around him safe and sound. I love you, Brandy. I love you more than anything else in the world. You didn't do anything to me. I came willingly, all the way, 'cause I fell in love with the cutest, sexiest, craziest girl in the world. All we did here, including the bad mistakes, we did together. You're a part of me, the most important part. How could you screw me up if I wasn't just as crazy as you?"

She grabbed me and kissed me, hard and passionate. "I love you, Sam Horowitz," she whispered sexily. "I love you a thousand times more now than when I married you."

It was kind of kinky doing it there in the wet grass, out in the open and all, but, damn it, if you couldn't eat and you couldn't sleep and the only thing that really meant anything to you was there in the same mood, it sure beat thinking.

The underwear and the cigarettes and lighter were okay, but the rest was a real wreck. That sun was *hot*, as hot as I had ever felt it, and I'd been in the Philippines and Hawaii in midsummer. That sun had done a real job on some of the clothes.

"I never knew jeans could shrink," I said glumly. They didn't look all that different, but there was a good two- or three-inch rise in the leg bottoms, and as for closing the top flap and zipping them up, forget it. I didn't regret the flannel shirt that much, not in this heat, although at least I could get it on—though not buttoned—but the pants were a pain.

Brandy's hadn't fared much better. There was enough give in the briefs and even in the bra to make them serviceable, like my jockey shorts, but as for the jeans and dyed tee shirt, forget it. Seemed that no matter what, we were stuck in our undies, and as for the boots, well, mine felt as wet as last night, although Brandy's were okay, only mildly damp, but still had some of that black gunk in them because they hadn't been rinsed out.

"Well, it's not a total loss," I commented sourly. "At least when we find some civilization we'll have our underwear."

Brandy shrugged. "Well, it's something. Our big problem isn't clothes, it's food. Wonder what grows in Oregon?"

"Apples, I think, and maybe potatoes, or is that Idaho? From the looks of things here, I'd say we'd better move or learn to eat grass."

The grass, in fact, *was* tall, going up to almost waist height in the lower areas. I knew it'd seemed bad last night, but not this bad. We picked up our soggy boots and walked up the rise to the nearly flat center of the big meadow, which was about where we'd come out, or woke up, or whatever it was we'd done, and Brandy looked around and frowned.

"What's the matter?" I asked her.

"This place. You got to use a little imagination, but it sure does look like the same area that plant was built in." She checked the sun. "If that's east, or sorta east, then let's go south a bit and see what we find."

"If there's a train yard down there, I'll believe anything," I responded.

It really was a vast area of grass, maybe a hundred or more acres, and it *did* kind of look like the lay of the land where the plant had been—if, as she'd said, you used some imagination. It was kind of like what the place would have been if the plant had never been built and this area never developed. There was even a steep downslope, but it led to the start of the trees at the bottom, not any rail yards. It was, however, a flat area, more or less, built up from the looks of it by occasional stream floods.

"You got any idea where we're heading?" I asked her.

"South is all. We can't stay around here, can we? Nothin' to eat but grass. South's as good as any."

I had to admit that much. There was no reason *not* to head south. We entered the trees and kept walking, but I still couldn't feel like this was all real. We'd gone from the bottom to an assignment to find a guy who skipped with mob money, trailed him to the house of some dame that looked like his identical twin, right down to his fingerprints, tracked them to a redneck town in rural Oregon that was the headquarters for a company that supposedly sold junk to TV ads and had a plant that was run with no workers, then saved our quarry from a gunman who turned out to be another twin, got taken to the cleaners by the town for our pains, and then we'd broken into that damned plant and wound up communing with Mother Nature in our underwear.

We reached a streambed that was still somewhat swollen from the results of the previous night's storms, and Brandy started walking east along it. There was no way I wanted to risk crossing that thing now, not at this point, anyway.

"This stream look familiar?" she asked me.

I shrugged. "I'm a city boy. See one stream, one forest, you see 'em all."

"There was a stream running alongside them railroad tracks. Looked kinda like this one."

"Yeah and we're gonna hit a road down to town just through here, I suppose."

"I doubt it. I really doubt it."

"So what's the point? What do you expect to find?" I asked her.

"Something. Anything. Something like—that area over there. See where it's sorta cut out by the stream?"

"Uh huh. So?"

"See that big rock there, stickin' sorta out of the bank? Look familiar? Use your imagination a little."

"It's been overworked the past week." Still, I did see her point and I didn't much like it. That rock was almost a dead ringer for the one jutting out across from the picnic table where we'd had that first meal from the cafe. There was also a kind of dip, or fold, in the land, more than a valley, that went off beyond it to our right and curved around and down a little, and the fold continued up something of a slope to our left. If I were going to build a road, it'd be along that fold for sure, even though it was a little creek of its own to the left and had been cut dry by the stronger stream to the right.

I stopped. "All right, I admit it looks a lot like

the same place, or the same place if people had never been here, but what's that prove? I bet there's a ton of places that look just like this all over these hills."

"Sam—when we took the walk up the tracks last night, I paced off the distance. You know I'm always just doin' that kind of thing in my head."

"Uh huh."

"Well, this is about three hundred and eighty standard paces from where we came down. That gate and sidin' was less'n four hundred yesterday. Face it. This place here is just where it would be if we were still in the same place, and that's too much for coincidence, 'specially with that big cleared area just up there right where it should be—only it ain't cleared, it's natural. There may be a ton of places around that ain't developed, but I betcha not a one has just this way."

I sighed. "So what are you saying? They didn't send us anyplace, they sent us back in time or something, before there were people here?"

"I don't think so. You ain't noticed nothin' queer about this whole place? Think about it."

I thought. "What do I know? I'm from the city, remember, and so are you."

"Don't have to be off the farm to see this. No birds, Sam. No birds, no squirrels, no animals or sign of animals around. Bugs, yeah—and I couldn't tell one bug from another, so I can't say if they're funny lookin' or not—but no birds, that I can see."

I looked around and up at the trees and the patches of sky, and I knew she was right. There were insects, yeah—crawling, buzzing around, all sorts of bugs, but if they didn't look like roaches, wasps, or bees, I was no better at telling one from another, either.

"Well," I said slowly, not really wanting to think much further on this, "we have to decide what to do next, then. We can say this is some kind of limbo where there's no company, no people, no animals, go back up to the clearing and hope that old Monocle-and-Moustache sent some kind of message and they'll come and pick us up before we starve to death, or we figure they aren't coming for us, and try and find some food someplace before we starve to death."

"Well, if they didn't come for us last night, with our pants hung out there like signposts and us not far away, then we can't count on them comin' any time soon. I figure we see if we can find some food or something, and if we can, we figure they'll be able to track us and come to us. Sure ain't much here to lose a scent 'cept maybe another big storm. I mean, *they* sent us here, so *somebody* knows and can find us if they want, but we can't count on it."

I nodded. "Okay, then—which way?"

"You pick it. I haven't had much luck lately."

I thought a moment. "Well, let's assume for the sake of argument that this *is* somehow the same place as we were, although how that can be I can't imagine. If we go across the stream and down *that* way, we'll have miles and miles of ups and downs and forests until we hit the river valley. That might be the place to play house, but it's ninety, a hundred miles, maybe. We won't make that without something to eat. Still, I remember the map enough. If this fold holds true for the road, going north is more of the same until we hit the river valley, only it'll be mostly uphill for a while. These are only baby mountains compared to the big ones around, too."

"So?"

"Well, no matter what, we curve around and get back to that river valley, right? That means the river runs north and south. You got to figure the shortest route down there is by going *west*, along this big stream, here. We've been thinking road, and we don't have a road to travel."

"Sounds good to me, but I sure hope we find something to eat real soon, or I don't think either of us will make it all the way."

We headed back up, and now that I'd come to accept her theory, at least as a working model, I could actually almost visualize building that railroad through here.

About a half hour beyond the big clearing, the slope started down, and the whole thing widened out. Suddenly, we weren't in forest anymore, but in a thick grove of very different-looking trees. I stared at them. "I'll be damned! Apple trees!"

They *were* apple trees, and while some of them were better along than others, there were some there with apples as ripe as you could want. We ate a few each, throwing caution and possible bellyaches to the wind, since they were either all right or they weren't. At least they were enough to give us some energy to keep walking for a while.

"Funny about those trees," I commented. "They're really kind of out of place here. I don't remember much about farming stuff, I admit, but it also seems kind of hot here for apples, and it always seemed to me that red apples were picked in the fall, not the middle of the summer."

"You think they *were* planted? To keep people like us alive?"

"Maybe. Let's go on a little and see. People can't live on apples alone, or at least I don't think they can."

The valley dipped down and widened out still more, and it was clear after a while that in fact this whole area wasn't totally natural. There were pear trees, and peach trees, and huge wild-growing clumps of grape plants, and while they weren't all ripe, some of each were. There was stuff there that shouldn't be ripe and there was other stuff there that I would swear shouldn't be there—the grapes, for one, and a whole grove of trees dropping walnuts by the score. Equally odd was the fact that only a small amount of each was ripe, with others clearly in a kind of line, going east, from ripe down to not ready for a long, long time. If you didn't pig out, maybe up to a dozen or so people could live here for months, maybe indefinitely, so long as nothing spoiled the crops.

"They shoulda put up signs," I noted. "Not everybody would come east."

"Maybe there's one like this in every direction," she suggested. "It might be worth finding out. If they have this stuff here to stash people who get into their system or whatever, there might even be others here, or there might have been others here."

Except for the sound of rushing waters and the buzzing of insects, I couldn't hear any sign of anybody else. "If there are others, we'll find them soon enough, if they haven't taken some of these and moved on. I almost doubt there's anybody else here, though. Doesn't look like there's *ever* been anybody in this place, except the ones who set this up." I sat up. "However, they can't keep a place like this up without some attention. Somebody's *got* to be by, if only to check it out and correct anything that's not right, sooner or later. Trouble is, that may be weeks, even months from now, unless old Monocle reported us and it wasn't filed for attention someday in the future."

"I'm sure we were reported, and I'm sure they know we're here, and just who we are by now. I think we're just stuck on a siding in the middle of nowhere. Face it, Sam—who are we to them, anyway? So they have our IDs and the cards and stuff like that. How long would it take *you* to have our life history if you had your wallet?"

I thought a moment. "About two hours, tops. Yeah, I see what you mean. They got more resources than we have by a long shot. So they find out we're both bankrupt detectives with no assets and no close family, nobody to even miss us, and that we got overeager, thanks to Little Jimmy. We're nobody back home, but to this company or whatever it is, we stuck our nose in and we know too much. If we didn't before, we sure as hell do now, although I can't think about what it is we really know. I mean, did we stumble into some deal where the Martian Mafia is trying to muscle into the Philadelphia drug trade? It's still crazy."

"Yeah, you're sure right on that." She undid her bra and panties and tossed them away.

"What'd you do *that* for?"

"I don't know. We had nothin', Sam, and we still lost what we had. Might as well be totally nothin'. I mean, face it—I think we're here, and here to stay. I always had a kind of fantasy to be stranded on a desert island or something, just me and men—a man—you—oh, all right. If we're stuck, we're stuck in a pretty place with a lot of food and water, and maybe we got a whole world to ourselves. I can keep washin' them things out, and weeks or months from now they'll fall apart anyway. Then what do we wear? Skins? There ain't no animals here, Sam, and even if there was, I wouldn't know how to trap 'em, kill 'em, skin 'em, or make what I needed to make into something that wouldn't feel and smell like rotten, dead animal. And if somebody comes, it ain't no more embarrassment to be naked than to be in a bra and panties. The hell with it."

"You're probably right," I agreed. "We're both city born and bred. I wouldn't know what part of what to even plant, and we're still guessing on what's ripe and what isn't. Fact is, we aren't just stuck, we're stuck *here*, unless they planted these groves all over the place. The damned thing is, we can't even get too adventurous. If we break a leg, or worse, there's no treatment here, no doctors, no phones or ambulances or cops. It's just you and me sitting around the garden, kid, depending on good old G.O.D., Inc., to keep us fed."

Brandy gave a little gasp. "Not if they leave us here forever, we won't be alone. My diaphragm's back in a room in a motel that just don't seem to exist no more. I always thought 'bout us havin' kids, Sam, but not caveman style."

I hadn't really thought about that angle, and, out here, there really wasn't anything else to *do*. Me, I was still trying to figure out how we could go to the bathroom without becoming real messy real fast. Shows the difference in the two of us, I guess.

I always dreamed of leading a life of idle luxury, but the fact was that this wasn't exactly my idea of things. I'm now convinced that Eve was easily seduced by the serpent because she was incredibly bored, and that Adam ate that apple willingly because there was nothing left to do. We didn't even have that way out, so there was no alternative to some careful exploring.

My boots finally dried out, and while it seemed kind of nuts to go tramping about the wilderness wearing boots and nothing else, the fact was that with the rocks and other unknown things in the ground, they were something of a necessity. We retrieved the clothes anyway, and fashioned some of them into crude sacks in which we could carry small amounts of food. It didn't give us much range, but it gave us some, meaning at least that we didn't have to plan on getting back to that little garden spot before dark.

Just *where* we were still bothered me. The best idea was that we somehow got flung back in time to before there were animals or people, but that didn't really wash when you thought about it. The land was just too closely shaped to the land we'd seen when it was civilized, even to that big exposed rock and this stream. If we were in the distant past or something like that, things would have to look very different.

We managed to cross that stream and then walk into town, or where town would have and should have been. Just beyond it was another of the groves, proving Brandy right again in guessing that it really hadn't mattered which way we'd gone. It was pretty clear now that old Monocle had in fact stashed us on a "siding," a place where you put people when you knew they shouldn't be riding your railroad but you didn't exactly know who or what they were. The real question was whether we'd eventually have an engine sent to move us or if we were on one of those abandoned sidings. The other question was how the hell you could move, or have sidings, when you didn't move, as it were.

The first night, both of us had muscle cramps and some blisters, but we'd managed to survey some of the area and we were learning to accept the situation a little. We had no trouble sleeping, huddled together on soft grass under the edge of the trees, although we did have a couple more little thunderstorms in the evening. Noisy and wet, but nothing like that tremendous storm that had hit us that first night.

There were bugs everywhere, but we got few bites of any kind. I guess if you don't have mammals around much you don't develop mosquitoes and things that drink blood, so the few bites we got were from ants or small spiders or something that just didn't like us or where we were sitting. I had this vision of black widows or tarantulas or something, but none of the bites seemed more than irritating.

The real question was how much exploring we were going to be able to do. Neither of us was in any decent shape, and the second day every muscle in our bodies ached. That more than anything was the real trap of this place for the overweight, out-of-condition folks from civilization. If you rested and relaxed the second day, you were back where you started from in terms of shaping up, but it was tough to force yourself to go anywhere or do anything when you hurt so bad and the basics of what you needed were so close at hand. So, out of necessity, we kind of pushed each other.

There were, in fact, at least four groves, the one up the "road" we figured was about where the motel would have been. We shifted up to that one partly because it was closer to the "company" site, and provided clear access to that huge meadow as well as better storm cover.

It's funny, though, how quickly you can adapt to something totally foreign if you don't have to worry about the basics. We had food, water, a very basic shelter with the trees, and each other to keep from going completely nuts. If you had to stash somebody, this was a good place to do it. You didn't even need weapons or fire to scare off the wild animals. There *were* no wild animals. As long as it stayed hot and humid, and deserted, there wasn't much need for clothes. Brandy still had her lighter, although her cigarettes were long gone, but we decided to conserve the lighter as much as possible in case we ever really needed a fire. We even abandoned the boots after a while; it seemed better to get the feet toughened.

After a while you no longer noticed the bites; you learned where was a good place to sleep and where wasn't, and what gave the best shelter when a storm came up; the heat and humidity seemed normal, and even crapping in the wild became second nature, although Brandy had more trouble with part of that than I did. Nothing around seemed poisonous, but a few stomach upsets taught us quickly what was ripe and what was not.

I had worn a cheap watch much of my life, but for some reason I hadn't put it on when we set out on that expedition. It was one of my many regrets; it would have been interesting at least to know what time it was, and what day.

"You know, I don't think anybody's comin' for us," Brandy said one afternoon. "It's been too long."

I nodded. "Yeah, I'm kinda getting to that point myself."

"I was thinkin' that the winters get real cold up here, I bet, no matter how hot it is now. We don't have the know-how to make stuff like clothes, even if there was something around with fur or if we ran into a whole mess of cotton plants. If we're gonna live, we got to move south. Real far south."

"Yeah, I know. I just haven't wanted to think about it much. I don't even know how far it is, but it seems like a hell of a long way. A thousand miles, maybe. If we walked ten miles a day, it'd take a hundred days if nothing else was wrong, and there won't be groves of trees around dripping with ripe stuff to eat, and there's pretty big mountains in the way, too. I don't remember the map much, but it seemed like the only flat land was from Bend—or where Bend *should* be—north, and that's the wrong way, babe."

"I know, I know. But if we stay around here much longer, we're gonna be too late to beat the snow. We took all the other risks. We risked goin' after Whitlock when we were warned off—even fired—and we snuck into that plant."

"Yeah, and it got us here." Still, she had a point. Stay here, and we had a potentially short lifespan. Move, and we either bought time or bought it quicker. I never liked being in the back with the meter running, and that was what staying was. We *had* to chance a move.

"All right," I told her, "we'll gather up what we can carry that might feed us for a couple of days before it goes bad, and we'll strike out west, toward that Bend valley. Once we're there, we'll see if we starve at that point or can go on. One day at a time."

"Yeah. One day at a time."

We rigged up some makeshift packs using the old clothes, but we really couldn't carry too much, and only the nuts weren't likely to quickly spoil. Still, we had to do *something*, and this was better than nothing.

We walked east along the streambed, past the grove we originally found and more or less into the wilderness. It was not easy going after a few hours; these were mountains, not little hills, and they were pretty much unspoiled except by weather and stream action. Some of the passages involved pretty narrow areas above the stream, and in some cases wading in the stream itself, trying to avoid slipping on the rocks or losing your balance. The worst part was that it was hard to tell how far we'd come. We might have covered ten miles, we might have covered one mile, for all we knew. By the end of the first day, though, we were in pretty rough country.

There was only danger in going on after dusk, so we found as level and as comfortable a spot as we could and settled in for the night. We were not fussy anymore, that was for sure. We snuggled up together in silence.

Finally I said, "What are you thinking about?"

"Just—thinkin'. Maybe thinkin' 'bout not thinkin'."

"Huh?"

"Somehow, some ways, we wound up with a whole world just to ourselves. Nobody else. No cars, no pollution, no slums or ghettos, no wars, no violence, no racism—*nothin'* but what we brought into it. Just Adam and Eve, more or less. I been findin' myself thinkin' funny the last few days."

"Huh? Funny?"

"Yeah. Right off, all I could think of was how everything was always against us. You know, the self-pity bit. All I wanted was back. Lately, though, I can't figure what I want to go back to. I stopped thinkin' 'bout that world. It ain't *real* no more. It's evil. Corrupt. And it sure ain't done us no favors, honey."

"You're getting another one of those dreams. I can tell."

"Yeah, well, what's wrong with dreams if that's all you got? We were okay back there. Hell, honey, we were *good*. We did our jobs real good, and it got us nowhere. Nobody cared. Bein' good just didn't cut it. So, here we are, with a whole world to ourselves. I know the odds against us, so don't start lecturin' me, but we got to think like we're gonna make it. If we don't, we sure as hell won't. And what if we *do?*"

"We survive. We try to do something with the rest of our lives."

"Yeah, but what? So we have a mess of kids, right? Can't hardly avoid it if we stay together. We got to forget that old world existed; make it a nightmare. The rules of this whole new world are what we say it is, the way we live and act and teach our kids. We got a big chance here if we just stop lookin' back and thinkin' the old stuff.''

I kind of thought human nature would run its usual course regardless, but I let her dream. It was better than thinking about the first broken leg or worse injury. Even appendicitis would kill her—not me, mine's gone—and just handling our first toothache might be too much for our level of skill.

Still, we went on until in about two or three days we reached the end of the mountains and the start of the great, broad river valley. It was really a sight to see, from a grassy knoll a couple of thousand feet up a mountainside. You could even see why they named the town Bend, from the way that river looped, but, of course, there wasn't any city. There also weren't any trails, but we tried to figure a safe way down. The whole river basin looked rich, and there were all sorts of trees, bushes, and other growths all over the place. Whether anything down there was edible, though, I didn't know. Without our mysterious Johnny Appleseed, I didn't know if there'd *be* apples or other stuff in the wild.

We didn't, however, get the chance. It was the damndest thing I ever ran up against, including that crazy thing inside the warehouse. It was a wall, a solid wall, that just wasn't there, but was.

By that, I mean that you couldn't see anything, and the wind came right through, and all was natural and normal in every way except that you couldn't move down that mountain beyond a certain point. It felt like thick glass or extra-smooth plastic. There was no sound when you pounded on it, and when we tried to beat against it with sticks, there was also no effect. Pounding it with a stone produced only a dull thudding noise, but if you threw the stone at it, the stone sailed right on through.

Brandy was so frustrated she was close to tears, and she finally knelt down and beat against it. I went over to her, not quite knowing what to feel like. Clearly, whoever had put us here wanted us to stay here. It was a wall that blocked people, and nothing else. I looked at Brandy, but there wasn't anything really to say. We'd reached the limits of G.O.D.'s county, and we could not go beyond. Even here they were going to make sure we didn't violate the terms of our bail.

6.

Of Seasonings and Secrets

I don't know how long we'd been in that place; any semblance of time was shattered after we discovered the Wall and determined to our satisfaction that it went pretty well around the place. Long enough for Brandy to grow back a fair amount of hair, and me the fullest, thickest beard I ever had. Long enough for the both of us to become slimmer, trimmer, yet more weathered and worn on the outside. Brandy wasn't built to be thin; she had a wide frame that was designed to be somewhat substantial. Still, she'd lost all her gut and much of the fat off her hips and thighs, and replaced them with hard muscle. It was a dramatic improvement, probably the best she'd ever looked or felt, although she was somewhat surprised that her breasts didn't shrink proportionately. I was delighted with that.

I, too, was as tight and as lean as in my Air Force training days, although my stomach showed the scars and stretch marks, as did hers, of past abuse. What was most startling, and next to Brandy's figure the most pleasing, to me was

that, incredibly, I started to grow hair again
where none had been for several years. It itched
for a while, but then it started to come in, black
speckled with gray (what the hell, it was *hair*),
and Brandy really was impressed. My beard, as I
mentioned, also came in very full and thick,
something that also surprised me because the
only other time I'd tried to grow one it had been
thin and uneven and scraggly. The new combination was very much to Brandy's liking, which was
a good thing since I had no way to shave the
damned thing off. The fact that being outside all
this time had turned my complexion quite dark
brown was an added bonus.

There were negatives, though. Constant exposure had weathered and toughened the skin,
which also aged it. Both of us certainly looked
older than we were, and we were developing lines
in our faces and skins. My vision was still pretty
good, but Brandy's, which hadn't been that good
when I met her, had deteriorated more. She was
having a hard enough time that she no longer
went to any lengths to conceal it. I had the
distinct and uneasy feeling that she was going
blind and she knew it.

We had our share of cuts and bruises and
scrapes, and even developed some small scars
from them, but we weren't ambitious enough
anymore to try anything really dangerous, and if
infection was possible here it sure didn't bother
us. It kind of figured. If there were no animals or
people on this world, then the local germs wouldn't
know what to make of us.

The feared winter weather just didn't come.
There were two temperature conditions within
the Wall: hot and hotter; and two conditions of

moisture: ninety-nine percent humidity and heavy rain. The storms varied in intensity and duration, but there was always one sometime in the afternoon and another in mid-evening. Although the days grew short, that didn't vary, and we realized that the Wall wasn't merely a barrier, it was a greenhouse. The streams began to run bitter cold, but the air temperature never cooled. We would occasionally go down to the Wall and look out at the mountains in the distance and see snow falling, and to touch the Wall it felt cold; yet just a few feet in, it was, if anything, hotter than earlier. At least, *I* could see the snow falling and describe it to her. She could see her immediate surroundings, although blurrily, but anything beyond a few yards was a total blur.

Interestingly, she adapted well to that, and insisted on keeping up our runs, our tree climbing, and the rest. She feared, however, even short separations. She liked to be near me, touching me, as much as possible, as if nothing but me was real.

Another casualty, though, was conversation. There didn't seem much point in reminiscing or discussing the past, and neither of us much cared anymore why there were at least three Martin Whitlocks of at least two sexes, or what that company did, or even how it sent us here. The Wall, and the unchanging sameness of the place we'd come to think of as the Garden, left little in the present to think about and offered no future except more of the same. Days might go by with us saying very few words to each other, since the routine rarely varied and where we went now we'd been before, yet I had never felt closer to her nor she to me. We didn't care about anything

else because there *wasn't* anything else. Because
we lacked the knowledge and skills to turn this
environment as our ancestors would have, and we
lacked the necessity of doing so, having food and
water and warmth and needing nothing else, our
whole civilized veneer was being stripped from
us. Thinking much only made things worse, so
you got so you didn't think much, just acted out
of habit and did whatever your impulses told you
when they spoke, within the limits of the environment we now took for granted. We realized that
we were sinking into a kind of comfortable
madness, a *bearable* madness, that, like animals
in a cage, we were consciously being trapped by
it.

There is no world but the Garden, whose
boundaries are the Wall. There is no other world,
no other reality. There is only Her and Me. I
found myself repeating that every time I thought
of something beyond the here and now, and I
really didn't want to stop it, not consciously.
I—we—both of us—had consciously surrendered.
Only the dreams remained.

*He was there at the stream, and at the trees, and
along the pathways, always there in my dreams,
with trenchcoat, slouch fedora, and dangling
cigarette.*

"Listen, sweetheart, you can't give in to this thing
or they win, see? You're a man, a private dick, not
no jungle savage. You can't sit around doin' nothin'
or you may as well be dead."

"Listen, Spade, don't you lecture me!"

"Hey! I made all the mistakes, didn't I? Even fell
in love with the dame that iced my partner, and
that's worse than anything you got to show. Now,
your old lady, she loves ya and depends on ya. You

gonna let her go down like this? She saved your neck a couple times, and she still feels all this guilt stuff about all this bein' her fault. It's your turn now, hot shot."

I turned to get away from him, but other figures stepped out of the woods and stared me down. I knew them all. Marlowe, Archer, the Continental Op, Nick Charles. . . . Everywhere I turned there was another, and they were all saying, "Your turn now, hot shot. You're the big brain, Sam, you're the top gun, Sam, you figure it out."

"What the hell can I do? I don't even know where I am or who sent me here or how! You didn't break out of jail, any of you, you were all bailed out!"

"There's always something, Sam, if you look hard enough," Spade responded. "You keep it up and something always turns up."

"Sam? Sam!"

"Uh, wha—? Leave me alone, all of you!"

"Sam—wake up!"

I opened my eyes groggily. It was still pitch-dark. "Huh?"

"Listen! Wake up and listen!"

I tried to clear out the cobwebs and listen as she said, and I heard something, something odd, off in the distance. A sound, like a cross between a hum and a crackling noise. I was suddenly awake. "The meadow! It's coming from the meadow!" I was on my feet in a moment and she followed. I looked around, unable to see a thing. "We ought to get over there—if we can find it in this darkness."

"*I* can," she responded, and took my hand.

It was about half a mile through the woods, but she led me like she had the eyes of a cat. It was no big deal in the daytime to follow a trail that was worn and blazed by you in the first place, but I hadn't realized how little she'd been depending on her eyes and how much on other things. She *felt* that path, and she was unerring and confident.

We reached the edge of the trees and I stopped her, and we both crouched down. There, up on the rise, was a pattern I had seen only once before and never expected to see again, outlined clearly against the darkness. Rotating, folding, revolving panels of blue light surrounding a mirrored darkness, moving around and around, folding this way and that.

"Think somebody's coming for us, after all this time?" she asked me.

"I don't know, but maybe we shouldn't wait to find out."

"Huh? What do you mean?"

"If they can come out of that thing, we can go in it."

"Yeah—but we don't know where we'd come out."

"Yes we do. Someplace other than here. Come on!"

We ran for it, not caring about the exposure or thinking about anything else. Someone had opened the cage door, and might discover that and close it at any moment. It didn't occur to me to wait to see who might emerge; the fact was, there was no certainty that *anybody* would emerge. It might be intended for us to enter, if we had the nerve, or it might even be that somebody else had to use this siding to get someplace else entirely and it might vanish for an eternity at any minute. I had to use their tracks, but by damn it was my train!

"Which way do we go once we're in?" Brandy called as I pulled her along.

"We went left to get here, so we'll go right," I told her. "Just hold tight. The odds are we're gonna get sidetracked again, but maybe this time somebody will remember us!"

Okay, Spade, you just keep that sucker there another twenty seconds and I'll take the leap!

We reached the edge, and it was still folding and unfolding into those impossible patterns with increasing speed. There was no hesitation; I went right in and grabbed Brandy's hand, tight.

We were once again standing in something that seemed to be a revolving door; but this time I wasn't scared and confused, I was desperate. Once again, scenes of landscapes seemed to flash by as various panels approached, but if you kept moving, kept walking through them, you didn't exit but continued on through that maze. All of the scenes seemed to be totally different than any I remembered, but it had been so long ago and a life away and I neither could be sure nor cared.

We were suddenly not alone in the maze of panels. She was tall, real tall—seven feet, maybe—and incredibly thin, and her face was white, not like I was white but like those Japanese dancers—only this looked like her natural color. Her lips, nostrils, and eyes were all jet black, and she was wearing some kind of long satin dress down to the ground, all a brilliant purple. She spotted us and started for a moment, then just nodded and went on past into the direction from which we'd just come. There was nothing else to do but nod back and give a casual wave with my free hand.

Rather than upset or unnerve me, our encounter with the strange-looking woman reinforced my feeling that this thing wasn't operating for us. I didn't know much about her, and wasn't sure I wanted to, but we owed that tall woman for this chance.

Suddenly we spotted another woman behind a panel, but this one was different. She was small, slight, wearing a uniform that looked like a cross between *Star Trek* and the Bolivian navy, and if you overlooked the spiked purple hair and the slight puglike snout below her eyes, she looked relatively normal. She was also sitting behind a table that looked like a mixing board, and she was wearing, of all things, a monocle.

We kept walking, but we were suspended nonetheless, unable to reach the next panel no matter how we tried. I felt Brandy tighten her grip as she realized what had happened—even she could see *that* far—and I watched as the woman saw us, frowned, and looked at her board. I got the distinct impression that our looks, even our nudity, didn't faze her in the least, but that the fact that we weren't on the timetable was simply not done.

She was a lot younger and, I suspect, a lot less experienced than the old guy we'd hit on the way out who'd sent us to the Garden, and I could tell she was trying to figure out just what to do. I stopped walking, as did Brandy, sensing my intent, and we stood there patiently and waited for her to make up her mind. She looked up and saw us standing there, and I gave her a disgusted look and shrugged. I could sympathize with her problem, but how she solved it was of vital concern to us. We weren't supposed to be there, but we were acting like we were, and not at all scared or withdrawn; nor did we, as we were, exactly look like major threats to the organization. We weren't, after all, totally black-clad individuals trapped in the system. Finally she activated her intercom speaker.

"Glifurtin sworking on ka pau maw?" she asked in a low, guttural growl, or at least it sounded something like that.

I hadn't the slightest idea what she said, but, what the hell, if she expected me to speak her language I had every right to expect the reverse. "G.O.D. Western Distribution Center, McInerney, Oregon, United States of America," I shouted back, surprised that I could hear my own voice.

She looked at her board and fiddled with a couple of dials. "Oh, English. How jolly quaint," she growled. "What line number? I don't have you on my board set."

"Beats me," I responded. "You people were supposed to take care of that. We just use this thing, we don't know how to run it."

She cleared her throat, which really sounded menacing. I now had a new definition for calling somebody a real dog. "Terribly sorry, there's been a mistake somewhere along the line," she replied. "I'll take a stab at it with what I see and what you gave me, and if it's wrong you can get them to reroute you." She pushed some levers and turned some dials and we were back off into the revolving doors of blue rectangles again.

Some of this network of whatever it was, was obviously on all the time, but not between all the right places. Of course, the Garden hadn't any machinery at all, or at least I didn't think so, but it might have been buried deep underground. The fat hairy man and the silver girl from what seemed so long ago had obviously gone in to turn their station on, either because it was needed as a way station to send somebody further, or because they were going to send some of that trainload of stuff somewhere else.

We stepped out of the pattern—not really of our own accord any more than we'd exited into the Garden—where the girl with the monocle had sent us. It was quite dark, and we were clearly inside a large building, but I knew almost immediately it wasn't our warehouse. The floor of the warehouse had been poured concrete; this floor was very rough stone, maybe stone block. "We're not home," I whispered to Brandy, "but the thing's still going. Want to get back on?"

"Why bother? She said she was sendin' us where they spoke English and where people looked like us. So what if it ain't home? What we got that we hafta go back there for, anyway? Let's see if we can get outta here before they find us."

"You're sure?"

"Nope, but so what? They ain't gonna send us back and just let us go. Next time might be someplace a hundred times worse, or maybe back to the Garden."

"But we have nothing!"

"And we got more back home? Come on."

It was nearly impossible to see in the place, so we ran into a wall before we knew we were at it. It seemed made out of even rougher stuff than the floor, more like natural stone. A cave or something like that. We went along it, away from the still-twisting display, until we came to a large double door. It was locked, and so were a number of doors we also found. There didn't seem to be any way out of the damned place.

We looked back at the transport display, but it

seemed to be slowing noticeably now, more or
less reversing its previous contortions, until, very
quickly, it was the simple cross, then the single
screen, then just a tall blue line, and then there
was only darkness. The vibrations and rumbling
of the great machine died down, then all was
silence.

A strip of light suddenly came on at the far end
and far up the wall, and I could see a little. It
appeared to be a balcony cut out of the rock wall,
and, moving a bit, I could see that there were
stone stairs cut in that side, leading up from the
floor. It was definitely not the place we'd left, but
it clearly served the same purpose. I could see no
other stairs, although there were massive doors
cut into the side where we'd tried to exit—doors
clearly locked and barred now.

"It looks like that stairway or nothing, babe," I
told Brandy. "They got this one designed for an
exit up top. Stay with me against the wall, and
let's get over there so we can find it in case they
turn the lights out again."

The funny thing was, there was just enough
light to see the whole expanse of the place, and
there was nothing really to see. The whole floor
looked as barren as the unadorned meadow back
at the Garden. Wherever the machinery was that
worked that thing, it was well hidden.

"I think we got to chance those stairs and that
door now," Brandy said worriedly. "You got to
figure they'll lock this place tighter'n a drum
when they go."

It was a good point, although I didn't at all like
the idea of going up there and being on the same
level as the operators, with it lit up like that.

The stone floor and stairs were cold, and we

climbed quickly to just near the top. I barely had time to think that before we'd had that long stay in the wild, neither of us could have made this climb without wheezing.

As expected, there was a door at the top; and, well down the balcony walk, there was a second, open door and to its right a viewing window just like back in the warehouse. As before, there was little time to think about our next move and no time to debate it; we bounded up and opened the nearby door and entered a narrow passageway, still of that same stone block. At the end was yet another thick wooden door, this one with a lock on the inside, and I threw it and we stepped outside.

It was still dark. I suspected they did all their transportation stuff when it was dark and there would be few around to wonder about the funny noises and vibration or get too curious about it. The area was lit up, though, with either torches or some kind of oil lamps. It looked pretty primitive, but nothing got around the fact that it was pretty cold outside and that there was a slight wind to boot. Not wintry or snowy weather, but it sure as hell wasn't the sort of weather you could be comfortable with if you had no clothes on, and I said as much to Brandy.

"We might as well go back and try and bull our way through, then," she answered, accepting the obvious. "We sure can't hold up out here for a night."

I turned, and immediately saw a flaw in the new plan. The damned lock was spring-loaded and the door was solidly shut behind us. I looked around, but there wasn't a soul to be seen anywhere.

"This is a kick in the head," I noted sourly. "All that crap we went through to keep from being picked up, and now that we decide it ain't worth it, we can't even get arrested. Can't even find anybody to arrest us."

"We could just hunker down here and wait for them," she suggested. "I didn't see no other way out of there. Be kinda hard to lie our way outta this, though. *Damn!* If we only had somethin' to pick that lock with!"

"We could freeze waiting for them. Let's see if we can find somebody to surrender to."

We walked along what I first thought of as a stone porch, and more of the place seemed to come into focus. It wasn't just a big stone building; this thing was a castle, like they had in Europe, and what we were on was called, I think, a battlement. All around I could see other buildings of dark stone, but aside from the fact that they all looked like travel posters of Austria, there was little to be learned from them.

Before we found a stairway or entrance, we heard the door open well behind us, and turned and went back. Two figures emerged, and after making sure that the door was secure, turned to walk away.

I took a deep breath. "Hey!" I called out loudly. "Help!"

The two figures stopped and turned, and we started toward them.

"We took a wrong turn and, boy, are we in trouble!" I yelled.

They stopped, then stared at us in wonder as we came clearly into view. I was afraid we might have another dog-girl or fat werewolf here, but the two at least *looked* human, although dressed in robes and hoods.

"Who the *devil* are you two?" the larger of the two demanded to know. "And what in heaven's name are you doing skulking about here like *that?*" He was a man with a very cultured British-sounding accent and a very pleasant voice. It was a relief to find somebody in this network who didn't speak gibberish first.

"I'm Sam Horowitz and this is my wife, Brandy," I told them. "We've gotten caught twice now in that damned transport system, and this time they shot us here."

The second figure gasped. "*You* came out of *there?*" It was a woman's voice, with much the same accent.

"Yeah, out of the blue lights and the folds. Can we explain everything inside someplace? We're *freezing* to death!"

"Yes, by all means, follow us," the man told us. "This is most irregular. Most irregular. The abbot is not going to like this one bit."

I turned to Brandy as we walked, and repeated, "The abbot?"

"I don't know. Sounds better than the Costello, I guess."

I knew what the title implied, and I think Brandy did, too. Abbots headed abbeys or something like that. Monasteries and convents and that kind of thing. With my background, I couldn't be sure beyond that, and Brandy was raised Baptist, but I kind of suspected we were now in some sort of religious retreat, probably Catholic or whatever passed for Catholic wherever this was. The Middle Ages for sure, but monks and nuns in medieval *Oregon?* Either history was real wrong or Columbus had a great PR man.

We went down some stone stairs and reached a wing of the big building behind the main body, and the woman opened a door and entered while the man held it for us. It wasn't tremendously warmer inside, but at least there was no wind.

The woman had gone on ahead, because we had a reception committee. There were three of them, each of whom looked about seven feet tall and three hundred pounds, and all three were wearing black robes with the hoods hanging down their backs, and all three had swords on thick black belts worn outside their robes. They all bowed slightly to the man, whose own robe was a rusty brown color.

"Take these two to a holding room without allowing them to be seen by anyone else," he ordered. "Sister Elizabeth will be returning shortly with some clothes for them. No conversation with them, no questions. I will notify the abbot and then return for questioning."

The three bowed again, then turned their attention to us. One of them motioned us to follow him, and the other two fell in behind. I didn't feel too great about all this, but at least we had shelter, and somebody who knew the score was being forced to pay attention to us. The only thing I worried about was whether these guys would just decide we were a complication they didn't need, and dispose of us, one way or the other. It was something I didn't care to think about.

We were taken to a small room lit by an oil lamp with a straw bed and straw on the floor as well. It had a door but no windows, and after we entered, the door was shut; but it was clear that two of the silent giants had taken up guard duty on either side of the door just outside. I figured it was more to keep the curious out than to keep us in. We had no place else to go.

Sister Elizabeth was back in a few minutes carrying a bundle. These turned out to be a brown wool robe like the man had been wearing, a black robelike dress like the sister's, and some boots. "I had to guess on the sizes," she told us apologetically, "but at least it will warm you."

She was a slightly built woman with a plain, very English sort of face, totally free of any makeup or jewelry, and her rust-colored hair was cut so short she didn't have to comb or maintain it, although it would never win any prizes for hair styling. While we tried on the clothing, I couldn't help but notice that Sister Elizabeth's gaze kept returning to Brandy, and I had a suspicion that she might never have seen a black woman before. I kind of hoped that she hadn't seen Jews down at the local Inquisition.

The clothes were baggy but serviceable; mine was thick wool and Brandy's seemed to be cotton, and while mine ended just below the knee and hers almost dusted the floor, it was still okay. The boots were a different matter—not just for size, but because we hadn't worn shoes of any kind in so long that they hurt and felt funny. They were soft leather, though, with a lot of give, and while both pairs were a bit large, they would do until we had the chance to get a better fit.

"What is this place?" I asked her. "A monastery?"

"It is the Mount Olivet Retreat in the Barony of Oregonia," she responded. "There is both a monastery and a convent here, as well as a seminary, conference area, and master library."

"Are you *really* a nun?" Brandy asked, echoing my own thoughts.

She seemed somewhat startled by the question. "Of course. I have been in holy orders for eleven years."

Her reaction was so genuine and so automatic that there was no reason in the world to doubt her. Still, it was puzzling. I could easily see a group like this using a monastery, convent, or whatever as a cover, even having some real ones around, but I couldn't see having real ones work that machinery. I mean, most of the folks we'd seen so far, like the pair at the warehouse and the woman who'd sent us here, weren't even a hundred percent human.

We were given no more chances for questions, though. The man who was with her, who she called Brother Michael, came for us, looked us over, nodded to himself, then said, "You will come with me now. The abbot was just getting ready for bed, but he insists on seeing the both of you at once. Come along, please."

I could tell we were hardly trusted, although what sort of danger we could pose to them was beyond me. I mean, they sure as hell knew we didn't have any concealed weapons or concealed anything else on us. Still, those big guards had eyes only for us, and passages had been sealed off to keep anybody from seeing us. Finally we reached an upstairs chamber, just about the time I was ready to take off those boots and throw them away, and we waited while Brother Michael went in and then returned. "The abbot will see you now," he said formally, and we all went in.

It was a comfortable office, large and well organized, with walls of bookshelves filled to capacity, a huge redwood desk and padded chair, and plush padded seats and benches. To one side was a large fireplace whose fire was dying but not dead. The room was very comfortably warm.

The abbot entered by a side door, looking tired. He was a thin man of medium height, with short gray hair and a pair of old-fashioned glasses. He wore a black robe over which was a gold chain with a round medallion hanging from it. He sat in his chair and looked us over carefully, then looked at the others. "Take the normal security precautions, but you may leave us alone," he said to them. It was a kind, gentle voice and the tone was casual, but clearly this was not a request but an order. They bowed, and all left, closing the door.

"Please sit down," he invited, indicating two padded chairs. His voice had more than a trace of Irish brogue in it. "I am Brian McInerney, bishop of Olivet and the abbot of this place. And you?"

"Sam Horowitz, and this is my wife, Brandy," I responded.

"Uh huh. Horowitz, you say? Jewish?"

"Born that way."

"You will pardon me, but the lady does not look Jewish to me."

"The lady wasn't born that way," Brandy replied a little coolly, "but she's pretty satisfied to be a Horowitz."

McInerney shrugged. "No offense is meant. I've seen a lot stranger than the two of you in my time, I assure you. However, the only people of color in this land are of American Indian ancestry, and interracial unions are quite rare and, I'm afraid, not socially condoned."

"It's not easy where we come from, either," I noted. Well, it was easy to see why Dog-woman sent us here. I'd said McInerney and Oregon and specified English.

The abbot sighed. "Ah, yes, and that brings up an interesting question, Mr. Horowitz. Just where *do* you come from?"

"New Jersey," I told him. "But in that world this place is the western distribution center for a company called General Ordering and Development, Inc."

McInerney nodded. "As you might surmise, I am familiar with the company. Why don't the two of you tell me how you came to be here—and doing an imitation of Adam and Eve, as I'm told. Before we can make any decisions regarding your future, I must know who and what I am dealing with."

"I have a lot of questions, too," I said.

"But *you* do not have *me* in *your* office in *your* world deciding *my* fate," he pointed out with unassailable logic.

And so I told him the basics of the story. At least, I told him that a rich man in a big city near ours stole a lot of money from a man in our city, and that both were involved in criminal activities, and that the victim hired us to track the thief down because his own bosses would not be very understanding if they found out. I told him we were private detectives whose work was taking jobs like this one, and how we'd traced our quarry, found his look-alike girlfriend, traced them here, and then gotten involved in the gunfight, the third Whitlock, and why and how we'd wound up sneaking into the plant and getting caught in that thing and sent to limbo. He sat there, listening intently, and never once interrupted until I was done and until Brandy had filled in some gaps.

He sat there about a half a minute more, saying nothing, then said, incredulously. "Do you mean to tell me that you do not have any idea what this is all about? That, even now, with two trips through the Labyrinth, you are as ignorant of the facts as you are stuck?"

We nodded in unison. "That's about it, Bishop," Brandy agreed.

"You understand that I am going to have to check this all out? That if any part of your story is false I will be able to determine it?"

"That's fine with us, sir," I told him. "Why would we lie about it?"

The abbot sighed again. "Mr. Horowitz, I am certain that you must realize that any organization of the size, scope, and power of the one that controls the Labyrinth will have its enemies, its opponents. Idealists, revolutionaries, and ambitious underlings seeking to topple its leadership or to compete with it are inevitable. Such activity is always ongoing, although lately it has been sharply on the increase. People have died, stations have been put out of commission, and a great deal of havoc has been raised. The only reason you are not in our dungeons is that I think you are telling the truth. A gut instinct, I admit, but born of thirty years of ministering to people."

"Then you're really a priest? As well as the— station master?" Brandy asked.

"Oh, my, yes! Part of this appointment entails also being the station master, as you put it. We are no false identity put on to mask them. Instead, we have an arrangement with them that works to our mutual benefit. This is not to say that they don't have their representatives here— they are all over the place, by which I mean the world and not here. I fear that the general accommodations here are too spare for their liking. They are a worldly bunch, I must say. This post is difficult to fill, you understand, for there are few who can deal with them and still sleep nights. I often am beset by doubts myself, but I must accept my Church's decision that our inter- action with them serves the common good." He yawned. "You must excuse me, it is getting quite late. For the moment, I fear I must place you under guard and keep you apart from the rest of the people here. So far, we have managed to limit the knowledge that you even exist only to those connected with the Labyrinth, the security staff, and myself. As the security staff are all under permanent rules of silence, I feel certain I can keep this quiet for now. In the meantime, I will arrange for Sister Elizabeth to get you some bedding and something to eat, and I will call for you when I know more."

He called for the guards, and that was the end of the interview. They took us back down to the floor with the small rooms, and Sister Elizabeth managed to find some blankets, a couple of scrawny feather pillows, and some sweet-tasting beer and fruit and pastries. It wasn't exactly heaven, but, right then, it would have to do. It was certainly no worse, and a good deal better, than I'd feared it might be.

They kept us down there for a couple of days. It wasn't all that comfortable, particularly after being used to some ability to roam, but the food was decent and it gave us a little time to reacclimate ourselves to the real world, or what passed for the real world, anyway. I kind of hoped the guards were eunuchs or something, though, since there were times when the sounds coming from the cell might have made celibates reconsider.

The rest of the time was spent simply comparing notes and seeing what we could come up with. We had a big picture now of what was going on, even if the details still didn't make much sense. Somebody, somewhere, had invented a machine that allowed you to travel between worlds. It wasn't between planets—we kept coming back to the same out-of-the-way spot in Oregon—but between different versions of Earth. How they could exist, we had no idea, but clearly they did; and it was the kind of fact you accepted by Sherlock Holmes's maxim: when everything else is eliminated, whatever is left, no matter how improbable, must be the truth.

The next question was, what were they doing on all these Earths? If they followed the usual human pattern, which was not certain, then just about every motive boiled down to wealth, power, or passion. From what we'd seen so far, passion was not one of their strong suits, which left the other two. Certainly they'd shown real power, and maybe they wanted to take over and run all those worlds—or maybe they already did, and we just were too ignorant to know it. Power was an end in itself, but there still had to be a bottom line someplace to justify all this trouble and expense on a permanent basis, and that left wealth.

They loaded railcars' worth of stuff into that warehouse back home, and it had to go some-where. Maybe natural resources from resource-rich places were being acquired and shipped to other worlds that were resource-poor, or who had wasted theirs. That was an idea, but what did the poor ones give? Interestingly, it was Brandy who came up with the answer to that.

"Knowledge," she decided. "They trade off both the raw materials and maybe finished products, and they get knowledge in return. Maybe just little stuff in some cases, big ideas in others. Just think of all the Edisons that might come up in a thing like this. And maybe other types of folks, too. Education, religion, business, philosophy—you name it. If most of these people are basically like us, stuff that works one place might work another." She frowned. "Yeah, and stuff you ain't sure of could be tried out on some world, or a lot of 'em, just to see how it *did* work. Guinea pigs, Sam. It's a real complicated operation, if you think about it."

She was probably right. I remembered back long ago some science teacher of mine putting down the sociologists and historians and all the other social scientists because they couldn't be scientific—you could never isolate all the vari-ables and repeat the experiment. Not with this, though. If there were a lot of Earths—who knew how many?—you could manipulate things, play God in the background, stand back, study, and see how it all came out. And all the time you were taking what you wanted from all those worlds, trading raw materials for ideas, finished products for raw materials or ideas—you name it. Wealth and power in spades, with all of us as

pawns in their games. But who had the ultimate
control? Where did all the best, the profits in
wealth and power, wind up?

"Simple," she said. "On the one Earth that
invented the—what did he call it?—lab'rinth?"

"Labyrinth. I think it was a giant underground
maze in Greek mythology, but I'm not sure.
Seems to me I read about it once. A place so
complicated that if you didn't know the way,
you'd wind up getting lost forever."

She nodded. "Like us."

"Yeah," I sighed. "Like us."

"What I can't figure is the mess that got us into
this in the first place. I mean, I can see 'em, now,
inside the Mafia, inside the drug trade, you name
it. But where do folks like Little Jimmy, Big
Tony, and Whitlock come in?"

I had given that some thought. "You heard the
abbot. Somebody's been playing games with their
operations. Somebody who knows the Labyrinth
and can use it, get access to it. People have died,
stuff stolen, even stations destroyed, he said. I
think we got sucked into something like that.
This company or something like that was being
taken and their operations blown. You'd have to
be real smart and real subtle to take on and
maybe hurt an operation like this. Think about
all those Whitlocks—male, female, you name it,
all with the same prints and stuff. Where could
they come from?"

She saw where I was going. "Sure! Other
worlds. But that must mean there's lots of worlds
with the same people in them!"

"Uh huh. So Whitlock is their man at the
start—one of the boss company's men. He wouldn't
be able to resist the combination of power and

wealth and being on the inside. That's his type.
But somewhere along the line, the other side,
whoever they are, puts the snatch on him. Maybe
they kill him, maybe not, but he gets replaced
with another Whitlock who's working for the
other side. He feeds information to the opposition, queers their deals, maybe for a while. And
maybe they got *another* Whitlock around on their
side, but the only ones they got are from worlds
where he was born a girl. I know that sounds
crazy, but it fits."

"Yeah, yeah. It's all crazy, but if it fits, it fits.
You're on a roll, Sam, now that we're thinkin' the
right way. Keep goin'."

"Okay, so the only other Whitlock they have on
their side is a girl, but she looks a lot like old
Marty, enough to pass, if you didn't get right up
close with somebody who knew him for years;
and they need a way to make the switch so *their*
Whitlock can report, get stuff, whatever, and they
also need a way so that if anybody catches on
and fingers Marty as a girl, it seems convincing.
Could be this would give our G.O.D., Inc. boys a
real perverse thrill. Marty takes off work, goes
down to Sansom, comes out later as a drag
queen, and everybody's happy—while the *real*
Marty is uptown making deals or making calls to
his bosses. If anybody noses around, there's the
dresses in the bedroom, and Minnie's big mouth
and that album, which, I bet, is part of the family
album of the girl Whitlock. It's so wild it worked
for two years, partly because nobody could dream
that they'd fake it that way, and partly because it
was so well contrived."

"Yeah, it hangs tough, I admit, 'cept for a
couple of extra problems, like Mrs. Whitlock and
the *other* female Whitlock."

"His wife's no problem. They got the real Marty someplace, remember, so there's blackmail, and she's got two vulnerable kids away from home. For all we know, they went the whole hog and switched her, too. She didn't seem all that worried, anyway. As for the other woman, well, they had to get their own girl out of there before it all fell apart and she was snared, right? Be kinda hard to explain her to the feds after the first physical, after all. So the big double has to get out, but keep in character, keep convincing. They built this whole transvestite thing as a cover, after all. Now the feds swallow it, we swallow it—but sooner or later somebody's gonna put Amanda Curry someplace while Marty was clearly someplace else. They need both a him and a her, so they send in another to be Amanda while the female double plays Marty. It worked. *We* were fooled. So was the hitter—the male Whitlock sniper. All the heat's away from Philadelphia and over in Oregon where it can be controlled. They probably even left that old business card behind the dresser in the apartment deliberately. It also explains why they delayed and then sat around here, and why they used the Curry credit cards all the way. Decoys, while they cleaned up the mess back home. And we were so damned proud of ourselves!"

Brandy seemed disturbed. "Yeah, Sam, it all makes sense, if anything in this craziness makes sense, but I don't like the other things it says."

"Huh? What do you mean?"

"Sam—if there are lots of Whitlocks, male and female, and we can talk so easily about maybe another Mrs. Whitlock, too, then—how many of *us* are there? Sams and Brandys, I mean?"

I hadn't thought of that angle. "Um. . . . Yeah."
Fat Sams, thin Sams, Sams who married nice
Jewish girls and sold cars in Harrisburg, Sams
who went on the pad. Maybe even Sams who
were nice Jewish girls. And Brandys who went to
college, Brandys who married middle-class black
guys, Brandys who wound up whoring for pimps
in Camden, maybe even Brandys who made Spade
& Marlowe the biggest agency in the area. I
couldn't imagine Brandy as a guy, but there were
probably some of those, too. The fact was, the
very idea that the two of us would ever even get
together at all, let alone hit it off and get
married, was pretty slim. Everything was against
it, and lots of how it fell together was pretty
improbable—like real life, I guess. Everything
was a string of both likely and improbable events
and turns, luck, breaks, or lack of breaks, you
name it. Everybody's life was like that, from the
small to the famous and the infamous. What kind
of impossible breaks did it take for a nerd and
loser like Hitler to get where he got, and stay
there? The odds were that in most of the worlds
like ours, he never got that far.

Now it was clear, at least, why we were under
wraps, and under suspicion as well. Even if they
found out that our story checked exactly, they
had to have a way to make sure we were the
same Brandy and Sam who went through all that.
If these people even had the same prints, I
wondered how it was possible to determine that
for sure. Maybe they couldn't. They sure couldn't
with the Whitlocks. If that was the case, then any
organization that played God with so many lives
and worlds, and played with creeps like Big
Tony, Little Jimmy, and the drug boys, might not

be willing to take a chance on who we were. We could be buried up in the mountains here on a world not our own, and that would be that. Back home, people disappeared every day and were never found again. If the abbot objected, or made some kind of moral protest, it would be just as easy to send us to some world like the Garden that maybe was the end of the line for a spur, not likely to ever be used again.

Whatever, it was sure that we weren't going to break out of here. Oh, I think maybe we could have suckered the guards, maybe gotten out of the building, and just maybe clean away—but then what? We couldn't exactly be unobtrusive—it was pretty clear that nobody around here had ever *seen* a black person before. No job, no real clothes—and not even any knowledge of what the regular folks wore for clothes. No, we were stuck, and any play we might make we'd have to make out of desperation.

It was well after dinner on the third night that they came for us. Two of the guards came in and motioned for us to get up and get ready to go someplace. We were more than ready, although we figured that they were just going to take us back up to the abbot. Instead we found ourselves outside in the dark—it always seemed to be in the dark, these days—and being marched toward a fairly fancy-looking stagecoach. The driver up top was an indistinct figure dressed all in black himself, and when we got in, we found ourselves shut up with a fugitive from a Robin Hood movie. Well, all right, the outfit was a dark purple and not forest green, and the boots and belt were a dull, dark red, but you get the picture, right down to the little three-cornered hat. I first took this character for a young guy, but on second look it was a real boyish-looking girl, no makeup, short hair combed and parted on the side.

The coach lurched forward and we almost found ourselves in the girl's lap. I used to watch all sorts of westerns and costume epics, with stagecoaches and chariots and all the rest, but I never realized how damned bumpy, rocky, and downright uncomfortable they were.

The girl smiled. "It takes some getting used to, but it's easier if you just relax." She had one of those low, husky kinds of voices that also could be either male or female. I was getting my fill of androgyny by now.

"And who might you be? Maid Marian?" I asked her.

She threw me a curve, with her reply, because she knew who Maid Marian was, and because she seemed to know things about our own world: "And you are the barbarian warrior with his Numidian queen, right?"

"*Touché!* So what's this all about before I get so seasick on this meat wagon that I can't make out what you're saying?"

"My name is Jamie," she said, and she had that same English-type accent as everybody else around here. "My occupation is somewhat like your own. I am in the security division, northwest zone."

"For the Company, the Church, or the local government?" Brandy put in.

"For all of them, to one degree or another. Someone wants to talk with you under more controlled circumstances, and we thought it best to get you out of there as quickly as possible, before they started getting ideas on their own."

"You mean they *do* have an Inquisition, then?"
I said. "I knew it!"

"An Inqui—" She paused and laughed. "That's
amusing. Surely you don't think that the place up
there is Christian, do you? Oh, there *are* Chris-
tians about, here and there, but they were never
the major force in this world that they were in so
many others."

Brandy looked thoughtful. "Come to think of it,
we never *did* see a cross. Not a one. Even that
abbot wore some kind of round medal."

She nodded. "I fear they are an odd lot,
although they have a great deal of influence in
this district. They worship a whole pantheon of
gods and demigods, and spirits of trees, animals,
fire, you name it. Oh, on the whole they're a very
moral and sanctimonious lot. They never sacrifice
anyone to the gods who doesn't go willingly."

Brandy and I gulped at the same time. "They
sacrifice—*people?*" she managed.

"Oh, yes. Not very often. Usually only at sol-
stices and equinoxes unless there's some special
need or occasion. As I say, they have a lot of
power and influence about, and everyone's a bit
frightened of them anyway, so they make perfect
allies. We maintain them and allow them a
measure of authority, and in exchange they run
the station for us. It works out rather well all
around, and has for quite a long time. You *do*
realize by now, I hope, what sort of operation
you've blundered into?"

"We sorta figured it out," Brandy told her.
"Not that it's clear or that we can follow everything or accept everything, and maybe we guessed
wrong here and there, but I think we got it.

There's a whole lot of Earths, and somebody runs the railroad between 'em.''

"The railroad is a near-perfect analogy," Jamie replied. "Yes, there are a *lot* of Earths. A lot of universes, really, all one right after the other, as far as anyone can find. They all exist basically in the same place, only removed so that what happens in one has virtually no effect in the ones on either side. There are occasional mild problems, which are usually taken as ghosts, spirits, premonitions, visions, or whatever, usually connected with an overlap between specific people or places. Some worlds that have destroyed themselves have bled their poisons as well, drastically changing or even destroying their neighbors at the same time. Well, on one of these worlds, a minor company—formed in a barn, basically, by some very bright people—discovered how to go between them. Such a discovery led to profits, and power, and what we have today."

Brandy peered closely at the woman. "And just what *do* we have today?"

"Why, the Company, of course. The biggest thing that ever was created, bar none. You've had a taste of it."

"More than a taste," I noted sourly. "You haven't been stuck in these hills for a year, living on apples and nuts, with nowhere to go and little or nothing to do."

She shrugged. "No one told you to break into the Company. No one took a sword to your throat and forced you into the Labyrinth. Occasionally there's a field disturbance and someone from one world suddenly passes through to the next, which is why all worlds have their mysterious disappearances and occasional appearances, but that didn't happen to you. I have read your file."

That got Brandy's interest up. "So there's a file on us, is there?"

"There is a file on everyone who ever, wittingly or unwittingly, got involved directly with the Company. I must say that you two look only vaguely like your pictures, though. That's one major reason we were wondering about you, you see. The boss finally had to trace you entirely through the network to verify your story, and that only makes us ninety percent certain. You could have been intercepted at any number of points, particularly since the time line of that siding you were on is quite fast."

I stared at her. "What do you mean by that?"

"Well, there's a centerpoint of sorts. Worlds go out in all directions from it. It's not the one that runs the Labyrinth—it's really not much of anything—but it's likely it's the prime world, the seat of creation. The time rate there is also the base rate, and it's quite slow, relatively speaking. The further away from the centerpoint, the faster the time rate seems to be for each given world. It's purely subjective—you never know the difference unless you travel often between them. Take this world, for instance. I have no idea of the true ratio, but it's probable that an hour here would be the equivalent of, say, a day in your home universe, or perhaps the reverse. That abandoned experimental botanical region the switchman shuttled you to when it was clear you were not authorized on the system—which is one of the standard procedures for such things—runs at a very fast clip. That's why it was used for organic experiments. You plant your seeds and they grow at a normal rate relative to their universe, but since it's hundreds of times faster than the universe of the planter, he or she just pops back over in a day or two, and it's a year later to the plants."

Brandy shook her head wonderingly, and I was feeling a little dizzy. "You mean," Brandy said, "that we spent a year there but maybe only a coupla days passed back home?"

"Yes, something like that. That's why it took so long to trace you, you see. The switchman's report on you hadn't even reached Company security for processing when you popped up here. I fear that switchman you talked into sending you here is going to get badly disciplined."

"You've been to our world?" Brandy pressed. "You seem to know a lot about it."

"Not *yours*. Good heavens, that would push chance too far. One like yours, anyway, and several more. Part of our promotional training. I must tell you that I wasn't all that impressed. All that dehumanizing machinery, the ugly smells, the coldness of the people, the crime and corruption and fears and tensions. . . . We've had three murders in this barony in the past four years, and all were crimes of passion. It's quite peaceful and quite secure. Oh, I suppose your medicine is wondrous, and perhaps the good of such mass communication and transport outweighs the bad, but somewhere along the line you seem to have lost your sense of values and proportion. Your woodland is vanishing, your animals and plants are dying, your water and air are fouled, and you live in houses like forts behind heavy locks and steel bars, and fear to venture out alone at night. Everyone was so upset, when I was there, that a bunch of fanatics had blown up some ambassador in some foreign kingdom; yet right then, people were getting robbed, raped, and murdered all around them, and everybody seemed to think that was normal. No, thank you. I like it here."

It was a hell of a speech, and I wished I could come up with a good, snappy retort, but I was still trying to find the flaw in her reasoning.

"Tell us about this place, then," Brandy invited. "What is *your* world like?"

"Oh, it's not organized very differently from anywhere else. There's an emperor here, one of several for all the empires about, and under him there are kings and a few queens who run countries within the empire. The countries are divided into smaller and smaller units under dukes, barons, and the like, each taking a sacred oath to obey and defend the one above him. The nobility accounts for about four percent of the population. Then there are the knights and their families, the heads of individual estates and the leaders of police and military, which are one and the same thing here, and that's another five percent or so. The rest of the people, except for the townspeople and traders and the like, are bound to the land. They work, and in exchange are given food, clothing, housing, general cradle-to-grave care, and protection from any bad elements."

"That's the kind of thing they used to have in olden days," Brandy pointed out. "I forget its name, but what it boils down to is that about ten percent have everything, and everybody else supports them as slaves."

"It's feudalism. That's the word," I put in.

"No, it's not slavery," Jamie argued. "In the world like yours that I lived in for a year there were several different forms of government. One was called a democracy, but in it about five percent of the people had about ninety-five percent of the wealth, and most of the political power. You got to vote for which of the two people put up by the rich you wanted. Then there were two other systems that differed in ways too subtle to matter. One had the government owning everything in common, and was run by a single party and a bureaucracy that amounted to about nine percent of the people. The party made all the decisions and lived quite well, and the rest of the people worked for whatever the party gave them. The third system was sort of like the other two combined, with the rich owning everything and being members of a party who all sat down together and decided what would be made, what would be sold, and at what price and profit, and what wages and working conditions would be. In all cases it seemed that you were talking about ten percent ruling ninety percent absolutely. I may be a bit dull on political matters, but I couldn't really see much difference deep down. No people in this land may be bought or sold. It is immoral. They remain with the land, no matter who becomes their lord."

I began to realize that they'd sent us a live one to soften us up. Trapping us in a coach with Jamie in the middle of the night was worse torture than sending us back to the Garden.

"And you? Do you belong to somebody's land?" Brandy asked.

"Oh, my, no! I'm the daughter of a knight. The *fifth* daughter. My parents were always preparing my sisters for marriage and position, and I was always down learning fencing with the squires and outdoing the boys at their own games. Why not? I never liked the idea that men were inherently better at some things than women, and, besides, by the time they got to me there was pretty slim pickings in terms of wealth or advancement possibilities. My father, noting my talents and having surrendered at his attempts to make a lady out of me, introduced me to a man who turned out to be a marketing representative with the Company. My contacts and position have allowed me to aid my family, so they are content; and my job suits my own proclivities, so I am content. The Company is male at the very top, but no one not born on that world can be on the very top anyway, and that takes both talent and relatives. There is, however, a considerable career path an ambitious and smart woman might take, and that is sufficient for me."

I was about to ask whether she liked boys or girls best, but Brandy read my mind and gave me a poke in the side. What the hell. Diplomacy was a part of the detective's art at times.

It was nearing dawn when we began to slow, maybe three or four hours out. I didn't know much about horses, but I figured we'd have to stop just to rest *them*. We were coming into a town of some kind, down low, and in the distance I heard an eerie and very mechanical whistle blow. "What's that?" I asked.

"A train. What else would it be except a train or the fire alarm?" Jamie asked casually. "They can't get steamboats this far upriver."

And here I was just getting used to the idea of being in the land of King Arthur or something. "You have steam stuff?"

"Oh, yes. We're not primitives, after all. Steam

is at the heart of the emperor's power, for only the emperor runs things of steam, and licenses and schools all those who operate such devices. When I was little I once had a dream of being the first female train driver, but that's just not done here. One of the empires over in Africa, I hear, is a matriarchy and there it's possible, but that's not the way of my own emperor or land. As I say, there are trade-offs, and I have found my own niche."

"Yeah," Brandy whispered a bit sourly. "Everybody born at the top thinks that way."

To my surprise we went right down to a small railway station, and then alongside the tracks, slowly. There wasn't a lot of light, but the trains used in this world looked more primitive than museum pieces, not even as fancy as the wild-west trains or those of the Civil War. The cars were all wood and looked like they belonged to an enlarged antique Christmas train set. Most were freight, but the last car was an old-time passenger car, and it was the only part of the train that was lit.

We pulled up to it, and Jamie reached over, opened the door, then hopped out and helped us both down. We were stiff and I, at least, was starting to feel my lack of sleep. I wasn't tired enough, though, that I didn't see a dozen or more black shapes lurking about the yard. Whoever this was, he carried a real heavy bodyguard.

The car was divided into two parts, a parlor area and a sleeping area, and we entered the parlor and took seats in lavish surroundings. There was gold trim and velvet seat covers and the curtains were fine silk. It was the kind of car old royalty must have owned in Europe back in the nineteenth century.

A man entered, wearing a maroon dressing gown, a pipe in his mouth. He was a large man, rather handsome with a full brown beard just going to gray, nicely trimmed hair of the same color and condition, and a large build. His gray eyes surveyed us with some bemusement, and he smiled and came fully into the parlor. "You must pardon my meeting you like this," he said to us in a voice that was full and sonorous and more classical American than English, "but I'm afraid I hadn't planned on fitting any of this into my schedule. This world isn't one where you expect your tea to be late or anything more complex than a toothache." He paused a moment. "Oh, pardon. Jamie, you wish to make the formal introductions?"

The security agent stood. "Sir, Mr. Samuel Horowitz and his wife, Brandy Horowitz. May I present the chief of operations for the northwest district of the Company?"

The man smiled and stuck out a hand. "Lamont Cranston, at your service," he said pleasantly.

7.

A Choice of Futures

There was a sense of total unreality about sitting in an antique railroad car, surrounded by a world still stuck mostly in the Middle Ages, and having the Shadow come up and introduce himself. I figured I needed sleep worse than I thought.

"You seem startled by my name," Cranston noted. "Have you encountered an alternate me?"

"Not exactly," I told him, "but if you can't cloud men's minds so they cannot see you, it'll be a big disappointment to us."

He frowned. "Invisibility? Haven't heard of that one."

"Your name was attached to a fictional detective who could, back in my world."

He laughed pleasantly. "Well, that's flattering. It *does* happen, you know. *Everything* happens, you see."

He sat down, and just after, we felt the car lurch and there was a loud sound behind us. They were adding cars, it seemed.

"Brandy, Sam—I hope I may call you that— just how much do you understand of all this?"

"They got it pretty clear. Surprisingly clear," Jamie assured him.

"I don't know how it's possible, but we have to figure there's a lot of Earths one on top of the other," Brandy told him. "And your Company can go between."

"Very good!" Cranston exclaimed, sounding quite pleased. "There's not merely a lot of Earths, there's apparently a number approaching infinity. An enormous amount have no human life at all, and many have no life of any kind. Others have developed rather differently, with different species dominating the worlds. We're in what we call the 'human' band, although that's misleading and an insulting term in many ways. It's just that the men who discovered the infinite worlds and the way to go between are from a world where people evolved much the same as your ancestors and mine did. We prefer to call the band the Type Zero band, and those Earths which developed quite different advanced forms are Type Ones, Type Twos, and so on. Each band is vast in and of itself, with uncountable variations of the same basics. Far too many for our people to even have sufficient numbers of live bodies to check them out."

I thought about it. An infinite number, with thousands, maybe millions, or more varying the norm. I couldn't really grasp it, even though I could accept the reality of it because here I was in another of them.

"The physics is far too esoteric to explain, if I could," Cranston continued. "It's a matter of perception, they tell me. I had it gone through a hundred times and it still made my head swim. All their histories date to the same event, a big

explosion that began the universe but also created an infinite series of universes, all overlaid
one atop the other. So much of all this development is chance, though, and none of them developed precisely the same way. In a sense, you
could just think of the history of the universe and
all the chance occurrences and improbabilities
that went into the way it is now, and then step
back and say, '*Everything that might possibly have
happened differently, did*'—somewhere.''

"And you're milking them all," Brandy commented.

"Well, yes, of course we are. Only a very
few—representative ones from the regions of more
dramatic departures in history, culture, and development. We have perhaps a dozen established
stations in your area of the Type Zero spectrum,
all well apart. Occasionally we can open a temporary station stop—a flag stop, we call it—when
we need something specific from a close neigh-
bor, such as someone's exact counterpart. That, of
course, breeds the curses of this network. You live
in constant paranoia in this job, never a hundred
percent certain if the person you're talking to is
the exact same one you think or someone else.
And, as you can well understand, any organization with this amount of power makes enemies.
Some just want the power for themselves. Some
believe we have an ideological mission to remake
all the worlds into whatever vision the group has
in mind. Others think it's immoral to do what we
do, or are troubled by our methods; and still
others want free and unlimited access to the
network with no restrictions, which would bring
chaos. You see how it is.''

We nodded, because we *did* see. "I know you're

in bed with some pretty disreputable elements back home," I noted. "I can see how that sort of thing would upset people."

The train lurched and then began to move into the dawn. We were clearly not going to remain in central Oregon much longer.

"Sam, Brandy—look. The Company is not heartless, even though it must sometimes seem pretty ruthless. We've seen the horrors humans can do to other humans in all their worst aspects, but we can't cure the ills of an infinite number of worlds. It simply isn't possible. We took the view, long ago, that we would not interfere in the development of worlds in any way that would induce dramatic change, with a single exception: We can't even hope to prevent mass destruction of humanity where it might occur, but when it is clear that a holocaust of that magnitude is about to take place, and that world adjoins worlds where it is not, we endeavor to stop it. That alone taxes our resources, but something like a nuclear exchange of massive proportions is so catastrophic it actually can bleed over, poisoning the worlds on either side for some distance, killing those nearest and dramatically altering others further away. That is something we feel we *must* do, no matter what the cost. If a world blows itself away, it is tragic and we can't stop it, but when it takes up to billions of others with it—we must try."

"That sounds admirable enough," I admitted.

"Otherwise, we establish stations and spurs, and that takes resident Company personnel. We're so stretched now, that often that personnel is of a different type, and thus can't even operate freely within the world. For what we want, we are dependent on setting up a network of natives, people from that world. In many cases, the most efficient way to gain access to whatever we want quickly and unobtrusively is to co-opt the criminal element, particularly if it is well organized and powerful. They understand wealth, power, and secrecy. I looked up your world. We've only had stations there for thirty years or so. The easiest way into the so-called Western World was through its criminal organizations, which were organized much like corporations. They act as autonomous subsidiaries of the Company, and only those at the very top know the truth—and they don't mind. Control them, and their inheritors, and leave everything else running normally, and we get what we want."

Brandy sighed. "Let me get this straight. You're sayin' that the *Mafia* is a wholly owned and operated subsidiary of this Company of yours?"

"Well, yes, among others. It's different here, because this society is far more simply organized. Here we simply need to control some key members of the nobility and influential religious groups. The biggest problem is being dependent on the slow transportation system and the very slow communications here."

"If they got steam now, they're about ready to explode into real technology," I noted.

"No, that's unlikely. Most of the basic research here has been done already. Most of it is suppressed, sometimes forcefully. The rulers here, those at the empire level, want no radical changes beyond what you see. I suspect we may have overdone it at the beginning, when we showed certain key people other worlds, worlds like yours. To them, those worlds are the stuff of nightmares."

There was little to say to that. "Might it be presumptuous to ask where we're heading?" I asked, trying to steer things to a more practical point. "And what you plan to do with us?"

"We are heading south to my beach house," he told us. "There we'll get you cleaned up, groomed, dressed, and whatever, and there you can be examined by staff personnel. I have a few ideas right now, but until we know more I won't be able to give much more information, I fear. We've hooked up a sleeper and a diner to the train. Just berths, I'm afraid, but they will allow you to get some sleep. Tomorrow will be early enough to discuss the future. Nothing is hurried here."

We were treated with every courtesy by Cranston and his staff while we were on the journey, but Jamie was there with us any time we weren't in the sleeper, and when we were, others outside and all around made sure we stayed there. They would talk about pleasantries or maybe the land or any kind of general things, but nothing specific, and certainly nothing more about the Company. Cranston kept to himself a lot, apparently working in his room, but he made appearances for meals and occasional drinks.

In the sleeper, Brandy wondered where all this was leading. "I can't get a handle on the man, Sam. He's the kind of man who don't mess with you unless you can do him some good, but what could we do for him in *this* place? Is he gonna ask us to kill somebody for him and take the fall, or what?"

"I don't know, babe. We have to roll with him for now, though, because he's the boss and there's no place to run. I know what you mean, though. He's too high up to mess with us for this length of time unless he has something in mind, but he's too low down in the Company totem pole to really do *us* much good."

Cranston's "beach house" turned out to be a monstrous Elizabethan-style estate overlooking the Pacific Ocean. It was, however, more than a little isolated, forcing us to ride south for most of the day and the next night on the train, then transfer to coaches and basically climb a mountain on a pretty poor dirt road for maybe thirty miles to get over to it. It had a permanent staff, but was clearly supplied by sea somehow, and not off that rickety road with the hairpin curves. The view from his terrace was beautiful, though, and his living room could hold four hundred families from a Camden project with room left over.

A staff was there, and no matter how they dressed or talked, it was clear from the outset that absolutely no one in or around that house was anything but a Company employee, and from some of the accents and what they knew, it was equally clear that few were natives of this world.

We were measured for clothing by people who'd done it a lot, and somehow some of that clothing was ready for us within hours of our arrival. While waiting, each of us was given a full physical by a doctor who knew far more about medicine than any doctor should in this world, and maybe more than a doctor would back home. The place had no electricity and was fireplace-heated at night, but that doctor had instruments that worked by battery power. He pronounced us both in excellent physical shape, except for Brandy's vision, and used a small device to measure her eyes.

We went back to the bedroom, a luxury affair with big, wide bed, fireplace, redwood furnishings, and the rest, and when the clothes arrived, so did a pair of glasses. They were round and seemed rimless, but the bridge and earpieces were a golden bronze color. They looked kind of cute on her, although they magnified her already big eyes somewhat. She put them on and, standing stark naked, walked to the mirror and looked at herself in wonder. "Sweet Jesus!" she breathed, and it occurred to me that it was the first time she was really seeing herself clearly in the reflection. Me, I'd been admiring her new head of hair since I came in. So what if it was mostly gray? It was *hair*, damn it, where hair hadn't been in years and where, I had thought, hair would never be again.

Just the exercise and the food of the Garden had dropped almost a hundred pounds from her, replacing most of it with good muscle. The only places she hadn't lost much were in her face, which was still round and apple-cheeked, and in her breasts, which had stubbornly refused to shrink much. Her ass and hips were tight, her waist very slender. I made her at something around 40–24–36, and she was something else.

Me, I had a full head of hair, although it was uneven, hanging down the neck maybe an inch, and a full and pretty ragged beard of the same color. I always had a lot of body hair, but it was uneven; now I had hair on my hair—chest, arms, legs, you name it. I'd slimmed down and firmed up pretty good myself, although it was still the same old nose and mouth and eyes that peered back at me, maybe a little more worn and wrinkled. It was easy to see, though, why we wouldn't match the IDs Cranston had gotten. Our own relatives wouldn't recognize us now. I had a sinking feeling they would, sooner or later, though. I remembered that when I got out of Basic I looked almost this good, and I'd sworn to myself I'd keep it, but it hadn't lasted six months after I was free to do what I wanted again. I was a born self-abuser.

"Oh, Sam, this is *dy-no-mite!*" she squealed. "If I ever thought I *could* look this way I'da worked at it. I sure as hell ain't gonna let this go, no sir!" She turned to me. "You don't look so bad yourself, you know. Get that hair and beard trimmed up and you'll be the sexiest man in *any* of these worlds."

We examined the clothes. They'd only sent up one set each, but what could you expect from six-hour tailoring? Brandy's outfit was all tan or beige, and mostly soft calfskin lined with thin fur, maybe rabbit, that also served as trim. She had a pair of those Robin Hood boots like Jamie had, the kind where the tops are kind of folded down, although with thick but not real high heels; a matching dress that wasn't quite knee-length but was cut real loose; a pullover wool and cotton sweater dyed to match the rest; and a thin calfskin belt that was more ornament than necessary.

My outfit was more along the lines Jamie had worn, but was even more Robin Hoodish in being a real dark green. Except for the boots—which were leather and had the same kind of turned-down-top design but which had lower, flatter heels than Brandy's—mine was all cloth, mostly cotton it seemed, with pants, a pullover shirt that nonetheless had a low cut exposing some of my hairy chest, and a thin black leather belt that also wasn't really needed. There was some stretch, but those pants and that shirt were tight. If anybody in this world had discovered underwear, it was for strictly formal occasions, and even though the pants were reinforced in the crotch, no lady would ever have to guess about my sex or how big it was. It was crazy—I hadn't had any problem being stark naked, but I was more than a little embarrassed at this skintight business. They also didn't seem to have invented flys. I'd have to peel this sucker off to piss.

We were called to dinner and served by a staff dressed out of some old English movie with the double-buttoned uniforms and knee-length jerkins and high socks and all that, even white-powdered wigs, but we dined alone. After, the servants took us into separate small rooms off to one side, and we were given hot scented baths, which we badly needed, and I got the haircut and trim I needed, and got the countless snags out, not without pain, while Brandy got her hair shaped and trimmed. She mostly did it herself, she told me; they just didn't know how to handle her kind of hair.

Finally, we walked out on the cliffside patio and stared into the darkness while the sound of the surf hitting the rocky cliff far below engulfed us. It was not at all lit, except for some reflections from the candles and oil lamps inside, but it was just light enough to keep from killing yourself and not enough to spoil the stars.

"Sam," Brandy sighed, "we've come so far to here, and none of it seems real. I think of all of 'em, this seems the least real, includin' that Labyrinth thing. I almost feel out of place here. I mean, what's a low-class pair of jokers like us doin' in a place like this?"

I nodded and sighed. "Yeah, I think I know how you feel, babe. I don't know what's up now, or whether anything is real. I mean, we're not only on another world in a fancy place, but it's Lamont Cranston's place, for heaven's sake! This is sort of out of our league, babe. We were back there playing sandlot ball and dreaming of making the minor leagues, while preparing to give up the game and get real jobs. Now we're in the majors, babe, but as utility men. Expendable and maybe useful. Don't kid yourself about the upper-class bit, though. You noticed this place? Even the *maids* got fourteen petticoats on, and the butlers could wait on the queen of England dressed like that. Us, they dress like Robin Hood and a B-western cowgirl. This may be fancy-made, hand-tailored peasant dress, but it's still peasant dress."

"Yeah, well, it's where we should be in this place, I guess. I know tomorrow they might serve us up for breakfast, but, right now, I just got no complaints. Hell, Sam, we never *did* have nothin' but each other, and that's what we got now." She paused a minute and looked back out into the darkness. "You know, when I started missin' them periods back in the Garden, I thought I was pregnant. That doctor says no, though. Says it was the food that did it, that I'll start gettin' 'em again. That's what made these bodies and your hair so right, you know."

I hadn't pressed that point when it was my turn, and I was interested. "You mean I'm going to lose it again?"

"Could be. Maybe not. Turns out that place was

designed to grow special food that would do funny things to your chemistry. Not all by itself, but with exercise and sleep and all, it'd pep up your sex parts, change fat into muscle, get your hormones really flowing, and it was supposed to be more or less permanent. Painless perfection. Even protects against most diseases and promotes healin', he said. That's one of the byproducts of working for the Company, I think. You know how old he said Cranston was?"

I shrugged. "Forty, maybe forty-five?"

"Seventy-one! That's the kind of stuff they got, Sam."

I swallowed hard. I was nearly perfect now, but if I looked like Cranston at sixty, let alone seventy-one, I'd feel more than happy.

"Then I asked him why they abandoned the Garden. He said the stuff was too unpredictable and had some side effects, like my extra-big boobs and all that fur on you. They got better, more reliable stuff now. The old boy only meant to stash us for a few days. Still, I'm almost glad, now, that we got stuck awhile, now that we got out. Bein' forced to eat healthy foods, exercise, get in condition. We'd never have done that on our own. Still, I can't handle that time thing."

I nodded. "Yeah, I'm still finding that one hard to swallow. A year there and we haven't even come up to our trial date back home. If that's so, I'd sure like to see the look on people's faces if we showed up there looking like this! Nobody said how fast this one runs, though. It's between the Garden and home, that's for sure, so it's probably fast, too. Not that it makes any difference now, I guess."

A butler emerged from the house bearing a

silver tray with two drinks. "A light liqueur before bedtime, sir and madam?" he asked politely. "It is the master's own special stock."

We shrugged, and took them, and the butler went back into the house. We sipped the drinks and relaxed, sitting on a redwood love seat on the patio.

"You know," I remarked casually, "one thing's really bothering me. That Garden made your vision worse, yeah, but you had lousy vision to begin with. How the hell did you ever drive that car without cracking up?"

She chuckled and yawned. "I always had my old pair of glasses in my purse. They weren't much for everyday—gave me headaches—and I never liked their looks, but I could drive with 'em."

I clinked glasses with her and we downed the rest of our drinks. "Well," I told her, "you make sure you keep wearing those. I like 'em just fine, but I like somebody who can see even more. You take 'em off in bed, when you don't need to see well." I yawned, too, and started feeling dizzy. The world started spinning. "Brandy?"

She slumped over into my lap, out cold, but before I could do anything I slumped over, too, and all was darkness.

If you ever had general anesthetic at the dentist's, you know how we felt for a considerable time. You're vaguely awake and aware that things are going on, that questions are being asked and being answered, things are being done to you, but you don't remember what, and you're only vaguely aware that any time is passing. Then, slowly, you come out of it, but you feel like you're drowning in the bottom of a well and you rise up, try and break the surface, and gasp for air as the real world breaks around you.

I sat up and opened my eyes in one quick reflex action. I was in bed, naked, in a bedroom that was smaller than the one at Cranston's beach house but still quite pleasant. It was still on the beach somewhere; I could hear pounding surf and the cries of seabirds outside.

I looked around, head still pounding, and saw Brandy lying there, still out, but murmuring agitatedly and occasionally kicking or pushing away in her sleep. My head ached, but I figured that was the mickey working its final revenge. A pair of French doors led out of the room to my left; a regular door led, I thought, to the rest of the house. I managed to get up and walk over to the French doors and look out.

We had certainly been moved a great distance. There was a small balcony out there, and beyond was the ocean, but not the rocky cliffs and chill foam of the northwest's Pacific; white, sandy beach led gently down to it here, and the breakers crashed onto a nearly pristine beach. Well out in the water, I thought I could see sailboats or something like them, and the whole place looked warm and summery in contrast to the chill of Oregon. I didn't know a whole lot about the Pacific coast or more than one little corner of Oregon, but I had the sneaking suspicion that we'd changed worlds again. How, and why, I didn't know. They certainly hadn't lugged us all this way down to Cranston's place just to take us back to McInerney.

I looked in the drawer and found clothes there, and in the closet. Not funny clothes like we'd been given at Cranston's but real clothes. Shirts, socks, pants, even jockey shorts with the label in them. Another drawer had women's clothes, including panties and large bras, and the closet had others, from informal to a couple of dresses that looked like they could be real interesting if filled with a warm body. Maybe there was a different reason why they only gave us one set of funny clothes.

Brandy woke up with the same suddenness that I had, and looked around, then groaned and held her head. I turned and went over to her. "It passes pretty quickly, babe. How you feeling?"

"*Oooh!* Badder than I felt in a long time!"

I let her come out of it, got up and walked back over to the dresser. Her glasses were on top, and I picked them up and brought them back to her. She put them on, and started to look around. "New place again, huh?"

"Yeah, more to our style, anyway," I told her.

In a few more minutes she was examining and then checking out some of the clothing. She found two boxes, one containing an assortment of jewelry and a cosmetic case, the other had a pair of watches along with a beard trimmer and comb set. Both watches were the digital-alarm type, one for men and one for women. They both said it was 10:34 on August 1. If that related at all to home, it had us gone less than two and a half weeks.

"Of course, it don't say what year," Brandy noted.

We slipped the watches on our wrists and began to get dressed, since that seemed the thing to do. Since we still seemed to be at the beach and the watches said it was August, Brandy went for shorts and a tee shirt and I decided on some slacks and a sport shirt. Shoes still felt wrong, but we both figured we'd better get used to them again. There was a pair of slip-on moccasins that fit nicely on my feet, and Brandy found some sandals. She debated the bra and decided not to, for now; although she'd always worn one and even slept with one for support, it had been a very long time.

"You tried the door?" she asked me.

I had to admit that I hadn't. "It just didn't occur to me," I told her, walking over and turning the knob. The door opened, without a problem, on a narrow hallway. There was a bathroom right there, with clean linen, and we took the opportunity to wash our faces and get generally straightened out. Then it was time to see just where we were and what this was all about.

There was a modern kitchen with patio doors that led out to a patio, of all things. A girl was sitting out there in a skimpy bathing suit, relaxing in a lawn chair and sipping on a drink. She saw us and motioned for us to come out. It took me several seconds to realize that the girl was Jamie. She still had that short haircut, and I think *I* have bigger breasts than she's got, but her body was lean, curvaceous, and unexpectedly feminine shorn of those boyish Robin Hood clothes. She had on sunglasses, which weren't a bad idea in that sun.

"Well, hello! Back from the dead, I see," the security agent said cheerfully in that London-cultured stage accent of hers. "There's coffee and tea on, if you like, or cold drinks in the 'fridge. If you're hungry I could do up some eggs and bangers or hunt up some fruit or sweet rolls. Won't take a moment."

Brandy looked at me. "Bangers?"

"I think they're sausages." I turned to Jamie. "I think some coffee and those rolls would do me. I think I've had my fill of apples and stuff like that for a while."

"Maybe some iced tea and some of that fruit," Brandy told her. "After what fruit did for me, I'm not gonna switch off."

Jamie hopped up and ran into the house while we took seats around a round lawn table shaded with an umbrella stuck up through the center. This was quite nice, but it sure didn't make any sense at all.

Jamie was back in less than five minutes with a tray that included what I wanted, and not only the iced tea but a whole bowl of fruit—apples, oranges, bananas, you name it. I tried the coffee and it tasted very bitter. I was about to complain about it, when I suddenly realized just how long I'd been between cups, even though I used to run on the stuff. I was always a black-coffee man, but this time I added some cream and sugar from a nice little tea service there and got it palatable.

Jamie took another chair at the table and relaxed. "So, how do you both feel?"

"Let me get something straight first," I responded. "You *are* the same Jamie that came with us south on the train?"

She laughed. "Oh, yes. Mr. Cranston recommended me for assignment to you for a while, and no one who is ambitious ever turns down a promotion."

"I thought you couldn't stand the modern worlds," Brandy put in.

"Oh, it's not standing or not standing, it's that one never has the choice of where to work if she wants the good jobs. I certainly wouldn't like to *retire* here, or spend the rest of my life here, but I certainly don't mind working here for a while. I admit I could get to like *this* sort of place very easily."

I nodded. "Just where *is* this sort of place, if I may ask, and what was all that about slipping us both mickeys?"

"Mickeys? Oh, some sort of slang, I suppose. We needed to know just exactly whether you were what you claimed to be or not. There was no way to check on a switch in Horowitzes, as it were, somewhere along the line, particularly since you *were* involved in some nasty business with the wrong element. We couldn't very well do much around the monastery, since if the Labyrinth is infiltrated we couldn't know who we might trust up there in case they wanted to falsify the results. The beach house was perfect, and we could get some good technicians there in a hurry without arousing suspicion or alarm. They put you through the most *awful* tests, I'm afraid, but don't feel singled out. I've been through them myself and will probably be through them again. Complete computer analysis of your entire body, psychiatric probes and analyses, various kinds of coercive interrogation, and all the rest. They know more about the two of you now than you know about each other, or yourselves. A great deal of who and what we are is in our genes and body chemistries, they tell me, and they can even read those codes."

"I gather they were satisfied," I said.

"Oh, yes. They're quite impressed with you,

you know. You tracked through that whole ugly Philadelphia business all the way to the plant, and then you infiltrated the plant, even though you had no idea what you were seeing. Then, faced with the evidence of something totally unbelievable, you accepted it and worked from there, even figured much of it out. That *is* impressive. They were also fascinated with you as a pair. In spite of vast differences in education, background, culture, whatever, the two of you have minds that seem to be very much alike. So much so that you almost know what the other is thinking when you're concentrating on a common problem. What one lacks, the other has, so the fit is nearly seamless. Yet you're so unlikely a couple to ever get together that you just prove the old rule that anything that might happen has or will happen."

Both of us liked to hear that, although I suspected I'd rather skip the downside of the report.

"The proof of that is in your intelligence and aptitude measurements," Jamie continued. "Individually, you're not exceptionally above average, either of you, but together you have near-genius aptitudes in certain areas, such as puzzle solving and deductive reasoning. They like that, which is why we're all here. 'Here,' by the by, is a small island in the Bahamas group that is wholly owned by the Company. You are essentially home."

The funny thing was, I wasn't all that sure I wanted to *be* "home." There wasn't a whole lot here for us, after all. "So why the Bahamas and all this, then?" I asked her.

"We'll know more when the Company personnel arrive, but I think they are going to offer you a job with the Company. Something in the line of work you've always followed."

Brandy nodded. We had been expecting this, simply because we survived and remained in civilization. "Jamie—you've worked with them for a long time. I can't say we aren't interested, 'cause if they're as thorough as you say they are, they already have a good idea we'll take it, but what if we didn't? I mean, I want to know if this is a real proposition or if we have a gun to our heads."

She was silent for a moment, then said, "Well, it's a bit of both, I suppose. They prize loyalty highly, for example. As Mr. Cranston told you, there's a good bit of paranoia involved in this job, and you survive and prosper by not fighting it. You have already caused a lot of trouble not even knowing the facts. You could cause a lot more now that you *do* know, or, worse, you might get an offer from the traitors working against us. They probably wouldn't kill you—they really don't like people working for them under that sort of coercion since they're so easily susceptible to being turned against the Company—but they would probably open a quick and temporary flag stop on a world without a station, very primitive, the sort of desert-island situation, and implant some sort of device that would prevent you ever traveling the Labyrinth again, and forget about you. I'm afraid, though, I can't see where your reservations lie. You are being offered a great opportunity."

"Their reservations, my dear, are that they are romantics and moralists at heart," said a man's voice behind us. We all turned, and even after all this time, both Brandy and I gasped.

Martin J. Whitlock IV, male, handsome, pepper-haired and nicely tanned, dressed in a colorful sport shirt and slacks and tennis shoes, walked over and pulled out the fourth and final chair around the lawn table and sat down. "Isn't that right?"

We both continued to stare. Finally I managed, "The *real* Martin J. Whitlock the Fourth, I assume?"

He grinned. "You tracked me down at last. Not, I'm afraid, anywhere near Oregon, though."

Jamie looked at him, and then at the two of us, and frowned. "You know each other?"

"Only by sight and reputation," Brandy replied. "So we *were* right about the decoy business!"

"It got more and more convoluted as it went along," Whitlock told us. "It was kind of insane to begin with, and so it fell apart in an insane way. We'll get to that in a minute. Just now we were talking about morality, Mrs. Horowitz. You see, Jamie, she's grown up in a pretty poor neighborhood where the pimps and the junkies battled for territory, and now she knows the relationship of that group to us. You were willing to work for that pig Nkrumah, though."

"That was different," she shot back. "That was crook against crook. You can't insist your clients be perfect, but if it was Nkrumah goin' after some poor sucker who skipped without payin' 'cause he was scared for his wife and kids, I wouldn'ta touched it in a minute."

Whitlock thought a moment. "You ever think of what organized crime really is today? I really didn't, until I analyzed it from a strictly business viewpoint, because that's just what it is—a business. It fills a gap in the system. People get up in arms about immorality, or want to legislate behavior, liberals and conservatives alike, and they outlaw all sorts of stuff—but it's stuff that a large number of people in society want. Take loan sharking, for example. Anybody with any job at all, even a fry cook at McDonald's, can get collateral credit for buying furniture, that kind of thing. Like any other bank, no loan shark will lend to somebody with no way or means to pay a loan back. They lend to the compulsive spenders, the compulsive gamblers, the people with long histories of stiffing credit companies, declaring bankruptcy, that sort of thing. Their own behavior has made it impossible for them to get credit. Nobody goes out on the street with a gun and says, 'You will borrow a thousand dollars from a loan shark.' They beat down the shark's doors with pleas. The shark sees they have the ability to pay, but the basic collateral is fear. These are people who *want* or *need* to be coerced, frightened, forced into paying back the loan."

"Yeah, and if you don't, they break your legs," she noted.

He shrugged. "That's why the interest has to be so high. If you have to enforce the contract, you remove the guy's ability to repay, and that cost is added on to everybody else's loan. It's a business, and a service people want. It's just based on a fact of human nature the churches and politicians want to ignore or pretend isn't there."

"So you make crooks out of them to get the payback money," I noted.

"Crooks don't borrow from sharks, generally speaking. If you have to stick up a store to pay back the shark, you're better off just sticking up the store in the first place and saving the interest."

"Yeah, well, what about drugs?" Brandy pressed.

"Another good example. About twenty percent of the country uses illegal drugs regularly. I suspect *you* have. Nobody is forced to use them; they do it by choice, and sometimes through self-deception. Nobody thinks *they* can get hooked. But they're so anxious to snort, smoke, or inject drugs into their bodies, they'll buy anything from anybody. Even the amateurs get into the act— and then we have bloodletting, and innocents die. Organized, with a steady supply at a stable price, we keep the victimization generally to those who victimize themselves. We don't force anyone to take anything; we just supply the demand because nobody legitimate would."

"And cause a crime wave so they can feed their habits," I pointed out.

"Yes and no. They got their drugs before there was organized crime, and they'll get their drugs from somebody one way or the other, because that's the kind of personalities they have. If the government legalized the stuff and doled it out, they'd stop that sort of thing. Otherwise, it's going to happen regardless. The demand is there. It's either a bunch of psychotic idiots or it's a business organization maintaining a constant supply."

He sighed and shifted in his chair. "You can do this with almost anything. No man was ever stopped on the street and had a knife put to his throat and told, 'You will go have sex with this prostitute.' Yeah, there are some forced into it, but you go talk to them sometime. You'll find most took it for the easy money, or because they have no sense of their own worth, or they're so insecure it's a safe haven. I know you once thought about it, Brandy. I've read your file.

Now, you were smart and attractive. You could have taken a basic job, a fry-cook job, got your GED, maybe gone to college or business school and gotten a career job. You know it. You think what your reasons were for considering going the whoring route, and you'll see what I mean. Yeah, people get trapped in those jobs, but people get trapped in lots of ugly jobs because they're stupid or don't think straight or have too many romantic visions. We don't trap them, they trap themselves."

He was pretty good at rationalizing, and I knew the arguments from old. They were the same kind of arguments vice cops gave for going on the pad, and many of them were valid. "You mean those kids who get kidnapped and forced into kiddie porn trapped themselves?" I asked him.

"Of course not. They're the dregs of the business and I wouldn't have anything to do with them. I have kids, too. If I found them under a rock, I'd turn them in. The problem is, when you're working a business that is predicated on the idea of supplying goods and services that people want but can't otherwise get, you spawn imitators, spinoff businesses, that fill the gaps even you won't. Somewhere there are organizations that kidnap blue-eyed blondes for the harems of Middle Eastern princes, but that's not us. It's just the proof that wherever there is a demand, somebody will supply it. General Ordering and Development doesn't even do the criminal stuff. They just use it because it's there, and it can't be stopped until human nature is radically altered. It's an unpleasant pattern that works well, world after world, because corruption is itself easily corrupted. There are countless worlds, and they don't have many people for them, but they can't take but so many natives into their confidence or their existence is blown, their operation compromised. Crooks take the money and don't ask questions even when the requests are pretty weird. Big crooks have resources, established channels of information—connections to almost every major business, industry, and government institution—and an insular, underground economy ready to use. We use it."

"You say 'we,' " Brandy noted. "I gather you're with the Company, but are you the native Martin Whitlock?"

He chuckled. "Sure. I am—was—one of the district managers for Company Operations. At the start, it was just the matter of getting huge accounts for the bank when we were expanding to full multistate operation. They sized me up, liked what they saw, and realized that my position was excellent for handling operations here in the east. I jumped at it, but it was pretty unnerving for a while. While I was training, they brought in another Marty Whitlock, and I mean another *me*. So close he knew all my friends and family. His whole life paralleled mine to an incredible degree, except for one important and glaring difference. He was gay."

I took in a breath. "Women's clothing, too, I suppose?"

"No, he wasn't a transvestite. In fact, he wasn't comfortable the way he was. He'd even married the same woman, but they'd divorced and had no children. It was pretty bitter, and Bobbie—*his* Bobbie—exposed him. She used a private detective to find his assignations and document them. You might appreciate that, Mr.

and Mrs. Morality. He kept most of his money, but he lost his job, position, social standing, that sort of thing. He became one of those rich bums with no aim or goals in life. The Company tracked him down, recruited him, prepped him, and we even tested him out experimentally. Nobody noticed. Bobbie—my own wife—knew. She had to. Meeting the both of us at once was a shock, but they can really razzle-dazzle you with their power and influence. She bought it, and the kids were both away. He was me while I trained, and old Whitlock never missed a phone call. Then, of course, I came back, and you can guess what he thought by then."

I nodded. "He liked being back in his old position, having his old family, prestige, contacts, and the like. He didn't want to give it all back."

"Right. Oh, they had a world for him, as a reward, that was right up his alley, a world where he didn't have to pretend anything, but he saw no reason to start again when he already had it. We didn't know it at the time, but he'd already started the ball rolling in his favor. Somehow, while I was away, he managed to discover somebody in the criminal end who was working for the opposition and could get word to others with access to the Labyrinth. He got back and dropped from sight, and we couldn't find him. That's when we came up with this insane plot. *I* didn't, but some big airbrain at corporate headquarters did, and just like the rest, I was trapped by that time, so I had to go along. I think it was because they had two other versions of me that I was recruited in the first place, but because of that, some think tank at headquarters—composed of people who never had to live this kind of stuff—

came up with using one of them, who, of course, differed from me in one even more vital way."

"Enter Amanda W. Curry—the W for Whitlock, I assume," Brandy said, nodding.

"Right again. We set up a command post in the apartment up in northeast Philly, with special scramblers and devices and remote phone hook-ups and all the rest. We couldn't use private detectives, because we had no idea where the other Whitlock was or what he was planning, and they'd always wind up fingering me. What we knew was that eventually he had to come to me. We used the mob, of course, to be our eyes and ears. Just told them my evil twin brother escaped from the asylum and was out to replace me."

"And they bought that?" she asked skeptically.

He shrugged. "Hey—these aren't exactly the intellectual cream of the crop. Mandy controlled the network, but *I* was director of operations, so it was my baby to control, and I knew the Company was mostly watching to see how I handled it. Of course, the way we had to give anybody the slip was the crazy one the boys back at headquarters invented. Mandy and I had the same parents, same society family and blue blood, same general aptitudes, so she was a natural to be their overseer on the project. When I needed to disappear, I'd walk over to Sansom, use a prearranged little hole there to get into deep disguise, while at the same time Mandy would also be there. Then she'd walk out as the drag queen Whitlock, and I'd get up to the apartment or out to track down leads I couldn't do publicly. My double worried me, but our big task was to find who the traitor was who'd given him the means, method, and opportunity for all this. That traitor was the key to finding him first, and also to making sure we were secure in the future. Mandy was about two inches shorter than me, but fingerprints don't lie, do they? And she was close enough to me in facial structure and the like to get away with it."

"She convinced almost everybody," I told him. "Confused the hell out of us, too. Still, the more I think of it, the less wild the idea really was. They didn't want to risk another double, but a female Whitlock was somebody different enough they could feel reasonably confident about; and you said she inherited your position, stock, and aptitudes, so she could run an intelligent investigation, understand your business and what you talked about and to whom. Still, in the end, it didn't quite work, did it?"

"No," he sighed. "They were too clever. I could be two places at once, but Mandy could never take my place in the office. When whoever the traitor was found out I was closing in on him, he moved. Left me a whole complicated string of red herrings that were very time consuming and very hard to unravel. It took time, so I arranged for a business trip as a cover—the Company's handy for that—and dropped out for ten days. As soon as I did, though, my double walked in—the very next day—and said the trip had been cancelled, and took up my spot in the bank. They prearranged this whole dope business—I would never have been directly involved in anything like that myself—and nabbed the two and a quarter million bucks that brought you into all this. We got the word almost immediately, but that put us in a bind. What could I do? Walk in and confront the bastard? You see what his plot was. Steal the money, vanish, which would bring me back with Nkrumah right on my neck. I would have to liquidate a lot of assets and cover the losses myself to save my own neck. He'd have made his point, and I would be as good as blackmailed. He could do anything he wanted to me. Ruin me, get me killed, *anything*. He could have it both ways. Be me whenever he wanted to, and be a bum playboy entirely on my assets when he didn't."

"And, if he ever got tired of it, he could bump you off anytime and replace you," Brandy added. "But I don't get why he didn't just bump you off in the first place. I mean, your wife knew, so she couldn't know if it was legit or not."

"Uh huh. I wondered, too, until I realized it was that crazy masquerade. Mandy confused them. They weren't sure if it was me or if it wasn't. We'd laid a pretty good foundation going back quite a ways, using Mandy's old family album pictures and stuff like that, so the servants weren't so sure, either. See, if Mandy was just me, it was a complication, but if Mandy was an alternate me then the Company would know the day after the switch was pulled. If he went along and dressed up as Mandy, and Mandy was really somebody else, then the jig was up, but if he *didn't*, then it was a radical change in behavior that would also be noticed, since Mandy was intimate with a lot of the gay and transvestite communities, and that was one part of my life he didn't share and couldn't fake. So, he finally decided half a loaf was better than none, and that he could find out the truth later and make decisions then. Either that or give it up—costing me a fortune, messing up my credibility, and running away with all that money as an untouchable. See what I mean?"

"But you didn't let him get away with it," I noted. "You pulled his plug instead."

"I saw no other way. I called in the federal bank people with a phone call—anonymous—to just the right people with just the right information. He had to skip before they caught him and hung him up to dry. His only chance then was to get me first. If I turned up dead, it would be a gangland revenge slaying, he'd be legally dead, and free to spend the money. Better than before, since he had contacts with the opposition, access to the Labyrinth somehow, and, being dead, he could hardly be disgraced. All he needed was my body, and all I needed was a trail far away from me that he would follow. That, however, necessitated using the fourth me—another female version, as you well know, because we needed a female me then. I made a fuss over getting the clothes from the lesbian center, which got them suspicious enough to follow me. I tell you, they were so incompetent I had a lot of trouble not losing them! Then we cleared out of the apartment, leaving the card. Right at the start, before I even called the feds, I called and made that Sunday reservation for San Francisco just to give an extra signpost and make it easier to find the pair going west."

"Uh huh." It was pretty much as we figured, but the fine details were not falling into place and it didn't make me feel too great. The guy had almost drawn us a map and detailed instructions, and we thought we were hot shit to have sniffed him along! It was pretty humbling.

"We needed another 'Amanda' just in case they were convinced that there were two of me, male and female. Mandy played me as a male, which she could do as long as you didn't know me, and the other one, who I understand was also Amanda—it was our grandmother's name—played herself. She had to look enough like me to make the whole scenario we invented fall into place. Of course, the joker was Nkrumah, who didn't roll over or put out a contract but instead set the dogs on us—pardon, no offense meant. You got to each of the points in the trail first. I have the feeling that after the first breakthrough, because you were related to Minnie, they all allowed you to be the stalking horse, and just followed the trail. One of the people along the way who you contacted or questioned is our traitor. He, or she, along with the other me, followed your leash as well. When you went up to McInerney, they followed, although I think they already suspected the destination. The two Mandys, I'm afraid, were the bait our security people used. That's why they hung around where they did, and why they stayed in the motel rather than getting out fast. The trouble was, you were the odd couple, the complication *we* couldn't figure."

I nodded. "Yeah. You knew we came from Nkrumah or somebody in that organization, but you didn't know if *we* were the hitters instead of the other Whitlock, or if we maybe were setting up the girls for the kill."

"Exactly. Little Jimmy initially just figured you to draw the heat away from his boys, but you got results and he let you run. We couldn't figure you—except that we could trace you to Little Jimmy's corner of the world, and that was good enough. The trouble was, we took our eyes momentarily off the ball while we, too, followed you. We figured you *had* to be with the opposition, knowingly. And because everything was concentrated on you, we let my counterpart and a contract hood who was free-lance but had done a lot of work for Big Tony's family get by. That hood knew his business. A real pro. No phone, no lights, and the girls in a room with no back exit in the middle of a concrete block of motel units. I was a crack shot in the Marines, and so, of course, was the other me. He would nail them in the room, or keep them pinned down until the hood could get right up to them and just shoot them down—all before security could get there, thanks to the train. Then you stepped in and saved them."

"I got the hood on sheer luck," Brandy told him. "I was blind as a bat, at that distance. Guess he just didn't figure we had that kind of firepower. One of your girls got—you—with a rifle."

"You can see, though, how it looked to security when they arrived. They still didn't know which side you were on, or whether you'd nailed the hood because there was no way he could tell which was which in the dark and at that distance. They figured the girls sounded the alarm, not you, Mr. Horowitz. Nothing was really clear, so they just rousted you until they could treat the girls and get the full story. By the time you reached our judge, we knew you'd saved them, but we didn't know why, or what game you were playing, so it was decided to buy time. Trap you there until we could find out everything about you, and what was going on and where you stood, and go from there. We just hadn't realized how resourceful you could be."

It made sense. It all hung together. Case solved. Except for a number of very puzzling details.

"You still don't know who that traitor was, then? He's still in place there, someplace?"

Whitlock nodded. "Yes."

Brandy frowned. "Yeah, but who called off the feds and scared shit out of Little Jimmy so's he fired us and scrammed? Who *could* have that kind of power and clout?"

"Good question. And everything in the east is stuck in limbo until we find out. Little Jimmy got out clean. We haven't been able to trace him at all. We didn't think he'd run, considering we offered to cover his losses. He must have had that escape route plotted for years. Either that or he's in a concrete barrel a mile down off Cape May."

I grinned, my memory going back what for me was more than a year, although to Whitlock it was still current events. "I think I can find him, if he actually got away and wasn't hit right then. I don't think he was. I don't know why—maybe—" I snapped my fingers. "Sure! Big Tony! Somehow he fed 'em Big Tony on a platter before he split. He tied up the mob for a day or two on that, and tied up any possibilities of Big Tony's mob making the hit then. He bought time that way. No wonder he was scared to death! He was so scared I doubt if he even realized it, but he told me where he was headed, generally speaking. I think I could find him, if he was telling the truth—and I think he was."

"Big Tony, of course, was a tool I sometimes used, but he had no direct knowledge of the Company and its reach. They would hardly use Big Tony's mob to hit Nkrumah—or would they? They had motive—the missing money—and they would be the perfect foils to do the opposition's dirty work with no traces. Hmmmm. . . ." Whitlock paused for a moment, thinking. "Interesting. You know he left clean. Didn't take the money. Hell, the *paperwork* wouldn't be done on it by now!"

"Clean. . . . No, not clean, and not with a slush fund, either, although I think he has one. Somebody else agreed to cover him first. That means he knows something." I had an unpleasant thought. "Once well away, though, they could hit him without it even making the papers. Save themselves money and a leak. They just got him out so he wouldn't turn stoolie to the feds. But the feds'd give him protection, and no money. He took the offer of a hideout and money from whoever it is, instead, but he's asking for a bullet now, if it hasn't been done already."

"You think he wouldn't guess that and maybe run somewhere else?"

Brandy laughed. "Sure, he'd take all the precautions, but he wouldn't run no matter *how* scared he was until he had the money. Money *is* life to Little Jimmy."

I thought a moment. "You know, if I don't shave, he wouldn't recognize either of us right now. Nobody drops a hundred pounds in this short a time, or grows a full real beard. Maybe, just maybe, there's a chance they haven't hit him yet, want to let things cool down first, up in Philadelphia; distance the hit from the rest of the stuff."

Whitlock smiled. "You *are* interested in the job, then."

Brandy held up a hand. "Uh uh, baby. Wait a minute. Yeah, we're interested. Real interested. But this is strictly free-lance right now. You can hire Spade and Marlowe, but you can't buy 'em. Not yet."

"Fair enough. Unlimited expenses, but one condition."

"Yeah?"

"Jamie goes along. You tell her what you need and she'll get it. She'll be the comptroller and contact on this. For obvious reasons I can't show my face anywhere right now, and I can't dare even try to clean up this mess until everything's tidy. I love my wife, you see. I love my children, too. I don't want them endangered or pulled into this, but I miss them. You have the vast resources of G.O.D., Inc. at your disposal. Find Nkrumah, if he's alive. Find that traitor. Let me go home."

I looked at Brandy, and she looked back at me and winked.

By God, the game was afoot!

8.

Taking on the Competition

We still didn't quite know what to make of Jamie, other than the obvious fact that she was holding our leash. We could pretend we were independents with a client again, but we knew better. We were there because Whitlock needed us; because all his money and power and fancy resources couldn't take him into the neighborhoods and classes where we worked best. What I mean is, you couldn't really penetrate Jamie's masks. She could accept without a qualm working for a company that at least aided and abetted half the crime in the Western World, yet she detested the crime-ridden cities and the atmosphere of fear that such activities helped promote. She seemed perfectly at home in our world, yet was a native of a place that had old-time steam trains, castles, baronies, and no electricity or working toilets. She had also seemed quite mannish, maybe more than a little butch, back in her own world, yet seemed girlishly feminine now. She was a bundle of contradictions, and when you saw that, you knew you never saw the real person at all, just whatever act or mask they wanted you to see at any given time.

Identification and papers were no problem; they'd brought all our stuff to the Bahamas as well, including our driver's licenses, P.I. licenses, and the like. I would have preferred ones with aliases, but we just didn't have the time. I certainly expected that if I found Nkrumah at all, he'd be stone-cold dead, but every minute wasted was one that might guarantee that fact. At least the Caymans weren't very formal, and we were already sort of in the Caribbean. Of course, I had no real idea of where the Caymans were, but I remembered hearing they were pretty loose and pretty poor.

I'd always wanted to fly as a passenger in one of those luxury business jets, sipping martinis at twenty thousand feet, but all they had on their island was a glorified Cessna with cramped quarters and seats that looked designed for the Army. The pilot was a big, black Bahamian man who looked like he'd been everywhere and seen everything and had never been impressed. He was very well paid, and he asked no questions of his passengers that had anything to do with business. He said to just call him Mike.

We flew over long stretches of water with just occasional tiny islands for hours, then came up on a huge landmass. Brandy leaned forward and shouted at Mike over the incessant engine noise, "What's that below we're flying toward?"

"Oh, dat's Cuba, m'um," he responded casually. "We hav'ta land there to get enough fuel to take us the rest of the way."

"Cuba!" both Brandy and I exclaimed at once. "You can't land *there!* We're Americans!" I had

visions of being forced down by Migs and getting
thrown in a Cuban jail for a year or two.

"No, m'um," Mike replied, sounding unworried.
"You are passengers on a General Corporation
plane on Company business. The government, dey
see eye to eye with de Company on lots of t'ings.
You bring hard currency, you be surprised how
nice dey be down dere."

I seemed to remember that the Mafia had tried
to bump off Castro once, but I guess the Cubans
didn't hold grudges. And, he was right. We didn't
land in Havana or anything like that but at a
small general aviation strip somewhere deep in
the country. Mike had been really pushing his
plane and must have had confidence he knew it
well; the gas gauge was right on empty when he
landed.

We used the opportunity to stretch and make a
pit stop—their johns were smelly and full of
flies—but both Brandy and I were more than a
little nervous around there. Although there were
mostly small planes in the airport, like ours, most
had military markings or coverings and a couple
had CCCP and a hammer and sickle on their
tails. Still, everybody treated us nicely, although
almost nobody spoke any real English, and the
plane was gassed, checked, and serviced efficiently.
Watching a bearded guy in military fatigues pump
fuel into a plane while smoking a big cigar, I had
to wonder just how much of a threat they could
be to anybody but themselves and helpless,
stranded travelers.

The Caymans, it turned out, were due south of
the extreme western tip of Cuba, really in the
middle of nowhere. Fortunately, there was only
one town of any significance on the main island,

and it didn't seem that big. This was not exactly
a place on the normal tourist routes. Because of
this, it was also quite poor, and money would
talk rather loudly and quickly there, even from
strangers. That was good, since we had no real
local contacts down there. Even G.O.D., Inc., it
seemed, had forgotten Grand Cayman Island.

We put down on a small airstrip well away
from town. The thing wasn't much; Mike said it
had been built by a crazy American who moved
there and collected satellite antennas years before. There were supposed to be the usual government formalities—the Caymans were a more-or-
less-independent country under the British Com-
monwealth—but there wasn't even a building
at the airstrip, let alone a customs and immigration man. Just a wind sock on a pole and
a tacked-up sign stating that all arrivals from
abroad had to check in with customs and immigration in Georgetown during regular office
hours. We were a little late for them today, so we
decided we'd hit them at our mutual convenience.

A Company official had phoned ahead on Jamie's
instructions. There were no Company personnel
on the island, but when you dropped cash on the
phone you could get a taxi to pick you up and a
cottage to rent. The taxi wasn't there when we
arrived, but just as we were beginning to think
about walking, an old and battered thirty-year-
old Chevy came smoking up the road and turned
in to meet us. Our coach awaited.

The driver, a good-looking black man who was
far younger than his car, got out and introduced
himself as Ben Swope. I noticed he had really big
eyes for Brandy, and I didn't feel the least bad
about that, even when she turned on the tease to

him. This whole "country" wasn't much more than a small town, and even in big cities the taxi drivers knew what was happening. Pair taxi and small town, and you have a really nice source of information.

The cottage wasn't much—one big studio apartment with a sloping roof, really, and a bedroom created by a wall divider—but we weren't looking for the Regency here, we were looking for a man.

Ben was *very* solicitous of Brandy, and helped with our bags, and Brandy gave me a wink and started really coming on to him. I knew she had to be dead tired by then, but this was business. Mike had to be taken into town, because he was staying at a small hotel there while he sorted out the paperwork and got some gas run back to the plane, and in no time Brandy had invited herself along. "You're real tired," she told me. "Maybe Ben can show me the sights."

I played along and let her go, which surprised Jamie no end. "You seemed rather cavalier about all that," she said after the taxi had driven away, Brandy in the front seat next to Ben.

"You're the client. This and stakeouts and long sets of phone calls and interviews are what the job is really all about. She's tired, but by tomorrow the whole town will know about us, officialdom will have to insist on checking us formally into the country, and we'll have to produce real IDs with our names on them. Names Little Jimmy and his cronies will know. The description might sound wrong, but how many salt-and-pepper couples named Sam and Brandy Horowitz can there be?" I paused a second. "No, don't answer that. I mean on *this* world?"

"You have a point, but he's very young and very handsome, and he is, well . . ."

I bristled at her insinuation. "Her kind, you were going to say. As opposed to your kind and my kind, you mean. I think you better get off any thinking of that sort while you're around either of us, or client or no client, Company or no Company, you will not be a part of this business and I mean that. There's enough native-born prejudice in this world. I don't have to take it from somebody who's imported."

She seemed genuinely surprised that I was offended by her comment. That was the nastiest form of prejudice, and the hardest to beat. The bigot who thinks he or she is a liberal because they don't mind eating in the same restaurant. Whitlock probably thought *he* was a liberal, too—after all, *all* his servants were black.

At least she didn't press it. For all I knew, a trained Company agent was a triple black belt and could beat me up blind and with both arms tied, but I think she sensed how close she'd come to getting belted. I had enough trouble with that kind of shit here; I sure couldn't ever accept it from somebody who worked for an organization that employed women who looked like dogs or seven-foot Japanese dancers or guys who had fur.

Yeah, I was worried about Brandy, but not in that way. She could handle poor Ben okay, but we were in a strange town on a remote island, and the only way off was a plane that couldn't get off the ground without a fill-up.

Jamie and I unpacked, and I, at least, took a nap. When I awoke, it was very dark, and nobody but me was around. Jamie had been busy, though; there was food for the small and very loud refrigerator, and I made myself a sandwich and drank a dark British beer, then went outside and looked around. I wondered where Jamie had gotten the food and why she'd gone back out, unless she was trying to make it a competition with Brandy. I hoped not. She might be a pro where she came from, but she was out of her element here and would most likely screw things up. It wasn't just waiting for Brandy and Jamie or anybody to show up that was getting to me, nor the fact that I was the only one doing absolutely nothing. What worried me was that time was marching on, and that if Little Jimmy found out about us I was sure as hell a perfect target.

I went outside into the darkness and wandered around for a bit, until I heard a car coming and went back up near the house, staying, however, in the shadows. It was Ben's cab, and he let Brandy out, and they had a very long kiss. That one really did make me jealous, I'm afraid; there's insecurity deep in the heart of every older man married to a younger and more attractive woman. She left him, and walked up to and into the house, and Jimmy backed out of the sandy drive-way and went back toward town. I walked up and entered the house.

Brandy turned, then smiled. "Sam! I was beginning to think everybody had deserted this place!"

"That was some kiss you gave him."

She smiled coyly. "Aw. . . . You care!" She came over and put her arms around me. "You know there's only one man in my life. God, I'm dead tired, though. Where's Jamie?"

"Good question. I took a nap, and when I got

up there was beer in the refrigerator and cold cuts next to it, but no Jamie. I been sitting around praying she isn't out there trying to be Supergirl and screwing us up."

"Yeah, particularly since I know where Little Jimmy's hidin' out."

"*What!* Thanks for the news bulletin! He *is* here, then?"

"Sure is. Right on schedule, too. Him and three foxy-lookin' ladies who seem to be his wives, bodyguards, and whatevers. A regular United Nations. One black, one white, and one Oriental, they say. I'll say this—he knows how to hide out in style. Seems he's got some relatives and old business pals around here, but nobody's real close to him."

"He's got a house?"

"Uh uh. Boat. Big sucker. Not a yacht, but you could make South America with it. He and his girls live on board—they're also the crew. I hope he's payin' 'em well. There's only one decent harbor and that's right downtown, or what passes for downtown here. This ain't exactly New York City. In fact, this ain't even Asbury Park. He's been layin' low but he's hard to miss, as you know. Callin' himself Joseph Mohammed, if you can believe that. He's spread the word around that he's some kind of Muslim and those are his three wives."

"He's one short of the maximum for the old style, but Little Jimmy always was cheap. Think he knows we're here?"

"Oh, he's spread some money all over to make sure of it. Ben got twenty whole American dollars to report any newcomers who show up without advance long-term reservations. The mob does move dope through here, but not on a permanent basis. A boat comes in, a bunch of men get off, they stay a couple of days, go out fishin' every day, then one night they meet a plane, and then when the plane goes, they go. It's fairly regular, but never the same boat, men, or plane. They got a decent commercial airport the other side of town. No jumbo-jet city, but it's all right for this place."

I nodded. "Any of these mob men in since Little Jimmy's been here?"

"Just once, for two days. Little Jimmy sailed away almost while they were gettin' off the boat, and passed 'em in the harbor when they sailed out. He's bein' *real* cautious."

"Yeah, that makes sense. Still, he wouldn't even stay around here if he had everything he expected to get. He's hanging loose, taking a risk here while he waits. This was where his slush fund was set up, and where he always probably intended to wind up. Now even here's too hot for him, but with two-plus million you can really disappear into Guyana, or maybe all the way to Brazil. Who's he waiting for?"

She yawned. "I dunno, but I don't think they're comin' tonight. I'm dead. I think tomorrow may be soon enough to go ask him, if Jamie don't spook him tonight. I'm done, Sam. I got to get some sleep."

"You go ahead. I'll keep the watch here for a while. I never completely woke up, though, so we'll see how long I last."

When my new watch beeped at four in the morning, I counted five beers and no Jamie, and dozed off myself in a chair.

*　　*　　*

I awoke when I heard the sound of a car pulling up to the house, and looked at my watch. It was about ten in the morning, and Brandy was still out cold. I went to the door and looked cautiously out. It was Jamie, driving one of those tiny English cars that make Volkswagens look like Cadillacs. She was made-up a little, but barefoot and wearing an oversized shirt and bikini bottom and not much else, although she took a shoulder purse out of the car and put it over her shoulder before she came in.

"Well," I said, "you look like you've been busy."

"Oh, it was most productive." She put the bag down, reached in, and pulled out a fist full of documents. "I couldn't get passports without your photos, but these papers will do in a pinch for here, and we are all clear with customs and immigration. You are a wealthy American businessman named Jacob Brodsky, and I'm afraid I took the liberty of making myself Mrs. Brodsky, and Brandy your personal secretary, since I wasn't sure what sort of line she was using with the cabbie and how long she wanted to maintain it."

I looked over the papers and they sure as hell looked official. "Pretty good for a night's work, but this names Brandy as Brenda Hawkins. That's probably not the name she gave Ben last night."

"Won't matter. I explained we were here incognito while the solicitors fended off some nasty lawsuits and cleaned up a few things, and they seemed to understand that easily. Apparently about two thirds of the foreigners on this island are using assumed names and this is a rather common practice here. They're honest enough that I think they would turn in really major

fugitives from justice, but not the passive sort
with lots of money and no danger to the community here.''

"And how did you accomplish all this?"

She shrugged. "It's a small town. I got bored
here and wandered in, found a grocery and got
the supplies here, then went back after dark to
see what the place was like. Everyone was *very*
nice, and someone pointed out a rather important
official to me. Since he was in a pub trying to
pick up girls, it wasn't difficult to get to know
him.''

I raised my eyebrows. "So I've got a cheating
wife now?"

"Perhaps. He *is* rather attractive, and it's been
a long time."

I couldn't resist. "Is he—your kind?"

She winced. "Please. I needed that lashing of
yours to remind me of the basics. I apologize.
That's really what sort of pushed me into action."

I wondered if it was really that easy. Still, I
had suspicions. "If he's attractive and important,
why is he picking up girls in a bar?"

She grinned. "I don't know. Perhaps you can
ask his wife, or, better yet, his three ex-wives."

"You didn't—press about Nkrumah, did you?"

"Oh, my, no! That would have set off every
alarm in the town. I mean, surely a strange white
woman asking questions about the likes of him
the first night in town would have caused him to
panic. I know my job. Do you know yours?"

"We know where he is, who he's with, and
what name he's using," I informed her. "I think
today we're gonna try and find out why he's
hanging around."

"Why *who's* hanging around?" I heard Brandy ask sleepily. She wandered in, looking shot to hell, the way either of us usually looked in the morning.

"Little Jimmy. Care to wake up and go into town for some brunch, and wander down maybe near the docks? We have a car now. Rented, I assume."

Jamie nodded. "At the airport. They almost fight with each other for your business. I left the keys in it. Who's going to steal it around here?"

"You want to sleep or come in with us?" I asked her.

"Oh, just let me change and I'll come in. I got some sleep last night, and I function on very little."

Brandy was never a big coffee drinker, but I made some while Jamie showered and changed, and Brandy drank almost as much as I did. The adrenaline high was gone now, and she was feeling the effects of first-night ambition. While this took place, I showed her the papers and briefed her on the cover story and identities. She was generally impressed, although she wasn't sure she liked my change in marriage partners— even though I could hardly blame Jamie for doing what I would have done, flying blind and handed an opportunity, myself. Since she'd told Ben she was Sandy Parks, from Philadelphia, we had the crazy situation of having cover identities for our cover identities. It kind of appealed to my sense of the perverse.

Jamie emerged wearing shorts, sandals, and a colorful shirt, and Brandy was now awake enough to get dressed herself. She, too, went for shorts and sandals, but picked a very tight tee shirt and no bra, a combination that left nothing to the imagination. It was kind of funny watching them, in a way. Brandy was dressing to show off her most outstanding attribute, and Jamie was wearing loose and oversized tops to hide her lack of same. Brandy was wearing a string bikini under her clothes, though, and I figured she might have something in mind.

The town was no tourist mecca; it was populated by real people, the kind the tour boats don't show you. It was Caribbean poor, and that was pretty poor indeed, even poorer than our old sections of Camden; but at least they didn't ever worry about a heating bill here, and even the most run-down shacks seemed to have cable TV along with five or six kids and two or three mangy-looking dogs, and about every fourth house had a car in front in some stage of repair or disrepair. The harbor area and marina were pretty nice, though, and the people were friendly, courteous, and English speakers all, so that helped. There were several restaurants near the yacht harbor, and we passed by the ones with native soups and great seafood and took the dingy one that would cook you breakfast anytime. An English breakfast, too, which was a real meal.

After, we took a leisurely stroll around the harbor area and got a fairly good look at Little Jimmy's hideaway. It was one of those large cabin cruisers with a lot of room belowdecks, and it looked imposing. It was docked all the way at the end of a large series of slips, and in its position, really at right angles to the dock, it only took hauling in the gangplank and undoing two lines and he was ready to roll. We didn't dare actually walk up the pier, but on the rear deck we could see the big man himself relaxing with a drink and reading something.

"Maybe I'll try gettin' up close," Brandy said thoughtfully. "I may remind him of somebody, but no way is he gonna recognize me."

"I don't like it," I told her. "Remember, odds are he knows just what he's dealing with now, even if he didn't before. If he gets one whiff of Brandy or Camden, he might figure you for a close double."

"He ain't that smart. Besides, he's got his girl guards around, and I'm gonna be strictly in a bikini. What kinda threat can he figure?"

I looked at Jamie. "Might be worth a shot," I said, "if we can get some support. You're the Company gal. Any way to wire somebody for sound wearing just a string bikini?"

Jamie thought a moment. "Yes, in a setup like this, I believe we have something in the bags that might work. Not good over any distance or obstacles, but from the boat to the shoreline, I'd think it might do. We might possibly arrange some cover, too. I'll check with Mike on that. Think it can wait an hour?"

I nodded. "If he's going anywhere soon, it won't matter anyway."

Jamie did in fact come up with what was required. It was a tiny little transmitter, powered by a watch battery and not much bigger, that could in fact be attached to a woman's watch itself. It required a small pickup unit with high gain, and an earphone, and was noisy as hell, but it might just work. Brandy took advantage of the time to make herself up a bit—nails, eyes, that sort of thing—and out of our old luggage, which had been transshipped to us, as I mentioned, she found the reddish brown wig. With a little work, it fit very nicely even though her hair had grown out quite a bit. Add dark sunglasses, and even I wouldn't recognize her.

We'd also gotten her father's magnum back, but it was impossible to conceal, the way she was going, and useless at any distance no matter what you've seen in the movies. I would be lazing on a bench at harborside, apparently listening to a Walkman-style tape recorder; Jamie and Mike would be elsewhere, with cover and support should it be necessary, Mike from somewhere on the rooftops and Jamie on a small rented one-person sailboat. Her versatility, considering that she was supposed to have spent most of her life in that medieval place, was surprising. I had a strong idea that Jamie's background was quite different than she'd let on, proper speech pattern or not. I grew up near two bays, several big rivers, and an ocean with lots of beach, and I couldn't sail one of those little suckers if my life depended on it.

"How are you going to arrange a meeting with him?" I asked her. "He never gets off that damned boat."

"I'm just gonna walk right up and say hello," she responded, and that is exactly what she did.

I'll tell you, she looked absolutely incredible when she walked out onto that pier, wearing about as little as you could and still be legal most places, sunglasses, the wig, and not much else; and despite being barefoot, she wiggled like she was wearing the highest heels around. There were men on about half the boats docked at the slips there, and she made an instant impression on all who noticed her. She stopped to talk to one or

another, passed pleasantries, asked a lot of dumb
questions, and kept her voice high and her vocab-
ulary low. It took a little effort before one of them
asked her where she was from, and when she said
she was an American, they asked *her* if she was
with the big boat at the end. She looked surprised. "That big thing's *American?* Ooooh! Gee, I
wonder if they're from anyplace I know?"

Little Jimmy had gone below, by this point,
and one of his girls, the white one, was up top
where the wheel was doing something. That
didn't bother Brandy a bit.

"Hi! Hey, up there! Hi!"

The woman on the boat looked puzzled, but
when she saw who—or rather, what—was hailing
her, she seemed to relax a bit.

"What d'ya want, honey?" the guard called
down.

"Lionel over there just said you was Americans.
I'm an American and I just thought I'd be
neighborly and say 'Hi!'"

"Well, hi, then, and good-bye. We don't want
no company right now."

"Well, jeez, it's just such a *gorgeous* boat—or is
it a ship? I just thought—"

"Well, don't think so much."

Whoever she was, she sounded like working-
class Philadelphia or very nearby. She wasn't
familiar to me, but I had a hunch now that all
three might be either whores (getting a little long
in the tooth) with whom he'd had relationships,
or maybe mistresses stashed around the area.
Either way, that made them addicts dependent
on Little Jimmy for their source in this remote
place.

Brandy pushed hard, stepping on the gangplank. "Well, sorry. All I wanted to do was see what a boat like this looked like. Jeez—it's real big."

"Don't you come on here!" the woman on the bridge screamed and started down. "Fuck off, sister! Now!"

At that moment Little Jimmy decided to stick his head up and see what the commotion was all about. He looked around warily, spotted Brandy on the gangplank, and had the expected reaction. "Annie! Enough! I'll take care of this!" he said sharply, stopping the woman just before she reached the gangplank herself. Annie looked uncertain, gave what must have been a real dirty and disgusted look in Little Jimmy's direction, and backed off.

The old loan shark hauled himself on deck and went over to Brandy. "My apologies, my dear. Annie can be a bit—protective."

"Well, jeez, I was only tryin' t'be *sociable*," Brandy responded, sounding little-girl hurt. "She ain't got no call talkin' that way."

"My abject apologies. I am Joseph Mohammed."

"Sandy Parks," she responded. "At least that's what they told me to tell everybody, and I kinda like the sound, don't you?" Somehow she'd made her way up the short gangplank and actually onto the boat in minute movements.

"It's very nice. It suits you. But that's not your real name?"

"*Nah!* My real name's *Brenda*, but I like this new one so good I might keep it. Don't tell nobody, though."

"Not a soul," he promised. "But why an assumed name, if I may ask?"

"Oh, Dave—I mean, *Jake*—is tryin' t'skip on

some dumb lawyers for somethin'. Oh, shit! This name stuff is so hard to keep *straight*."

"I'll keep your secret," Little Jimmy promised. We were pretty sure that by this time of the afternoon he had at least the full cover story on us. "Would you care for a drink?"

"Gee, you mean y'got a *bar* here?"

"And a bartender. *Nan!* Vodka and tonic for me, and—you?"

"I guess a daiquiri is a little much, even for *you* out here."

"One daiquiri coming up. Banana all right?"

"Yeah, great. Gee, this is *somethin'*. I mean, Dave's got a lot of dough—oh, damn! I mean *Jake*—but he don't have no boats. Just b'tween you'n me, he can't swim." She turned. "That's him, just sittin' there listenin' to that borin' music on his Walkman and readin' business magazines. Can't do much else right now. I mean, his *wife's* around someplace."

Little Jimmy did not require diagrams. "You know, I have the oddest feeling that we have met before," he said, and I tightened. "Could that be possible?"

She shrugged. "I dunno. I been in Dallas the past coupla years, but I was born in Philadelphia. Where you from?"

"That *is* a coincidence! We might well have met."

"You from Dallas, too?"

"No, Philadelphia. That area, anyway. I *thought* I heard it in your voice."

Well, Nan, the black one, came out with the drinks, and the pair on the deck continued to small-talk and gossip. Little Jimmy had a few trick questions that only a Philadelphia-area person would know, which was easy enough to cover, and he seemed to lose his suspicion as she spun a very convincing life story that was almost all inference. The biggest inference was that she'd met me while doing some hooking nights, to pay for secretarial school days, while I was in Philadelphia on business, and that I'd finally taken her on as a secretary—officially. There was a suspicion that my wife suspected, but since she was frigid tended to tolerate it so long as the fiction was maintained around her.

"Perhaps it's not all one-sided, my dear," Little Jimmy told her. "That wife picked up no less than a government minister last night in a bar and they went off together."

"*Oooh!* She *did?* That slut. Wait'll I tell Dave!"

"Oh, I wouldn't do that. Save it until you or he needs it, like maybe she decides on a divorce or something. You seem a smart girl. Play it right."

"Yeah, thanks. Maybe you're right. You know, it drives him *nuts* to pretend, but we gotta. I mean, be real. He's white, I'm black, and his business is in *Dallas*, for crissake! I ain't complainin'. I mean, I'm treated real well. All them Dallas rednecks only get uptight if there's a piece of paper and all, and I don't need that. Hell, half of them bigmouths got dark girls in their closets."

Nkrumah chuckled. "How well I know. It's tragic, though, that such a thing still exists in our day and age. I was born poor and illegitimate, and my mother spent her life on welfare. I promised myself I'd have everything the white man had but that I would use whitey, like he used us, but never depend or work for him. I did pretty good, too. The money for all this is all mine, but its sources are very thoroughly integrated."

And Little Jimmy was off with his grandiose bragging. He was retiring, he told her, because the kind of business where a black man could make this kind of money got dangerous sometimes, and he figured he had enough to quit while he was still young enough to enjoy things. Brandy was getting both tongue-tied and giggly in the heat; I suspected that the drink she had been given had a proof content high enough for spontaneous combustion. Back when she was fat she'd taken booze real well, but after a year on the wagon and now thin, I remembered that even the ale in that monastery had made her real mellow. It was getting time to break this up.

The only question in my mind was whether or not to force the issue now or wait a bit and hope we could catch whoever he was going to meet. I figured the best time was the present. With this boat, there was every chance that the meet would be at sea, probably at night, and he'd be impossible to track and all hopes of any answers would be gone. Besides, if he got hit, it wouldn't do us any good at all. Right now I had Mike somewhere in back of me, also wired, with a nice rifle and telescopic sight, and Jamie skirting around in the harbor. We'd learned about all we were going to learn from him at this point, including the fact that he intended to be around for a while yet. This had already accomplished what we needed: to get us access to Little Jimmy while he was tied to the pier, and in broad daylight.

"Oh, oh. I fear your man has grown a bit jealous," Little Jimmy said. "I think perhaps we should say *adieu* for now."

Jamie was just coming around again and I gave her a hand signal. Mike had a wire, so I knew he'd be on us. I walked straight up the gangplank and over to Brandy, my back to the sea, and looked at Little Jimmy. "Hello, Nkrumah," I said, real friendly-like.

I never saw somebody jump like that. "*Annie! Nan! Suzy! Stations!*"

Annie up front came up with a pistol from nowhere, and Nan opened the door and showed a real-nasty-looking M16 rifle, the kind that can fire fifteen rounds in a half second and kill with any hit to the body. I still didn't see Suzy, but it didn't matter.

"Now, is that any way to treat an old friend and ex-employee?" I asked him, trying to keep the confidence in my voice. "I'm not even armed. If I wanted to hit you, I could do it at any moment. I got a sniper trained right on your fat head right now, just as insurance. Girls, you can get us, but we can sure as hell get him—and what good'll that do you? Relax. It's talk time."

Little Jimmy stared at me. "Horowitz? *Horowitz?* Is that really you?"

"Aw, I thought I'd fool you with the beard."

He started to relax a moment, then grew tense again. "That beard isn't fake. It's real. I can see that. Nobody grows a full beard that size in a few weeks! You're not Horowitz—you're one of *them!*"

"Wrong, wrong, wrong," Brandy put in. "Little Jimmy, for a man with the smarts, you sure been actin' stupid and careless of late."

I could see it in his eyes and in the tremble in his hands. The man was scared to death. "You—you're Brandy! But you're not the Brandy I knew!"

"Still wrong," she replied. "You hired the two of us, and you fired the two of us, right here, in this world. Only thing is, after we got canned we took a little trip right outta this world, and things go faster there. We're back now, though."

Little Jimmy started to get a little of his confidence back. "So, you tracked me down. So what? All I have to do is give the word and you're dead, right now. I don't know what this game is, or who's paying you, but you have *my* retainer. I own you until the fifteenth."

"No, Jimmy boy, you releasd me on the phone and told me to bank the retainer. Remember?" I said calmly. "And can the threats. I got a sniper on you, and if Black Beauty in there opens up with that cannon she'll mess you up as bad as me."

"I—fired you?" He started looking around. "You're bluffing on all this, Horowitz. I don't know which one you are, but I've got you."

I sighed. "Girls, don't get itchy, or this will end real bad real fast. Hey, Mike, if you can hear me, see if you can put one where it'll be a nice demo but not spill any blood, huh?"

I waited, and for a couple of seconds I wondered if Mike was really there at all, but suddenly there was a distant firecrackerlike pop and Little Jimmy's latest vodka and tonic got blown to smithereens. I tensed, but the girls looked far less confident now than before, and Little Jimmy let out a screech and fell back.

"Sorry to scar your fine table, here," I told him, "but I think I've made my point as well as you made yours. Standoff. Except you're the target of our man, and I don't think the ladies here would find much profit in shooting us if you're blown away. In fact, ladies, I suggest that if he makes that necessary, you not shoot at all—or you will surely wish that you were as dead as he was. We have a client who's got a lot of people and a lot of resources and don't care much about people except as lessons."

Little Jimmy composed himself, and both Brandy and I started to relax a bit. If we were going to die, we'd have been dead by now.

"What do you want here, Horowitz?"

"Just information. Seems we got hung out to drip dry by you and your crowd, Nkrumah. I don't like setting up people for hitters, and I don't like getting in the crossfire."

"That was your own damned fault and you know it! I *told* you to take the money and split!"

"Yeah, well, we all got taken for a ride anyway, and your hitters shot a fat zero. They're both gone, and their targets, both decoys, are alive and away, and so are we."

"*Decoys!* But . . ."

"The man's still around, Little Jimmy, and he wants to go home, only he can't, 'cause he's got a backstabber in his neighborhood and we still don't have the whole picture," Brandy told him. "You got the missin' part."

"I don't! I was used, just like everybody else!" he replied. "I didn't know who, or what, was involved here! Who the hell *could* have even imagined such a thing?"

"But you know now, just like we do," I pointed out to him. "Only we found out by falling right out of this world. You didn't. That means between the time we searched Whitlock's apartment and the time we talked to each other that last time when I got to Bend, you learned more than a little. You found out the whole damned thing."

"I swear I knew nothing!" Little Jimmy protested, and finally his side came out.

He had been picked up, while leaving his office in Camden, by some of Big Tony's boys and taken for what they said was a meet. He was scared it was a one-way trip, that Big Tony was going to finish him off because he'd lost the money and was now undependable, but it wasn't Big Tony they took him to see. Instead, it was Whitlock himself, clean-shaven and distinguished looking. Except, of course, it wasn't Whitlock—not the one he thought. The double freely admitted he was a double and had switched places with the other one while that other was "playing games in queenie-land." He said he knew that Little Jimmy handled a number of investment accounts for Big Tony, that he was something of a laundry for the mobster, and he wanted the names and dates and information on those accounts and transactions. Whitlock Two offered him his money back—in exchange for Big Tony.

Little Jimmy shrugged. "I mean, what the hell? I never liked those white Italian bastards anyway. Kept people like me on the fringe of the real power, took us out when we got too uppity for them. Big Tony thought blacks should be back picking cotton except that they were profitable, but a hundred times he called me nigger to my face and I took it. I had no choice but to take it. Not then. But I was *ruined*. Wiped out. I knew I couldn't keep the news from Big Tony much longer about the money, and I knew what he'd do to me even though it hadn't cost him. Waste one nigger, you set an example. I had a way out, so I

took the deal. I gave him Big Tony, and he gave
me a list of safety-deposit boxes spread all over
the Caribbean, each containing some of my money,
and the authorizations. I went home just long
enough to pack, and then *Whitlock* was there! At
my house! Only he had a three days' growth of
beard!"

"The *real* one," I commented, nodding.

"Yeah, that's right. Or, I think so. Who the hell
knows anymore? He tells me what kind of thing
I'm up against. He tells me where the doubles
come from. He tells me he doesn't work for Big
Tony, that Big Tony works for *him*. He offers to
make good my money, and keep me out of this
mess, if I tell him what I know. Of course, I'm
scared to death at this point, so I agree to go
along with him and lie low for a while, but as
soon as he leaves, I *split*, man. I hit my stash
fund, then I started taking a quick tour of the
Caribbean. The first two banks, the money was
there; but when I hit the third, in Barbados, they
acted like they knew me on sight, and insisted
that I'd been there only an hour before—dressed
differently, but otherwise the same. I went from
there to Martinique—same story. Finally I skipped
down to Kingston, made certain I hadn't been
there before, and waited."

He sighed, paused a moment, then continued,
"I staked out that bank for four days. On the
fourth day, I saw—"

"Yourself," Brandy guessed. "You watched you
goin' into the bank."

He nodded and buried his head in his hands.
"Yes! I knew then that what the Whitlocks had
told me was at least partly true. They're taking
us over! One by one, they're taking us over,

replacing us with exact duplicates! I made for this island and this boat, which I'd prepared long ago, and which the ladies here helped maintain, and I've been on it ever since. *I don't want to be replaced!*" He stared at us. "You *think* this is your world, but are you *sure? Are* you sure of *anything?*"

"No," I admitted, remembering Cranston's comment that paranoia was part and parcel of this business when you knew the truth. "But I'm as sure as I can be. So what are you going to do now? Sit here on this tub until the money runs out? Sooner or later you're going to have to get involved again in some way to keep the money flowing."

"I *am* involved. You said I fired you."

"Yeah. Over the phone, when I called you from Bend."

"Horowitz—the last time we talked was the call you made after leaving the apartment in northeast Philly. They picked me up that night, and the other Whitlock was at my house when I got there in the wee hours of the morning. I was *gone* after that. As God as my witness, I never talked to you after that. *He* did."

That explained a lot. I suddenly had as much sympathy for Little Jimmy as I was capable of having for weasels and skunks. All he really knew was that he was screwed with the mob, and that there were two Whitlocks who'd used him. He bought the real Whitlock's story only as much as it helped him keep from going nuts, but he really didn't know that much. I was convinced of it. They'd pulled in another Nkrumah to cover and make a more orderly exit, but then what? The new Little Jimmy had the same greed as the old one. He'd made for those boxes to recover as much of the money as possible. He couldn't stay too long in Camden himself because the heat was on.

"*He* was waiting for me in my hotel room in Kingston that night," Little Jimmy told us. "I couldn't arrange a plane out that day. When I entered, *he* was there, with a gun."

"*I just wanted to meet face to face,*" Little Jimmy Two had told him. "*My intent, I admit, was to kill you. That would make it easy. You—I—would be legally and permanently dead. No hunters. I really intended to do it, but I can't do it. It's odd, but I can't. I hadn't really realized that until just now.*"

"What—what will you do with me?" our little Jimmy asked him.

"*Go to your hideaway. You have sufficient funds for quite a while. Stay there. Vanish there. So long as you do, you will live. If you show up, or get made by anyone, though, you will seal your own fate. I will not have to do it, thank God. Just stay out of our way.*"

"And you been here ever since?" Brandy asked him.

He nodded. "Not moving off this boat, or out of the company of at least one of the girls at all times, so they'll always be confident that it's me."

I had a sudden bad feeling about this. "Nkrumah—where's the third girl? The Oriental one?"

"Huh? Around, I don't know. Nan?"

"She went out earlier this mornin'," the woman with the M16 responded. "Haven't seen her in a while. We're low on a lot of supplies."

I was suddenly real nervous again, but I had to make an insurance position known. "Girls, there's no way you're going to shoot us all and survive, and you know it. You want to tell me who's working for who, and maybe get us all out of this?"

Little Jimmy looked like he'd seen a ghost. He turned and stared at the pair. Clearly he hadn't gone far enough with this replacement bit. He didn't have all the story.

"We was only suppos'ta keep him happy," Annie, the white girl, told us, still holding the pistol. "You got no idea what kinda life we come from, mister."

I nodded. "I think I might. Who hired you? Who brought you over?"

Both of them looked uncertain as to what to do or say. Finally it was Nan, with all the firepower, who said, "Gritch. Sol Gritch brung us. We was in his stable, y'know."

I looked at Brandy and Little Jimmy. "Name sound familiar?"

Both of them shook their heads no. We suddenly had a new player in the game, and that was something I didn't like at all. "He from Camden or Philadelphia?" I asked.

"Sure. He's big in southeast Philly. Everybody knows Sol."

There, maybe, wherever "there" actually is. Not here.

"You never saw nobody but this Gritch?" Brandy asked them.

"Sure. Lots," Annie replied. "But nobody else we knew or cared about."

I had a sudden, unpleasant thought. "You had to come in through the Labyrinth. Where was the station?"

"The what? You mean that dizzy thing. Up in

the middle of nowhere. You know, near Penn State."

There was a sudden spray of bullets and we all hit the deck. I saw Annie fall, and I felt a sting in my left arm. "Stay down!" I yelled. "Brandy! You okay?"

"Yeah, for a moment. Who the hell—?"

"Mike!" I yelled, hoping the microphone was still open. "Can you make the shooter and, if so, nail the bastard!"

There was no rifle fire, which meant that either they'd taken Mike out or he couldn't get a bead on the shooter. Suddenly there were three sharp reports, not rifle shots but pistol shots, and the sound of a body somewhere forward falling into the drink.

"Nan!" Brandy yelled. "Can you toss out that cannon to one of us without coming up? They're sure to wipe us out!"

"To me!" I shouted. "You're half tight and haven't got your glasses on!"

Nan seemed uncertain as to what to do, but finally tossed the M16 out onto the deck. I crawled to it and got it; the pain in my arm was getting real irritating, but better there than in my head.

It was clear now that the shots had come through the windshield from the bow; that's why Annie had taken it and why I'd gotten nipped. I was almost in a direct line from her.

I made my way warily forward and up the ladder to the wheel. Annie was splattered over half the side; she was out of the game for keeps. Keeping down, I cautiously peered out of the shattered windshield, but could see no one.

"Anybody alive up there?" I heard Jamie's voice call from the water side.

"Yeah, some of us!" Brandy shouted back. "You got 'em?"

"There was only one. The Chinese girl or whatever she was. She's meat now. Came up out of some hatch up there, crawled up, and started firing before I could react. Sorry."

I relaxed a little and made my way back down to the others. Brandy turned and then gave a little gasp. Little Jimmy had been between Annie and me. We went to him, but Brandy didn't need her glasses to see he'd done his last deal. One of the slugs had gone right in the back of his head.

Brandy suddenly looked at me. "Sam! Oh, my God! You're hurt!"

There was the sound of a European-style police siren in the background, and a lot of yelling and screaming.

"Only a flesh wound," I said bravely, and then passed out cold.

Mike came to see me in the small hospital. As the only registered member of our party not under arrest, he was the only one who could. I was sort of under arrest as well, but that amounted to a cop on the door and a search of all unofficial visitors. I figured that with all the shots flying around, the cops had never known Mike had been any part of this.

"Dey questioned me for a little, but only about all of you folks," he told me. "I tell dem I'm just a charter pilot and dey pretty much believe dat. I wasn't able to see either of de girls, but I made a few calls on de Company. Some folks will be in tonight if dey can get Company planes. I worry about dem two, though. Dis sorta t'ing just isn't done here."

"They'll hold up," I assured him, hoping the authorities would at least obey the normal procedures until help arrived. "Brandy's had a lot of experience with cops and Jamie's a pretty tough customer."

"I'll say! I didn't even *see* dat girl wid the gun. Angle was wrong. Sorry."

"You did your best. It's too bad she had to be killed, though. She was *their* agent here, that's clear now, although even the other girls didn't know it. She had the answers. What about the surviving girl, Nan?"

"Oh, she's okay. Dey got her under protective detention, as dey call it, tryin' to get more information, but dey don't t'ink she was a shooter. So far she's givin' dem the straight dope on the shooting, as far as I can tell, and odderwise clammin' up. Says she was a whore wid Little Jimmy, dat's all. She don't know nuttin' else."

I nodded. "That's good. I just hope we can get some big shots in fast, and, if so, they're the right ones. You heard the whole thing?"

"Yeah. I already tell dem dis Sol Gritch character. Dey will do a big check on him. We should know what we can know by de time dey get here."

"In the meantime, you make sure Nan stays in protective and doesn't get released or taken away," I told him. "If the opposition doesn't get her, then they can't know what we learned before their agent wasted Little Jimmy." I paused. "Mike— how much do you *really* know about what's going on here?"

He grinned. "I don't know nuttin', man. I'm

just a poor charter pilot for a big, big company, dat's all." With that, he turned and left, leaving me with the feeling I was being had. He sure was a pilot, and a good one, but he was far more than that. I wondered if even Janie knew how much more.

The bullet had taken a small chunk out of me but had only grazed the bone. My main trouble was loss of blood from moving around after being shot, although I knew I was going to have a pretty useless left arm and probably lots of bandages and antibiotics for a while. No matter what, I had to trust to Brandy, Jamie, and Mike to keep things from getting out of hand at this point. I was sure as hell stuck for the moment.

I was awakened in the middle of the night by the sudden turning on of my hospital room light and the entrance of two men who looked about as natural on Grand Cayman as Brandy and I at a Ku Klux Klan convention. They were both white, young, well built and trim, and wearing suits and ties. They looked like Secret Service agents.

"Sorry to awaken you, Mr. Horowitz," said one, "but I thought you'd want the details as soon as possible. We're working with the local authorities now to get the release of both your wife and our agent, and hopefully the outworld girl, too. I'm Bill Markham and this is Tod Symes. We're with headquarters security."

"I assume you mean the headquarters in Davenport."

He chuckled. "Where else? Or, then again, is that a question I should ask, all things considered? We are who and what we say, I assure you. There are ways to determine that, and you and your wife as well."

That was news. "Oh? How?"

"It's a small encoded implant. Don't worry—we'll show you all that sooner or later. We're on the same side in this, after all."

I was beginning to wonder who was on whose side anymore but I let it pass. "You run down this Gritch character?"

"As much as we could. As soon as the call came in, we hopped a Company jet and got here. We've tracked a Sol Gritch here in the Philadelphia area, but he died nine years ago and was a real-estate speculator and slumlord. We're now running a trace on him in other probability lines, but we don't have much close to this one, so it'll take some time. That's where they can get us easy. They go into worlds we don't cover that are pretty close, and do some development of their own. There's over sixteen hundred lines in which all the principals in this case exist in roughly the same positions, so you can see how needle-in-a-haystack it has to be when you don't have anybody there, not even a station."

The concept was staggering. Sixteen hundred lines in which there was a me, and a Brandy, and a Whitlock, and a Little Jimmy, and maybe all the others. Not the same, maybe. Maybe we weren't married, and not to each other, in all sixteen hundred, but we all existed there. Of course, the opposition would have, if anything, a worse manpower problem than G.O.D., Inc. There was probably only one of those they were using, the one in which they also found the gay Whitlock and the Nkrumah clone, but it would still take time.

"Mr. Horowitz," Markham said, sitting in the lone chair, letting his silent partner stand leaning against the wall, "do you have any idea now what this is all about?"

"As much as I can, without knowing the full facts of this Company opposition," I answered truthfully. "This is no band of radical nuts or malcontents. You know it and I know it. They have free access to the Labyrinth, so they have probably got the right Company credentials, and their moves are being dictated by somebody high up within the Company structure. We might sneak in and get trapped in that thing without you knowing it, and we could have even gotten out of that monastery if we'd had to, but something this elaborate can't depend on sneaking into warehouses, monasteries, castles, or whatever, whenever somebody needs to be moved. Besides, we could get in, and out, but not control where we were going. These people can. You want to tell me just what the hell is *really* going on? Maybe if you do, I can give you the rest."

Markham sighed. "You're right, it's bigger than a few rebels and it's nastier. The fact is, why does anybody want to be a senator, or congressman, or the cabinet secretary? The pay's good, but it's not great, and almost all of them can do better in private business. And I hope you're not going to say to serve the public or advance ideals. Otherwise, I'll have to tell you the truth about Santa Claus and the Tooth Fairy."

"Power, pure and simple," I answered. "That's why so many of them quit when they reach their limits. I'm not dumb. I grew up in the U.S.A."

"General Ordering and Development is probably the largest corporate structure in human or nonhuman history, but that's still what it is. A corporation. It runs as a business. The kind of people who run it run it because they like the power. They enjoy it. They *need* it. But there can only be one president, one chairman of the board, only so many board members, and even a limited number of vice presidents, although it looks like an infinite number to me. As in most corporate structures, the old men remain and refuse to give up power until they drop dead, and others are promoted as much on family or connections as on merit. In fact, often at the *expense* of merit. It's a familiar structure to all large corporations."

I nodded. "So somebody's trying to hasten things along, or get even with the top boys for not noticing them. They're the most dangerous, because they're smart and motivated more by revenge than even greed."

"Exactly, although we think this is very much a strictly business situation. You see, in many cases such large numbers of people would simply go out and form a competitive group. Often their new ideas and new slants would be so good they'd eventually sweep the old company aside, although not without a lot of nasty fighting. The problem here is that it's of necessity a monopoly business. The Company controls the Labyrinth, and there is only one Labyrinth. As far as we know, there can *be* only one Labyrinth, according to the physics involved."

"Huh! Seems to me that if you knew how it worked, all it'd take is a big machine hidden in a deep hole with lots of power to it and a camouflage structure on top."

Markham shook his head. "No, it isn't that way at all. Mr. Horowitz, there *are* no great machines under those warehouses and castles. If you think a little, you'd realize that, since you escaped the botanical station through a flag access stop in the middle of land with no buildings, people, or anything much else. They had to open the flag because you weren't at a dead end; you were in the way, and a switch point needed to be created that spanned thirty-seven worlds, in order to get somebody from here to there. You said it yourself: power. It takes incredible power. The lone master machine exists in a universe where there is almost limitless power—and nothing much else. All the rest are the mechanics needed to make the process a controlled network. Stations to channel access. Switch points to save time and increase accuracy. The worlds aren't in a straight line. They are at all angles to one another, including angles we can't even imagine."

I saw the problem. One machine, one network, and the competition couldn't really touch that network without fouling themselves up as well. "Then the only thing you can really do is try and take over the Company."

"Exactly. What they're doing now is running a competitive operation on our own network, using worlds we haven't touched, and building an organization of people recruited from those worlds. An organization that is now well organized enough to start hitting us in vital spots. It's not a general war; it's an endless series of little wars. The operation here is fairly large, but it's not vital. It's on the periphery, so it's lightly defended compared to some other worlds, where, naturally, the bulk of personnel and resources are channeled. Because we depend heavily on organized crime in the West here, it makes it even easier to go in and make alterations at the level where things actually get done. If they succeed here, then we have to either divert major resources and personnel here to fight them off, and leave a more vital point undefended, or we have to declare them a winner and abandon further development. Either way, they win. Corporate heads roll. Things are reshuffled. Key people move up."

I got the picture. No wonder G.O.D., Inc. took such a liking to the Mafia. Hell, it *was* the Mafia, the prototypical Mafia on the grandest of all scales. All the godfathers jockeyed for control, and if they were frustrated working with the system, they fought it, sometimes violently. Board members themselves probably double-crossed fellow members if they wanted to move one way and the old guard shot down their plans.

I sighed. "All right, all I can do is figure what happened here. They fingered Whitlock, probably when he was tabbed and investigated before being handed the east-coast coordinator's job. For some reason, they had burrowed into one of those sixteen hundred other worlds, and so they had a match—a real good one, considering their replacement Whitlock. A Whitlock loser who was common enough that he'd drool to be a winner again. And they have this State College access to the Labyrinth. It's pretty wild, real wilderness, all around there. Mind telling me why you used Oregon with a State College station?"

"We don't have a State College station. There's a semipermanent flag stop there for eastern access, but it's not a full operation and it's totally automated. We're checking out traffic to and from it now, but that takes time. See, we can't handle a full station unless we can secure it through a tremendous number of worlds. When

you're dealing with truck- and boxcar-loads of
stuff, you have to make sure it ships right, point
to point. Other points of entry for our convenience are automated flag stops. Just sidings, as
it were. Of course, if we'd wanted to get the
Whitlock women *out*, we'd have used State College, but we wanted them to be followed and take
pursuers as far away from the east coast as
possible."

I nodded. I was feeling very weak and tired but,
damn it, I'd paid for this stuff with a year of my
life and some blood, and twice this other crowd
had tried to shoot me.

"Tell me this," I said at last. "If Big Tony gets
twenty years in Atlanta, and his organization is
fragmented, who is most likely to get control of
his territory? Between loan sharking, prostitu-
tion, and particularly narcotics, he controls maybe
a billion dollars' worth of business, I figure.
That's a hell of a lot. Enough even for a seat on
the mob's own inner council." That was the
board of directors, more or less, of the old-line
organized-crime families.

"We thought of that. The most likely candidate
is Al 'Big Nose' Norton, who has a hell of a share
of Jersey and wants more. He's got the muscle,
the contacts, and the resources. Of course, he isn't
Italian, but that's not a hundred percent prereq-
uisite anymore, as you know."

"Anybody named Norton who can take a hunk
of Jersey can be anything he wants," I responded.
"If Norton moved in without much opposition
and takes over, we can assume he's the object of
all this. He's theirs, whether he knows it or not. If
something happens to him, or they push a dark
horse in to take over, that'll be the man they

wanted. He gets all that territory and power, and the only price he pays is that, with a seat on the inner council, he'll be able to figure just what the Company wants and what it's doing, and feed it to the competition. It's really pretty smart, and it involves leaving few—outworlders, you called them?—here. Maybe only one as a contact. Figure they originally thought of the replacement Little Jimmy for that, but when he got greedy on the payoff money and then didn't hit his double, he was out. Of course, they still have their original agent in place, the one that saw all this opportunity and put the wheels in motion."

Markham was interested. "What? Who?"

"The one who made Whitlock as a Company man, then was able to use the State College flag stop to get the other Whitlock—and whoever else he needed—in, and work this through. He'll be their chief agent here, with a pipeline into the Company's local operation, and organized crime as well. The one who'll eventually mastermind whatever bigger things this is leading up to. Right now we have the heads of the competition, which are untouchable because they're too removed to pin anything on. This Gritch character is obviously their agent in general charge of the operation, working with cohorts inside the Labyrinth system so he has nearly unlimited access. Those are your problem, or your superior's. Big Tony's successor is the end of the line. Sure, we can take *him* out, but will we ever really be certain that whatever successor Big Tony has isn't theirs? Only if we find this missing man, their resident agent."

"You know who it is?"

"No, but there's only a handful of people it

could be. You see, at some point he—or maybe
she—had to emerge from that shell of protection
because everything was going down too fast. The
connections are Whitlock—and Brandy and me. If
I can get a little strength, and you can spring us
all, I think I can nail that agent."

Both of them were all ears. "Nail that agent
and we'll know which mob leaders are theirs,
now and in the future," Markham noted. "Also,
we'll be able to trace and shut a nasty leak,
maybe trace it right up close to the source."

"Yeah," I responded. I had some trouble with
the ethics of all this—I didn't like the idea of
being a mob P.I., no matter what mob it was, and
it really didn't matter overall which side won to
me, except that if I nailed this bastard they might
stop trying to put holes in me. Still, I couldn't get
out of my head this vision of a fancy Main Line
home on an acre or three or four, with twin
Mercedes out front, which would be a nice home
for Brandy and me, or the vision of Spade &
Marlowe's office suite on the top floor of the
poshest office building in Philadelphia.

Damn it, I decided, Brandy had been right all
along. Playing it honest and true had gotten us
broke and desperate. Yeah, I don't think I could
deliver innocent lives to these corporate multi-
worldly mobsters, but so long as it was nailing
one set of trash for the other, it didn't really
matter. It was something to nail a bastard, even
if other bastards were paying me to do it.

Out of ignorance, we'd been suckered into all
this and fallen off a cliff. Well, we weren't
ignorant anymore. We knew just who, and what,
we were dealing with. It was time for Spade &

Marlowe to show just what kind of detectives they really were.

By the next morning, Markham's people and money had sprung all three girls, and Nan had been taken immediately into the Company's protective custody for interrogation. She alone knew what our elusive Mr. Gritch looked like, and we wanted a composite. Brandy came to see me almost immediately, after getting a shower and a change of clothes.

"It was pretty bad in there, even by Camden standards," she told me. "You don't have no constitutional rights in a system like this. What the judge says goes. I thought this was a democracy!"

"It is. It just isn't our kind. Were they rough?"

"Standard good-guy—bad-guy routine, hours and hours, with threats of violence but no real violence. They wanted the truth, that's all, and I couldn't give it to 'em, if they'd have believed it anyway. The worst thing was, they made us stay in our bathin' suits. Can you believe that? And Jamie was drippin' wet when they took us in to book us! She fell in a couple times on that sailboat while tryin' to keep us in range."

I thought for a moment. "You see the dead girl's body? The shooter, I mean?"

"No, but they told me about it and I didn't want to. Five slugs, all in the back. A real mess. Not much blood, though, 'cause she fell in the water."

I sighed. "Brandy, I think it's time we went home."

"Huh? You mean Camden?"

"Or something like it. In a little more style. As soon as they say I can get out of here, we go. I think I now have as much of the story as it's possible to know without the guilty ones filling in the blanks. The trouble is, I can't prove a thing. I think it's time to take a leaf from old Phil Marlowe's book. Go get Bill Markham and tell him I also have to talk to Whitlock. I think I have a way to get him back in the good graces of modern society again."

"I usually follow right along with you," she noted. "Sometimes ahead. But I can't figure you now."

"Oh, let's just say that maybe if I can never love this line of work, I can at least be good at it."

9.

The Agent in the Muddle

It had been less than five weeks since this insanity had begun, at least on the world where it had started, and now the drama was drawing to a close, this time at a Holiday Inn off I–95 in Ridley Park, Pennsylvania, just south of Philadelphia International Airport.

Agent Marshall Flynn Kennedy hadn't changed any in that time, not even his suit, and he walked into the lobby and directly back to the elevators and punched the up button, then got on and rode up to the eighth floor, then got off, walked down the hall, and knocked on 832.

"Who's there?" a muffled man's voice asked.

"Agent Kennedy, DEA, sir," the federal man responded.

The chain was slipped off the door, which opened to admit the agent. When it was closed again, the federal man shook hands with the real and authentic Martin J. Whitlock IV.

"We've had quite a time with you, Whitlock," Kennedy noted. "I'm glad to see you've gotten some sense. Frankly, we weren't sure if you were even alive. The last we heard, you had skipped off to the west coast dressed, ah, unusually."

"A friend, Mr. Kennedy. Two friends, both of whom resemble me because we're from the same family. I assure you this is the way I normally look, on and off the job. I'm just tired. I want to get this over with. My wife and kids must be frantic by now, and I miss them."

"You understand that it'll never be like it was. Turning state's evidence against mob figures makes you and yours a real target. Everybody will have to be relocated."

"I understand. What they do is up to them. I'm a target now, with no real place to go. At least this way I can see them, in protected circumstances, explain things to them, give them the facts and the choices. I have—alternatives—for my future." He gave a slight smile at that, as if it were some private joke.

"You are absolutely certain you can hand us Big Nose Norton as tight as we have Big Tony?"

"Tighter. I can trace and document his entire money laundry, start to finish, and hand you his entire distribution system as well, for all of central Jersey."

"Very well. I have a car and some protective personnel downstairs. We might as well go now and get this ball rolling."

"I—I thought we could handle much of it here, informally," Whitlock told him nervously. "I really don't want to be in some solitary cell guarded by officers until this is over. This was not part of our agreement over the phone, Mr. Kennedy."

Kennedy reached in his coat and pulled out a .38 revolver. "I'm afraid I must insist, Mr. Whitlock," he said evenly.

Whitlock stared at the gun. "That's not necessary."

"I think it is. Now turn against the wall here, please, hands behind your back." The cuffs went on quickly and professionally. "Now, let's leave this room, nice and quiet-like. I don't want to make a mess here, or even a fuss, but I can be *very* painful if I have to be. And no heroic escape attempts, please. I have men at your home, looking after your wife. Her future depends on your cooperation."

Whitlock turned and stared at him. "You! It was you all along! Nail Big Tony and put Norton, your boy, in on the inner council. Why, you corrupt son of a bitch!"

Kennedy smiled. "Now, we both know it was more complicated than all that, but you have the general idea. There's nobody better placed for this than a federal officer, is there?"

"You're going to kill me!"

Kennedy shrugged. "Not right away. Savor the moments, Mr. Whitlock, not the expectation. We all have to go sometime. I couldn't just let you come in with all you know and blow Norton to hell in the federal record, now could I? This has been messy enough, but I can still grab the brass ring."

They went out and down the hall, reversing Kennedy's trail. There were some raised eyebrows in the lobby, but Kennedy just said, "Federal officer. This man is a fugitive from federal warrants. Don't worry, it's all over before it started," and continued on out the door.

A big blue sedan pulled up almost immediately, and Kennedy opened the door and Whitlock and he got in. There were two other men in the car, both real mean-looking.

"This is Georgio, and this is Frank," Kennedy told Whitlock as they drove off. "They are both highly reliable employees of Mr. Norton's with years of experience."

They drove north into the city, then took the Walt Whitman Bridge to New Jersey, and then up I–295 for a while before exiting to the west. They finally stopped at an old factory site, now abandoned, right on the Delaware River. They stopped, killed the lights, and then the three men and their handcuffed prisoner got out.

"Mr. Norton uses this place a lot," Frank explained. "It's nice and quiet and deserted, and there's big old oil drums over there right along the riverbank. We got a couple of eighty-pound bags of Sacrete in the trunk, but we don't like to start mixing until the barrel's already full and we're all right on the water. You understand."

"You're not going to get away with this, Kennedy," Whitlock said, sounding pretty brave. "The Company knows that Norton was the object. We know all about Gritch and the Nkrumah double. They'll take Norton out just like you took out Big Tony, only cleaner, and they'll just appoint my successor to handle the likes of you."

Kennedy chuckled. "Sure. Like you handled me, right? Hell, even *I* never expected you to just call up and walk into my arms, but I made myself the logical one, didn't I? As for Norton—he'll stay. My unit at DEA here is attached to the Federal Organized Crime Strike Force. *Tsk tsk tsk.* All you nasty mob types for me to handle. Norton gives us the Philadelphia council chairmanship and a seat on the inner council. We are well positioned to protect Norton, and also to nail anybody you might send up against him. He's not the only inner-council member we've got, you know. With maybe a little bloodletting, he tips the balance our way. Boys, I think it's time we got this over and done with. I promised my girlfriend I'd be in early tonight."

Car lights went on, illuminating the quartet, and I stepped out from behind one set. "Who created this whole crazy mess, Kennedy?" I asked. "Machiavelli?"

Kennedy's hand went to his shoulder holster, but the two mob men had theirs out first and rather noisily. Both of their guns were pointed not at me but at Kennedy, and he realized it almost immediately and relaxed.

"Horowitz! You son of a bitch, it's always *you*, isn't it? My biggest mistake in all this was not just throwing you in the slammer that first day at Whitlock's house."

I shook my head slowly. "No, no. You have much too big an ego, you're much too clever for *that*. That's your problem, Kennedy. It was just too damned complicated a scheme and involved too many people. It was so intricate it was bound to fail."

"It almost worked!"

"No it didn't. You blew it right off, when you didn't figure the drag-queen masquerade. It was so outrageous it confused the shit out of you. You didn't know if you had one Whitlock or two, and your pretty plans for replacing the eastern regional director of the Company with a double went right down the tubes. Then you decided to put the screws on Nkrumah when it all started coming apart, and he handed you Big Tony, just like you hoped. But you couldn't just finish him off. That got me wondering. Why let Nkrumah live, and why bring in a double who'd tell me just where he ran to? It hit me just the other day. You didn't just need information, you needed Nkrumah, because Big Tony had to be nailed legitimately. But old Marty, here, went to Nkrumah after your boy finished with Little Jimmy, and the big fart skipped the country. You were left without a live body to swear on those affidavits and give testimony before legal witnesses, so you imported a double for him to do that. But the double really was another Little Jimmy, heart and soul. He looked at the bills here and saw they were the same as the bills on his world, which must be pretty close to this one. He knew he'd do his thing here, then go back home—and he wanted Little Jimmy's restitution money, too. So he told me about Grand Cayman, hoping I might point the Company that way or maybe go there myself and get him knocked off. How am I doing?"

"Pretty fair. When you deal with trash, you have to expect treason and greed sometimes."

"So Little Jimmy Two runs down to pick up that payoff money and runs smack into Little Jimmy One," Brandy continued, picking up the story. "He knows he just should blow Little Jimmy One away, but he finds he can't do it. It's like blowin' himself away. So Little Jimmy One panics and runs for the Grand Cayman hideout. That's where it gets a little fuzzy. Why'd you keep him alive at all, let alone pay him off and send three girls to guard him?"

"Simple," Kennedy replied. "Big Tony's boys figured immediately who had fingered their boss and went gunning for him. They nailed our Little

Jimmy thinking it was the original. That left me with only the original, and I was going to need a live body at the trial."

"So you told Gritch to get you three identical beauties to the ones Little Jimmy expected on his boat, and Gritch had already prepared a whole list of duplicates, if need be, from his world. Right?" I put in.

"You got it." Kennedy turned to the two mob toughs. "These are, I take it, not the same pair I've dealt with before."

Brandy grinned. "Yeah. Two can play at that substitution game."

"Can you tell me how you figured it was me?"

"That wasn't so hard," I told him. "It had to be somebody who knew the whole tri-state mob scene intimately, and was in a position to make things happen in it. It also had to be somebody who could find out who we were working for, and pull that switch of Nkrumahs. We talked to nobody about Oregon until we were in Bend, and at Bend I made only two phone calls. One was to the phony Nkrumah, the other to you. It was you who told me that Little Jimmy didn't even appear on the federal warrants list. The only reason for that was if he was a state's witness—but I knew Little Jimmy was splitting because he'd just told me he was, and with his ripped-off money restored. You might offer protection, but not even Big Tony would be worth a two-and-a-quarter-million-dollar restitution. Then the fake Whitlock shows up in McInerney to blow away the real one, who isn't there, and with him is one of Big Tony's best soldiers. Now, who knew they were there? I only told Little Jimmy—and both the real and the phony split—and you. And, of course, there was Nan's composite of Gritch, supplemented by Bill's detective team up at State College and some old photos from the obit files. It was a long time ago, for me, but that guy sure looked like a dead ringer for that fellow in the car with you the first time we met, the one who never got out. I have a thing for faces."

"But you weren't positive," he noted glumly, "so you fixed up this charade. Whitlock offering to deliver Norton to us on a platter. It made sense, since the Company's only way of getting things back to normal was to block Norton in a way that didn't seem to directly involve them. I figured Whitlock planned to deliver the goods, then split to one of the other worlds. Big Tony was already out on bail and sure to fight, and he figured he'd bumped off Nkrumah so there'd be no star witness at his trial. Whitlock, here, could deliver both—but wouldn't. He'd just deliver Norton. We can hit Big Tony now, but without Norton it's nowhere. I had to take him out once and for all, like I tried to do from the start."

"Frank, can you get the key from old Kennedy here and get poor Mr. Whitlock outta them handcuffs?" Brandy asked. "Thanks."

"So now what do you do?" the agent asked us.

"First," I replied, "we go back to Philadelphia. I have to admit, if you hadn't taken the bait, or if you'd just let Whitlock come in and send Norton up, we were stuck. I didn't have a shred of concrete evidence on you, and we couldn't just take out a federal officer without getting things *real* messy. With Big Tony feeling free, and Norton poised for a hit and a takeover, though, I figured that handing you all you needed to wrap it up in a nice package would be damned near irresistible—and it was. We taped the hotel-room scene, by the way, and our people are in place now to get it. There's nothing said there about the Company or other worlds or anything. It's strictly a picture of a dirty cop about to blow away a major witness. The U.S. Attorney is going to love it. Spout all you want to about other worlds and doubles and all that. That might just get you an insanity plea that'll work, but I doubt it. But before we head for Philadelphia, we're going to stop by a few friends of ours from the Company and they're going to give you a little implant."

Kennedy looked nervous. "What are you talking about?"

"Well, as you may know, the way the Company makes sure its people are its own people is by implanting a tiny little encoder in the body. Brandy and I got ours a few days ago. It's painless. But you can also stick a code in there that will make the Labyrinth a mess to you. Your friends won't pull you out, because you blew it in spades; but even if they did, and you got to a flag stop and got in, it still wouldn't matter. The Labyrinth would kill you. You better get used to the idea that you're going to spend some time in Atlanta, Kennedy."

"Yeah," Brandy added. "About twenty years, but probably a lot less, since that place is just *full* of busted drug kings. You might even have sent some of 'em there. They're gonna just *love* you."

I had to laugh, and she looked at me oddly. "What's so funny?"

"Ever since I became a cop I had this fantasy of lining up a bunch of folks in one place and explaining the case and the pleasure of unmasking the guilty party. This isn't exactly a drawing room, but, you know, that's just what we did."

"I'm glad you got to fulfill your ambition before you died, Sam," said a voice behind us. We all turned, and there was Jamie holding a semiautomatic rifle, an Israeli job we'd brought along in the car just in case. "Everyone just drop your guns on the ground—*now!*" Guns dropped.

"Jamie! Thank God!" Kennedy sighed, and made to move over to her.

"Hold it, Kennedy! You stay with them!" she ordered.

If anything, Kennedy looked more stricken now than he did when we turned the lights on him. "Jamie—what? We can still *do* it! Don't you see? These two pests, Whitlock, all out of the way. We can still win!"

"You idiot!" she snapped. "We lost our chance the moment Whitlock escaped. Who do you think we're fighting? Some little mob brain? It's the *Company*, you fool! This only had a chance of working if everything seemed to happen naturally. Whitlock going bad and skipping, Big Tony getting sent to prison by straight testimony of a middle-level hoodlum, all that. I don't think it *ever* had a prayer, considering that idiotic but effective drag-queen masquerade. These two are ten times the detective you are! You didn't even *know* about that business until it was already in motion, and then you couldn't penetrate well enough and quickly enough in two weeks to determine what these two could in forty-eight hours. We can't have this, Kennedy. You know too much."

"The last of the players in this particular little

game," I said. "Good old Jamie. Too bad, Jamie. I was getting to like you."

"I was getting to like both of you, but that's neither here nor there. This isn't a time for friendships, Sam. This is strictly business, and I'm assigned to clean up this mess. This should do it. A mob hit where Whitlock was about to turn himself in to the feds. Sorry, everyone, I'm on a schedule." She pulled the trigger, and the night was filled with two seconds of horrible bursts and a tremendous amount of smoke that made the scene look eerie as it reflected the headlights. Kennedy dived for the ground, screaming in terror. The rest of us just stared at her as she pulled the trigger.

We were still staring when the clip ran dry, only Frank and Georgio had their own guns back, although it wasn't really necessary.

"They wanted me to bring an empty gun," I said, "but I figured you might notice an empty clip. You're good at that. So I had them find me some blanks. A whole box worth. It made better theater, anyway."

"You bastard!" she screamed.

"Hey! Do you know how tough it is to find a box of blanks for an Uzi semiautomatic?" I noticed her glancing about. "I switched the ones in your handgun, too, so don't try for the bag. Besides, even if you did, it wouldn't make any difference. Bill Markham has boys all over here, including the only exit."

She dropped the gun. "I should have known," she said. "I wondered why you didn't tell me about this until it was under way enough that I couldn't do anything but ride along."

"I didn't want you tipping Kennedy. If he'd been a good boy, though, we'd have fed you something and seen who you ran to. Still, I can't take all the credit. Philadelphia is my turf, Jamie, and I already knew you were with them even before we left Georgetown."

"What?"

"I had to do something, just lying there in the hospital. My arm still hurts, by the way, thanks to you. So I thought, and I had it figured, particularly after Markham filled me in on the background of the Company wars. The plot I had mostly figured when we talked to Nkrumah. What didn't make sense was why the opposition would want to kill him, and the girls. He was worth more to Kennedy, here, alive than dead. He was better dead for the Company, but in that case *I* was the Company. Then it hit me. So long as we were talking, exchanging information with Little Jimmy, nothing happened. Nothing. But when we started fingering those *girls*, and talking two of them into maybe switching over to our side—then the lights went out. Then when Bill and Tod sprung both of you, and Brandy complained that the cops had kept you in your bathing suits and that you had been wet, it fell right into place. I got Bill to insist on a full autopsy on the third girl, Suzy, the alleged shooter. With five big holes in her, and a coroner's office like they got in Georgetown, the cause of death was too obvious to be worth looking twice at her. You counted on that. But she hadn't died from gunshot wounds. That's why there wasn't tremendous bleeding. She'd been strangled. Strangled maybe fifteen minutes, maybe more, before she allegedly shot me and the others."

"As soon as that autopsy report came in, I had no trouble runnin' with Sam's logic," Brandy added. "When an operation this big goes bad, the only thing you can do is minimize your losses. Take out everybody who knows somethin' they shouldn't, leave a mess but a *tidy* mess, and get out."

Suzy had been in the bow for some reason when I'd come aboard, and she'd stayed there when Mike fired that shot, going below for her pistol and coming back out on top. Jamie had spotted her there and moved her sailboat close in. Suzy hadn't noticed, since her attention was entirely on us. Jamie was quick and agile. She had gotten up on the boat silently and caught Suzy by surprise, and swiftly and silently strangled her with some professional hold, then took her gun and remained. Nkrumah was irrelevant, but when the girls had not only begun to come over to our side, but had brought up Gritch and others they didn't know but had met, she knew she had to act, and fast. She emptied the clip through the windshield, hoping to get all of us, but the angle was wrong and the gun unfamiliar. Then she had to be convincing. While I was creeping forward, she lowered Suzy's body into the water, then took her own gun and shot it five times. She couldn't shoot it on deck because it would make holes and a bloody mess. Then she dived into the water to make the falling-body sound, and shouted back up to us.

"You got all but Nan, I have to give you that," I told her. "And Nan you planned to take care of, if and when possible, but the cops were too tight, too quick, and too strict. It all didn't matter,

because both Brandy and I survived and we
already had some of the information. That meant
a total clean-up. When we headed back for Philadelphia, you just waited, contacting Kennedy and
alerting him that we were there. We were on your
list, but last, since we were doing the dirty work
of unearthing your victims for you." I looked off
in the darkness. "Bill, you want to come in and
take charge now?" I shouted.

To be perfectly frank, I almost expected another double cross, another hail of bullets, this
time real, but it didn't happen. Markham and his
people were right there and very professional.

We sat around a posh office on the fourteenth
floor of one of the newest office buildings in
Philadelphia. The one office we were in was
bigger than both our old office and our old
apartment combined, and was only part of a
complex that went two floors down and two
floors further up. This was the eastern regional
office of G.O.D., Inc. The irony was that most of
the people who worked here knew nothing more
about the Company than that it sold mail-order
merchandise by phone and that it had large
investments in other areas worldwide. Still, the
remarkable thing was that almost everything that
went on here was totally legitimate, and exactly
what would be done if it were just the company
it pretended to be. Only a very few knew the
truth here, and, most remarkably of all, there
were none here that were not native to our own
version of Earth. Only in Oregon and, we were
led to believe, in Japan and Mongolia, were there
any permanent party personnel who were not
natives.

Bill Markham sat there, along with Dr. John Koken, the vice president of the eastern office. Koken ran the legitimate side, while Whitlock ran the darker side of the business from his bank. Whitlock, too, was there, along with Brandy and myself. Curiously, in the hierarchy of the Company, Koken was senior and set policy for the whole region; Whitlock was in effect his deputy, while Markham was one of the top men running the eastern security apparatus on both sides.

"It was quite audacious, really," Koken noted, sipping coffee. "We have a lot of weaknesses, the greatest being our sheer size, but we tend to forget that they have weaknesses as well. They are far fewer than we, and that is their major problem. Like the terrorist, they can cause a disproportionate amount of trouble and tie up resources, but also like the terrorist they have few clear-cut victories. I think they needed a clear victory, if only to energize the others who must labor in slower and less productive mischief. The only way a small group gains that sort of victory against a major force is by sheer audacity."

"But it failed," Brandy noted. "It was so much of a mess, I just can't see how it could have succeeded."

"It almost *did* succeed," Whitlock pointed out. "It still almost worked. They managed to remove me and indict Big Tony, as well as cripple Big Tony's business and foul up ours. The truth is, you two really turned it around. It was sheer luck, in the end, that kept things from going bad."

"I can't believe we were the decider here," I responded. "I mean, this thing was blown from the start when they couldn't replace Mr. Whitlock, here, with their man. They missed killing him, and they failed to trace him or to figure out that crazy ruse. The other Whitlock figured that at the start; and so, really, did Kennedy, who ordered them to stiff Little Jimmy and pressure him to turn over Big Tony. The trouble was, they picked a slick but greedy bastard, and, thanks to seeing double, an unreliable goat. It fell apart from that point. The most they had was a temporary victory. They had nobody to make the charges against Big Tony stick, and if Norton tried to muscle in while Big Tony was fighting this, the whole council would have crushed Norton. The ones behind this knew it, too, the moment they got the real picture, and that's when they decided to send Jamie in to clean up the mess and get out before you went too far and learned too much."

"What's gonna happen to her?" Brandy asked. "Or is that better not said?"

Bill Markham sighed. "Information is more critical than examples and lives to us at this stage. Over the years we've learned that, and we've established a consistent policy. Anybody who's caught and can deliver really substantive new information of real value to us, higher-ups and the like, and is totally cooperative, can buy his or her life. I don't care if it's Hitler or who, it's absolute. We don't promise a rose garden, but we promise life and integration into some society. Jamie's been very cooperative. *Very* cooperative. She was simply young and very, very ambitious and very impatient about climbing the ladder. Our system was slow and she thought she was underused and underappreciated. They look for ones like that, and they offer them more adventure, more thrills, and more automony and authority. Instead of being a resident agent on a series of worlds, she willingly became a free-lance assassin and clean-up artist. She has absolutely no loyalty to anyone but herself. She's buying a future."

"Yeah, what kind of future?" Brandy pressed. "Alone in the Garden or something like that?"

"No. Right now we're thinking of a world that's been more or less culturally and technologically stuck in the tenth century since, well, the tenth century. In that world, the Islamic empire wasn't stopped at the gates of Vienna, and overran Europe and much of Asia as well as Africa. It's an old-line, old-time fundamentalist Islam that keeps a rigid system and breeds its conquered opponents out of existence. There's a sheik, a prince, deep in the Songhai Empire on the Niger River to whom we owe a minor favor. He finds white-skinned women exotic, and he has a pretty good harem. We're inclined to ship her there and treat her with a blocking code so she's stuck there. If she can make her way in that world, fine. We think she'll be in hell for a while, then crack and accept it. That's only fair. She has a lot of blood on her hands and she was pretty cold about it. Even now, her only remorse is that she failed."

"And Gritch?" I asked.

"We haven't got him yet, but we have enough information now that we've identified the world they're using. It's only nine away from this one, which means it's pretty damned close to ours. I think, once we have some of the major players in the game there reined in, we'll find the network and how it works, and take it over."

Brandy licked her lips nervously. "Are—*we* there? Sam and me?"

Markham cleared his throat. "It's not always a good idea to know those things."

"I want to know," she replied.

He sighed. "All right. You're there but Sam's not. He was killed in a riot in the Phillipines when in the Air Force."

I felt a chill. That scene was always with me, in my dreams, my nightmares, and even awake. All those white bastards stood back, not willing to risk their lives for a Jew, and that one black sergeant took control and saved my ass. How everything turned on little things. Had somebody given that sergeant trouble? Had somebody in that world who was white inflicted a serious psychic wound that was not delivered here? One that stayed his hand, kept him from risking his own neck to drag me out of there?

"What am I—there?" Brandy pressed. She was really adamant. "Are my parents still alive? Did I finish school, or what?"

"All right, then, here it is. Your mother died, same as here, same way and same problem. You were even wilder there than here, but when your father found out he gave you an ultimatum to shape up a hundred percent or get out and never come back. You went across town at age seventeen and became a hooker on a pimp's string. You still are, with a big heroin habit to feed."

"My daddy woulda killed me if I did that!"

"No, ma'am," Markham replied. "He killed himself, instead." He paused a moment while an extreme pall set in over the room. "I told you it's best not to know. Somewhere, somewhen, almost everything that might have happened did. Somewhere, too, your father, maybe even your mother, are still alive, have a successful agency, and you're a college grad with a career, husband, and maybe kids."

That cheered her a little. "What about Sam and me? How many worlds do you think we got together on?"

"Very few. I can say that without checking. The odds are just astronomical against it. More than one, sure, but I'd be surprised if it was a dozen out of hundreds or more where both of you are alive. The funny thing is, Kennedy says he actually called for a switch team on you two, but then you showed up trim, lean, different looking from the time on the siding. There was no match; and since you had nothing here, and the real you were with the Company, there was no percentage and no way to do it, even if they could have recruited and briefed a pair in that length of time. They had doubles for most of the others prepared, but nobody figured on Nkrumah hiring you, not even Nkrumah Two. It wouldn't and couldn't, because in that world everybody *else* was the same, but Sam was dead and you were a hooker, so there was no detective agency to think about going to. See?"

I *did* see. "Variables," I said. "Too many variables. All the big shots were the same, or real close to the same, but we were the one thing in this world that related to them that they didn't have. Our presence hadn't affected their development up to then; we were *zilch*. We only took on any importance when Little Jimmy came to us here."

"Even then, who knows what woulda happened if that old switchman or whatever he was hadn't sent us to the Garden?" Brandy mused. "I mean, a lot of these things are dead ends, right? We coulda rotted there. Only 'cause we happened to be there and I happened to wake up and hear it when they opened up that Labyrinth gateway, did we get out at all."

"That, in fact, is what we're here to discuss," Markham told us. "It was no accident, Brandy. You were meant to hear it, see it, and escape in it. That 'garden,' as you call it, *is* a dead-end siding."

I sat up at that one. "Now, hold on. Who was that seven-foot snow-white girl in the kimono, then?"

"That was when you were back on the main track. It's a short siding. You see, they needed you. They looked over the mess and they decided it was going down a failure, and the only thing they could do was send somebody in to take out those who knew too much, protect Kennedy if possible—waste him, too, if his cover was blown—and make sure nobody went any further than here. For that, they needed a way to get Jamie here, as a company agent, so she'd have the resources and cover to track these people down and know what we knew. The old switchman's report was filed with the nearest full station, as is procedure, so immediate action could be taken if need be. Otherwise, the station is supposed to send the report on down the line. They didn't. Instead, they arranged for one of their own to work the nearest switch set and convincingly send you to them with no record being filed."

"The dog-faced woman," I said.

"Uh-huh. We didn't know that for sure, since even Jamie wouldn't know the switching personnel, but we inferred it, and when we found she'd been recently certified and changed to that switch and watch, it was pretty easy to figure."

I nodded. "I figured if Jamie was their hitter, then her boss had to be Cranston. Too bad, with a name like that."

"That beach house, which in our world would be on the Sonoma County coast north of San Francisco, is a training center for younger operatives. He runs it because it's a quiet world and a stratified one, and so it's pretty easy to train people there without much danger of exposure. Now that I think of it, it's kind of odd that Cranston seemed happy there for so long and never pressed for promotion or reassignment, but that's hindsight. We probably have a large percentage of senior staff that get in a life they really like and want to stay."

"Cranston had it pretty good," I noted. "With some amenities hidden from the rest of the folks, I could get used to that lifestyle myself."

"Still has, but not for long," Markham noted. "So far we've covered all the entrances and exits, and he hasn't been tipped that Jamie was caught. If he finds out, he'll skip, and he has the means to do it. He's pretty wary; I doubt if we could con him into coming down to headquarters line, since he's always had to fight to get an appointment there before, and he's sticking pretty close to his house until this is done. He built the place, and it has a staff of twenty-four plus various students. We have no idea how many are really competition, and we don't know what's built into that house, but he has a flag stop in there, that we know. That's how he got you two back here. Our worry is, if we slip up and can't take him, he can use that flag to enter the Labyrinth. We don't know how desperate he'll be. Some of them are pussycats, some are *kamikazes*. We don't want to lose him if we can avoid it. We want *his* boss, and he's the only one who knows who that is."

"But you're going after him."

"Sure. Want to come? We sure can't use anybody from the local organization there. We don't know who's who."

Brandy looked at me. "Want to go?"

"I shrugged. "More getting shot at. Yeah, all right. I can see that *you* do. I have a bad feeling about this, though. Every time we've gotten involved in this activity, something nutty happened. We've been lucky so far, but how long can it last?"

"Don't mind him," Brandy told them. "He's always like that. That's his way of saying he wouldn't miss it for the world."

I looked at him. "The fact that we're invited seems to imply a few things. First of all, you really don't expect to nail him alive, so you can afford a couple of rank amateurs along. Second, you want to check us out."

"You're wrong. I *do* want him alive. I could have him killed pretty easily. That's why this is delicate. He is under no such restrictions."

The place was heavily guarded, but we had enough people to take out the major spotters and replace them convincingly with our own people. The trouble was, there were so many people in and around the house, and so many potential traps, that a full reconnaissance just wasn't practical. For the same reason, we couldn't come in through his basement flag stop, since we didn't know his alarms there and couldn't know what signals the automated equipment would give if an entry were made. What we could do, however, was issue a command that effectively shut down the flag stop from the Labyrinth side. Since McInerney and his cult were never in on Cranston's treason, since they deliberately remained ignorant of what was proper and what was not, we used the Oregon station for our own entrance, then had that temporarily shut down as well just in case.

Cranston's beach house location had been ideal for hiding the Company school and Company activities, but its very isolation in this world also made it relatively easy to cut off. Brandy and I were again dressed all in black, but this time professional outfits that were a lot nicer than that plastic, which the Company had been shipping to some other world from ours, that had gotten us into the plant at the start.

It was quiet and fairly still, but we slipped into the main hall and saw one of those liveried butlers making his way downstairs with a tray full of dirty glasses and dishes. We crept up to him, and I held him while Brandy took the tray and set it down. The gun in his back made him very cooperative.

"Company security," I whispered. "Cranston still awake?"

He nodded. "Y—yes."

"You have an intercom or speaking tube to reach him?"

"Yes—in the pantry."

"Anybody else in the pantry?"

"No, not at this time of night. Please—what is this all about?"

"If you have to ask, then you wouldn't believe

the answer or you already know it. Either way, just don't sweat it, and do what you're told. If anything bad happens to us because of you, something *awful*'s going to happen to you first. Understand?''

I had real hopes it'd be the guy who slipped us the mickey, but you can't have everything. The kitchen and pantry area was dimly lit and deserted as promised, though, and the tubes were all there—and all nicely labeled. He could still double-cross us if Cranston wasn't in his study and somebody else was, but it was his funeral if he did and he knew it.

"Mr. Cranston, this is Jameson," the butler said into the tube after giving a whistle. "I think you had better come down to the library, sir. There's something wrong that I think you'd best attend to in person."

"You said that just like we told you," I said approvingly. "Good night."

He looked puzzled. "Good night?" he echoed, and Brandy hit him with the juice right in the rump through all those clothes. That stuff, whatever it was, was quick. Maybe three or four seconds and he was down for the count.

We hurried into the library and concealed ourselves behind the drapes, guns at the ready. Cranston might just as likely send his people in first and we knew it. He didn't, though, coming down the stairs and walking straight into the library. He stopped and looked around, puzzled. He was wearing that same silk dressing gown we'd seen him in on the train.

"Jameson?" he called.

"Who knows what evil lurks in the hearts of

men?" I asked, stepping out, pistol pointed at him.

"De shadow do," Brandy responded, and stepped out herself, also armed.

"I thought it was Helen Gurley Brown," I responded.

"Horowitz?" Cranston was genuinely surprised. I think he might have expected somebody, but not me. "*Both* Horowitzes?" He paused a moment, then sighed. "I surmise from this that Jamie blew it. She always was a hotheaded little psychopath, but she had the most experience in a world similar to yours of anyone available to me right then. I assume the house is surrounded?"

"Yes."

He sighed again. "Mind if I get dressed first, then? Where can I go?"

"Yes, I mind, and I don't want to find out where you can go. Hands where I can see 'em, please. Now, just turn and walk the eight feet or so to the front door, and the nice men outside will take care of you."

Brandy glanced at me. "Pussycat," she whispered.

At that moment a series of shots rang out, ricocheting all over the library. We jumped and tried to find the source, but in that split second Cranston was gone.

We ran out into the hall after him. There was the sound of people moving around upstairs, and lots of queries and complaints, but I was pretty sure Cranston hadn't gone back up. He was headed for the flag stop, and as we saw in the pantry, you got there through the wine cellar.

Our own people were entering and taking up positions, so that left us to give chase. I had no idea who'd fired those shots, but whoever it was, wasn't apparent, and also, thankfully, was a lousy shot. It was probably some kind of automatic device triggered somehow by Cranston.

We had just entered the wine cellar when the bottles started to vibrate and there was the sound of loud and very big machinery beyond them. One of Markham's men came in behind us. "That thing's been shut off! He *can't* be going in!"

"Well, he's doing it!" Brandy shouted back.

"Don't lose us!" I said to the agent. "And make sure your switches are secure! I'm going in after the son of a bitch!"

"We're going in!" Brandy responded, and we went down the corridor, smashing some wine on the way, just in time to see the figure of a man in a silk gown enter what was unmistakably a small version of the Labyrinth. There was a fair amount of electronic equipment here, and some panels were exposed that had been built into the cellar wall. Somehow, Cranston had broken the seal and reopened the siding, giving him an opening to the first switch point. Brandy and I ran right into the blue lines of folding and twisting squares, running at full speed.

The trick was to keep Cranston in sight, because if we lost him he could go anywhere. That meant keeping no more than one cube length behind him. Fortunately, he'd stumbled very early on that dressing gown, while we were in good shape and dressed for this. We had sight of him, but we had been warned not to fire a shot in the Labyrinth unless we were in the same cube as Cranston and couldn't miss. Otherwise, the bullet would exit into some world and keep going until it was spent or hit something—or somebody.

Cranston reached the switch point, the same

point where we'd been directed to him by the dog-faced woman, and that was what I was counting on. No matter what, he'd have to run in place for a while until the switch was set and thrown, and that would give us a chance to be in the same cube as him. He'd thought of that, though. Now he stopped, turned, and showed that we weren't the only ones with guns. His was a shiny, crazy-looking thing but I had no doubt that it was lethal and that Cranston would have no moral compunctions about shooting into an adjacent cube.

I hesitated, but Brandy stopped, braced, and fired anyway, disregarding instructions. Then, again, better a chance of a stray shot somewhere than a shot in me, I thought, and stopped to aim my own.

Brandy's volley struck home at least once, though. Cranston reeled and fell back, his own shot, an emerald-green beam, going wild, and when he recovered there was an ugly red stain on his left side. He'd finally have to get a new dressing gown, after all.

And then he was gone, exiting through one of the intersecting cubes, and we rushed forward. Brandy again saved me, because she immediately saw that the only way Cranston could have turned his stop back on, let alone made it past here, was if somebody in his crew had taken over the switch again. She ran in and immediately fired her last shots in the clip at the transfer cube, not even looking at who she might be shooting. By the time I got there, there was the figure of a small, middle-aged man reeling back with a number of holes in him, while another figure lay slumped over the controller board.

Cranston had to have his own communications channel through the Labyrinth; he'd activated it as a precaution before coming downstairs, and obviously when he reached the cellar he gave the orders to take out the switchman. We should have covered that, but we'd been assured by those who were supposed to know that the flag stop was closed off.

Brandy pointed up, unable to convey sound in the medium, and I looked and saw a fleeing figure, tiny but in the cube. We concentrated on it and went for it, entering just as he exited to the next spot.

Now, though, it was getting tougher. There were worlds showing on some of the cube-faces, worlds that were dark, worlds that were green, worlds that were desert, worlds that were blasted heaths. There were sometimes as few as six facets, sometimes many more, showing, but all but two always showed worlds, exits into reality. The Labyrinth twisted and wound about, but there was only one way to go, to stay in it. We only kept up because Cranston had been slowed by his wounds. He was losing blood fast, and he couldn't keep this up very long. He knew it too, better than we, and he risked a look back to see us gaining on him.

Then, unexpectedly, a very dismal and dark cube-face came up to his right and he took it. We ran in, now only twenty or thirty seconds behind him, and exited out onto a world. Wherever it was, the exit point was outdoors and in the midst of a violent thunderstorm with tremendous wind gusts and driving rain. It was warm, but that didn't make it any less miserable.

Thunderstorms, I thought as the rain soaked

through me in a moment. Why is it always thunderstorms?

We were on a beach with tremendous waves coming in, and up between the beach and dense growth was maybe a couple of hundred feet worth of driftwood. It was a sea of dead trees, jagged and twisted and not very wet. I never saw anything quite like it, but it sure as hell made it hard to spot Cranston. We both stopped.

"It must be a safe house, something like that, for them!" I shouted to her over the roar of the storm. The lightning and thunder were fierce. "Somewhere here he's got enough to hole up until his buddies check here and pick him up!"

"Not without a doctor, he don't!" she shouted back. "Move in and get some shelter behind that driftwood! So long as we're between him and the Labyrinth, he'll have to come to us. No use trackin' him in this storm!"

She was right; we could do nothing until the storm passed, but we were in better shape than he was. Even if there was a superhospital just beyond the jungle line over there, he'd never get through with that wound in his side, not in this crap. I doubted if even *we* could. He was just taking a breather and trying to get some temporary treatment for his wound. I knew how he felt. My left arm was still killing me off and on— mostly on, right now—and this hadn't done it any real good. They'd told me to keep from using my left arm for a while and not to get the bandages wet.

Our shelter was more theoretical than real, and that storm showed no signs at all of letting up. Only the realization that there were green trees here kept me from thinking that this was a world of perpetual storms. I couldn't even tell if it was light or dark, but the frequent and violent lightning flashes, some hitting within our line of sight, gave the whole place an eerie sort of strobe-light effect.

Then, slowly, the storm started to fade, the wind going down to less-than-gale force, the lightning growing more intermittent and further away, and the rain almost completely stopping. Brandy took her reserve clip off its belt clasp and pushed it into the pistol-grip bottom. She looked up at the sky. "It's still night," she said. "I think we wait 'til mornin'."

"Suits me fine," I replied.

"I'm sorry, but I cannot wait that long," came the gasping voice of Lamont Cranston from above us. We turned as one and looked up at him, as he stood there, that crazy gun pointed down at us. He had removed the dressing gown and tied it around his midsection in an attempt to stem the bleeding, and it wasn't doing the full job. If we looked like hell, Cranston looked like a walking dead man.

"If you want to commit suicide, go ahead," I told him, "but don't include us in this." His gun was wobbling, and he looked strangely not quite at us, a fact Brandy, too, couldn't miss.

"I'll make it," he gasped. "I've been worse off than this before. Just throw the guns out there in the sand."

We did it. It didn't seem worth a move. I was wondering how much longer he could remain perched on that huge driftwood log. The rain had stopped, but the logs were wet and there was a really strong runoff at the bottom. I wasn't sure which would kill us first—Cranston's gun or possibly the shifting logs.

"I know a little about wounds, Cranston," I said. "Air Force training and police training. I can help you a little. Maybe keep you alive until help arrives. You may have been worse off before, but you were younger then, and in much better shape."

"Maybe—I won't—make it," he managed, wavering, "but I'm—going to do—what I should've done—when I first—laid eyes—on you."

He was right above us, very close, but Brandy and I were both in a depression between the logs in front of him. I slowly moved my hand toward my belt and got my own backup ammo clip. Brandy, noticing, suddenly moved away from me to my left, and I took the clip and threw it at Cranston as hard as I could. It hit his chest and bounced off, but it made him, for the slightest moment, forget his balance. He fell, backward, away from us, and we heard him cry out. I went for the guns, but Brandy moved to one side, climbed up, then looked down. "Forget it, Sam, unless there's wild animals around."

"Huh? What?"

I returned, but with the guns, and climbed carefully up on the logs and looked down at Cranston. He'd fallen on a sharp, slightly twisted tree limb and it had gone right through his chest. He looked pretty gruesome, but he also was very dead.

"It's a mercy," I told her. "He was walking dead anyway and he knew it."

She sighed. "G.O.D. just wasn't on his side," she said.

I helped her down, and we started back toward

the Labyrinth. I took Brandy's hand and squeezed it. "Case closed, babe. End of the line. But it sure was a hell of a ride."

She squeezed my hand back. "Sure was. I'm sorry I had to kill him, though. It ends the trail to the big boys."

"Doesn't matter. You don't nail that type with Cranstons. Not in this league. It's like Big Tony. He took over when somebody killed Larry Groziana. Norton was ready to take over from him, and there are a hundred Nortons in the wings waiting for anyone of 'em to slip. They're like weeds. That type's the worst that's in all of us, but you can't even pull 'em out by the roots. No matter what, they always grow back, and the little guys never notice the difference. A hundred loan sharks will take up where Little Jimmy left off. A hundred Cranstons, and their Jamies, will rush in to fill that void. In the meantime, the dope's still sold, the girls still sell themselves, the gamblers still get taken. I think that, deep down, is what makes some cops go on the pad and others quit like me. It's when you wake up one day and you realize that it never ends. Only the faces change, and the victims."

She stopped. "This beach never ends, either."

"Huh?"

"Sam—we didn't come this far in that storm. There ain't no Labyrinth no more."

I stopped, and looked up and down the beach. It was light enough now to see pretty far, and she was right.

"I wonder if this place has apple trees?" Brandy asked no one in particular.

No, it didn't have apple trees, but it *did* have

coconuts, and bananas, and other kinds of fruit. It appeared to be an island somewhere in the tropics, not very big but big enough for two. There were exotic birds, and some mean-looking insects, but no people. None that we could find.

It wasn't, however, quite as primitive as the last time. We found a hut on the third day, not far inside the tree line, constructed of bamboo or some kind of wood or plant. It wasn't much, but there was a medical kit, a map of the island, something that looked like instructions which were unfortunately in a language like no other we'd ever seen, as well as some blankets and straw mats. Clearly this was where Cranston had been heading, and where he never had the strength to make, particularly in that storm. We hung up the clothes and went back to nature, but we kept the guns loaded and at the ready, including Cranston's oddball. The hut was too far from the Labyrinth point and too well concealed to be official. If Bill Markham's boys couldn't trace us with those gadgets they implanted in us, then sure as hell somebody from the other side would be along to see whether old Lamont was ready to go. There was no way anybody could know which of us survived.

"You know, it's almost a shame that's true," Brandy remarked. "This place is one I could get used to. Tropical warmth, plenty of food, ocean breezes and the ocean to play in, and no Cranstons, Jamies, Little Jimmys, or nobody else. Only one person who talks English better than me, and I still got you to myself with no competition."

We used the hut, but didn't sleep in it except during the occasional storm. We wanted to see them before they saw us, and we'd spent a year in more primitive conditions than this, only ending that two months or so before this. It was almost like coming home.

But this time it was only a few days before the Labyrinth opened again. Four figures stepped out, all dressed in black as we had been, and fanned out along the beach. One of them had some kind of gadget, and discovered Cranston's decomposing body where we'd left it in about five minutes. They looked at it, then they turned and looked the other way.

"Hey! Horowitzes! You can come home now! All is forgiven!"

It was Bill Markham.

"Over here, Bill!" I shouted. "If we'd known it was going to be you, we'd have dressed for the occasion!"

There were a lot of handshakes and then a tour of the island, including the hut. The writings weren't foreign to Markham's expert.

"It's a general guide to the island," she told us. "Says what's good to eat and what to avoid, how to use medicinal herbs for this or that, and all that kind of thing. Done on a laser printer. Impossible to trace."

"We weren't sure which crew would come," I told them. "We were ready for the worst."

"Yeah, only this time we weren't gonna jump back in that damned hole," Brandy nodded.

"We'll stake the place out now in case anybody *does* show up from the other side," Markham told us. "The only thing we can do." He sighed. "Well, I was afraid Cranston might be tough. Too bad you had to nail him, but at least *you* nailed *him*. Okay, you passed. Now you got a decision to make."

"Come again?" I said.

"You can stay here and forget about everybody and everything except yourselves. We'll monitor any entries, but we'll never interfere. This place is somewhere in the Hawaiian chain, we figure, only real north of the state, up toward Midway. Not a bad place to be."

"Or?" Brandy asked.

"Or, you can come take a ride on my railroad. Be warned, though—this train's strictly for employees only."

I looked at him. "And what do we go back to?"

"An office in the city. Nicer than the ones you're used to. A full agency, maybe with staff, that can handle independent cases, but has one prime client on permanent retainer. I think, between Whitlock and the Company, we can steer a bunch of needy clients your way. Some real training, though, before that happens, in the less orthodox areas of detection you seem pretty good at, with the understanding that you'll be called upon now and then to use that training for your fat retainer. Interested?"

I put my arm around Brandy and looked at her. "Interested?" I asked her.

"Couldn't be otherwise," she replied. "Can't go against no act of G.O.D."

I looked out over the waters, where clouds formed strange shapes in the western sky, and I swore I saw them, saw them all, there in the clouds. Saw them looking down at us and smiling. Spade, the Op, Marlowe, Archer, McGee, all of them were there, and they all understood.

I looked at Brandy. "You know, Mrs. Charles, we ought to have a dog. After all, we're joining the upper classes now."

"*Oooh, Nicki!* You say the most *wonderful* things," she responded.

Bill Markham stared at us, half convinced we'd gone mad. I looked at him and gave him my best Bogart.

"Louie," I said, "this could be the start of a beautiful relationship."

Brandy frowned. "He wasn't a private eye in that one."

I pulled her close and kissed her long and hard. When we broke for air, I said, "It ain't the job that grabs ya, baby. It's the romance. . . ."